Bernice Rubens was born in Wales and later read English at the University of Wales, of which she is now a Fellow.

Her writing career began w... the same time she started wor... time, the author alternated between writing novels and films, but for the last decade she has concentrated solely on writing. Her novels to date include the 1970 Booker Prize winner *The Elected Member*, *A Five Year Sentence*, which was shortlisted for the same award, and *Our Father*, winner of the Welsh City Council Prize. Two of her books have been successfully transferred to film: *I Sent a Letter to My Love* and *Madame Sousatzka* – the latter directed by John Schlesinger and starring Shirley Maclaine. *Mr Wakefield's Crusade* was made into an acclaimed television series. Many of her novels are available in paperback from Abacus books.

Bernice Rubens' other love, apart from writing, is playing the cello.

'I read *The Waiting Game* avidly, in one evening, and I found myself pondering about the characters for several days after I had finished it' *Literary Review*

'Rubens is a sharp observer, a sympathetic chronicler of human weakness' *TLS*

'Wicked wit [and] black humour . . . powerful' *Sunday Telegraph*

'Bernice Rubens writes with both humour and sympathy . . . an ingenious novel with a compelling and chilling plot' *Express on Sunday*

BERNICE RUBENS

The Waiting Game

ABACUS

An *Abacus* Book

First published in Great Britain by
Little, Brown and Company 1997
First published by Abacus 1998

A CIP catalogue record for this book is
available from the British Library.

ISBN 0 349 10902 8

Typeset in Ehrhardt by M Rules
Printed and bound in Great Britain by
Clays Ltd, St Ives plc

Abacus
A Division of
Little, Brown and Company (UK)
Brettenham House
Lancaster Place
London WC2E 7EN

In Cyril's Memory

PART ONE

One

People who had made their home at The Hollyhocks often said that they lived on the road to Paris. And indeed they did for the coast was but a few miles away, at Dover, with its ferries to the French capital. The whispered mention of Paris gave their address a touch of class. And class was what The Hollyhocks was all about.

The brochure stated simply that The Hollyhocks was a Home for the Aged. Class was not mentioned or even hinted at. Nothing so blatant. But if you weren't gentry, you didn't stand a chance of admission. Matron saw to that. Though of no pedigree herself, she could smell it in others. And she could sift it from those other smells of ageing that were common to everyone irrespective of breeding. But class was different. A rare aroma was class. It soft-pedalled those other effluvia that alone were offensive to the nose, and occasioned disgust and intolerance. That extra perfume of class made them bearable, and generously ascribable to simple nature.

Though Matron ruled the roost at The Hollyhocks, the king-, or rather the queenpin, was Lady Celia Suckling. Lady Celia had not sought that position, for she was a woman of retiring nature. It had been thrust upon her, chiefly by Matron who was a sucker for titles and salivated while serving her. Lady Celia claimed to be a direct descendant of the seventeenth-century poet Sir John Suckling. Though no one at the Home had ever heard of such a poet, they took Lady Celia's word for it, and showed the awe that they thought was due to such an ancestor. Whatever her lineage, she was titled, and that title, whether she wished it or not, was her obvious claim to head of house. So in all matters they deferred to her. At every meal they sought her culinary assessment. After every news bulletin, they pressed her for her political opinions. Lady Celia did not relish this role and preferred to keep her opinions to herself. Yet she did not wish to appear snobbish and so she offered the best that she was able. In truth she had no political opinions, and even less culinary knowledge. But she engaged politely in any conversation that was offered her, all the time wishing to God that she was in her own room and able to telephone her partner and hear the news of the day's business. After a decent interval, she would retire early from the common room, and the other residents would almost bow her out, understanding her special need for sleep; after all, she bore the heavy burden of title. Yet despite all the deference, the bowing and the scraping, in their heart of hearts, most of the residents hated Lady Celia with a passion. They hated her because an almost animal instinct informed them that she would outlive them all. From information gleaned from a more than willing Matron, they had learned that Lady Celia's mother had made a century, and that her grandmother too had received a telegram from the Queen. Or the King as it was in her day. Moreover, on her nightly rounds of The Hollyhocks' corridors, Lady Celia's door was the only one in the establishment behind which Matron could hear no sigh. But of all the residents of The Hollyhocks, it was Jeremy Cross who hated Lady Celia the most.

Jeremy Cross was a professional survivor. In his early seventies he had suffered a heart attack, and two years later, a minor stroke. A hip replacement had followed and at the age of seventy-nine he had enrolled as a Hollyhocks member. He had brought with him a list, written in his shaky but triumphant hand, which he had pinned to the inside door of his wardrobe so that it was available for his daily viewing. It was a list of names, but in no alphabetical order, for Death is not concerned with such niceties. Heading the list was one David Gross. Heart attack. Seventy-four. The second culling was Deborah Winters. Stroke. Eighty-two. The third name was written in red ink, clearly a victory, and announced the death by road accident of a John Tilley, aged forty-two. There followed a group inscribed in purple ink, a death from AIDS group, all of them under forty. Then came a number of octogenarians of male and female gender, all of which indicated that Jeremy Cross had enjoyed a wide and varied social circle and had outlived them all.

Since he had been at The Hollyhocks, only one name had been added to his list, that of Cissie Thompson who, at ninety-four, had been scythed by 'natural causes'. But there was still much hopeful room on the sheet of paper which no doubt Jeremy Cross had every intention of filling. His waking thought each morning was, 'Who, if anybody, will I survive today?' Followed by a fervent and whispered wish that it would be Lady Celia Suckling.

He regarded Lady Celia as his arch-enemy. In the common lounge each evening, he would cast his eye over The Hollyhocks' membership and with confidence he assured himself that he would witness each of their departures. Until his eye settled on Lady Celia's chair and watered with fearful uncertainty. He stared at her and at each part of her body, those which housed her liver, her heart, her bowel and her intestine. All those vulnerable bits and pieces and he wished them ill, singly, slowly and with infinite venom. If she looked in his direction he would grant her a flashing smile. Then he would engage in animated conversation with Mrs Elizabeth Webber, aged ninety-five, who showed visible and certain promise of imminent demise.

One evening, when all the residents were lounge-assembled, Matron made an unnecessary call for silence and announced that a new resident would be arriving the following day. She hoped that everyone would make her welcome. Matron knew that there was always a certain unease when a new resident arrived. He or she was a threat to a closely woven circle, and a period of adjustment was entailed before a new boy or girl could be found acceptable. But when on the following evening Matron brought Mrs Thackeray into the lounge for formal introduction, it was clear from her visible breeding that she would fit in very nicely thank you. She was one of them and within minutes, she was plied with polite questions as to her provenance.

Jeremy Cross viewed the new body, assessing its durability. Sadly it seemed spry enough. So he turned to talk to Mrs Elizabeth Webber, now in her ninety-sixth year, assured that soon enough, she would no longer be a target for conversation.

Mrs Thackeray made an early night, shortly followed by Lady Celia who was, by breeding, entitled to her beauty sleep. On the latter's retirement, there was always a sense of freedom in the lounge, as if tongues could now be loosened, manners relaxed, and feet no longer wiped. And now with the new resident out of hearing, a review of the impression she had made was in order. But there was not much to comment on. Mrs Thackeray had given little away.

'She seems a nice enough lady,' Mrs Webber said, an opinion with which they all readily agreed, possibly because they were too tired for debate. Slowly they made their way back to their rooms. Jeremy Cross was the last resident to leave the lounge. He made a point of it every evening, as a deliberate gesture of his own survival.

Upstairs in her new quarters, Mrs Thackeray sat on her bed. Old age is not a blessing, she thought. It is simply a reward for having looked both ways before crossing the road. Well, she had certainly done that. Ever since she could walk. Her mother had drummed it into her day after day. 'Look right, look left, and right again,' was a mantra that had orchestrated her childhood. Even when she was grown, that sacred text rattled her ear at every crossing. She would not even risk the gravel path that led to her mother's front door without mouthing that injunction, though it was barely wide enough to accommodate a harmless bicycle. And where had it led her, that constant and offensive awareness of her own mortality? To The Hollyhocks Home for the Aged.

And why had she needed to come at all? She was sound in body and mind. Her gait was slow but firm. Her hearing was tuned to her own convenience. She wore glasses only for driving. Yes, she could still drive in her manageable Mini. Why this sudden need to uproot herself?

It was Seven Pillars, that home she had lived in all her married and widowed life. It had been her father-in-law's home and his father's before him. Generations of Thackerays had lived and died there, but despite its name wisdom had rarely dwelt therein. In her own remembrance it was a house of ignorance and abject misery. And after years of miserable reminders and infinite moments of sour recall, she had had enough. She'd sell it, she decided, and bury the rotten breed of Thackerays once and for all. Her husband would no doubt turn in his grave but Mrs Thackeray didn't give a damn about what her late husband was doing in his vault. She only regretted that he'd not retired to it earlier. Four years into their marriage would have been a good time, but she had had to wish him dead for nigh on thirty years before he obliged her.

The trouble had begun in their third marital year. She was pregnant. And fearful. Fearful that her child would be a girl, and that if it were, she would have to go on trying until a legitimate heir was born. Her husband had made that very clear. In hindsight she understood that it was this very fear that had provoked her miscarriage, though at the time the doctor ascribed it to a fall, with the cheery injunction to try again. It was the same as falling off a horse, he said, and advised her and her husband to remount. But Mr Thackeray was disgusted with his wife's failure, considering her of poor stock. One evening, Charles Thackeray, of a long and tedious line of gentry breeding, took a whip to his wife, and with absolutely no provocation had beaten her on the buttocks while she was prettily poking the fire. When she had turned around, as much in pain as astonishment, she saw that her husband's face wore an ill-fitting smile, and she had noticed a sudden and distinct stain on his trousers as the whip fell from his hand. It did not occur to her to connect the one thing with the other, but she knew instinctively that something very shameful had occurred. He had left the room quite quickly then, and she didn't see him again until breakfast the following morning. She received no apology. Nor did she expect one. Though from that day she studiously avoided ever poking the fire in his presence, she endured almost a score of years of his whipping, staining and smiling, with a growing bile of disgust and hatred. Until one merciful day, when he had taken his whip elsewhere and flaunted it with stain and smile in sundry back parlours of timed tenancy. Five years later he was dead of gangrene, occasioned by an acute and untreated dose of syphilis. Her hatred of her husband flourished still and after so many years he remained beyond even pity. Sell she must, and let others inherit the misery of Seven Pillars.

She wondered what to do with the furniture. In her mind she toured the rooms of the house. She started in the bedroom, that primary site of shame. The four-poster had belonged to his rotten mother. That would go in the sale. Especially that. And his mother too could turn in her grave. Then there was the drawing-room with the chaise longue, the whatnot, the Biedermeyer day-bed, the Chippendale table, the French cabinet, all of them Thackeray inheritance, straight down from the great-grandfather of the tribe. And the monogrammed silver too. And the plate. That curled contemptuous 'T' that stained the lot with its proud sense of property. All of it would go. By the time she had done with dispossession, the Thackeray family vault would no doubt be subject to an earthquake. And to hell with the whole lot of them, she thought. So she had put the home and its contents on the market, packed her clothes and personal effects, and driven off to The Hollyhocks without a single glance behind.

Two

When she came down to breakfast the following morning she hovered, uncertain, at the dining-room door.

'Over here,' she heard.

She noticed a hand that was raised, gesturing an empty seat beside the caller. It was Mrs Helen Green who issued the invitation. A new resident needed befriending and Mrs Green took it upon herself to fulfil that need. Mrs Thackeray was grateful. Gratitude was a banal talent of hers. She'd exercised it most of her life and it had got her nowhere. With a number of murmured 'thank yous', she took the seat that had been offered her.

'I'm Helen Green,' her protector said.

'I'm Mrs Thackeray.' She felt it too soon to offer the intimacy of her Christian name, and though the Thackeray handle
was sour enough, it would have to do for their initial exchange.
Mrs Green took the hint and did not press her further. She was
not offended. She put the reticence down to Mrs Thackeray's
shyness and uncertainty in her new surroundings. She herself
had felt exactly the same when she had first arrived, and some
weeks had passed before she felt she could reveal her full provenance. Eventually, the other residents had learned that she'd
been born in Edinburgh, but on her marriage she had moved to
Dover where her late husband had owned a fleet of freight ves-
sels. He had died almost four years before, and now, nearing
eighty, she had accepted the fact that she could no longer live
alone.

'You'll be very happy here, Mrs Thackeray,' she said.

'I hope so.' She turned to smile at Mrs Green and was struck
by the scar on the woman's face, a scar ill-concealed with
powder. It intrigued her, and she wanted to know how she had
come by her disfigurement. But she could hardly ask such an
intimate question when she herself was unwilling to give even
her Christian name. There would come a time, she thought,
when in exchange for that name she could ask about the scar.

That time came but a week later. They had breakfasted
together every morning and slowly Mrs Thackeray had thawed.
Between the grapefruits and the scrambled eggs, they had
achieved between them the intimacy of strangers, that closeness
permissible towards the end of one's life, when there is too little
time left to apologise for, or to justify one's past mistakes.

It was in this generous light that Mrs Green talked about her
daughter, and as a consequence gave away the cause of her facial
scar.

'Call me Mildred,' Mrs Thackeray said.

Mrs Green smiled and launched into her story.

'I haven't seen Liza for over twenty years,' she said. 'I have heard that I have two grandchildren, but she has probably told them I am dead.'

'Children can be very cruel,' Mrs Thackeray said, though with no personal experience of such cruelty. But old people are wont to say such things, having forgotten their cruelty towards their own parents, as those parents have forgotten theirs.

'Liza wished me dead all right,' Mrs Green insisted.

Mrs Thackeray tried to interrupt with some insincere rebuttal, but Mrs Green insisted on her daughter's devilment.

'I remember the first time she said it to my face. She was only ten at the time. We were in the kitchen and we'd had an argument. She lost her temper and she flung a saucepan at me. Caught me here.' She caressed her cheek. '"I wish you were dead," she said. No apology. Nothing. Not even remorse.'

'But she was only a child,' Mrs Thackeray said, trying to gild the monster Liza must have been.

'That was no excuse,' Mrs Green said. What she did not say to Mrs Thackeray was that her daughter was a regular chip off her mother's block and that she herself had done worse in her time, much worse, without remorse, and even with a hint of pleasure. She and Mrs Thackeray were not close enough for such sharing, and never would be. Any more than Mrs Thackeray would divulge her shame of the smiling and the staining and the whipping of her early marriage. Yet there was enough to keep them merrily gossiping. The other residents of The Hollyhocks and their stories kept them giggling for hours at a time, and their own stories of their past lives, those that were tellable, counted for hours between them of gentle consolation. Each woman felt she had made a friend for life, or what was left of it.

A few doors down the corridor, Mrs Alison Hughes, a long-time resident of The Hollyhocks, was entertaining her daughter and her great-grandchild. Mrs Hughes was an exception to the filial cruelty rule. She herself had been a good daughter, as was

Jennifer, her own, and Sylvie too, her grandchild who in her
turn had taken the cue from her mother. Little Minnie, now
three years old, Sylvie's first-born, was displaying her latest
drawings to her great-grandmother's non-critical and loving
eye. Minnie attended the kindergarten that was a few doors
down from The Hollyhocks and Mrs Hughes would listen out
for their playtime laughter and picture her Minnie as the centre
of attraction, her little face creased with merriment. Minnie had
drawn a portrait of her great-grandmother, unrecognisable to
anybody, least of all to Mrs Hughes.

'My eyes look closed,' Mrs Hughes said. 'Am I sleeping?'

'No,' Minnie laughed. 'They're closed because you've seen
everything there is to see.'

Mrs Hughes hugged her tight. Little Minnie had drawn her
soul.

At supper that evening, Mrs Webber's chair was empty.
Matron explained that she was feeling tired and had asked for
a tray in her room.

'She'll be as good as new in the morning,' she said with a
little laugh, which put the other residents at ease for the 'tray in
the room' routine could be a sure prelude to that which none of
them wished to think about. Jeremy Cross was undisturbed. He
himself had had trays in his room in his time, and had survived
to tell his tale. So dinner was consumed with its usual gossip
and relish except by those on Lady Celia's table, who in her
presence were wary and ashamed of both.

In the common lounge, in Mrs Green's occasional absence,
the cause of her scar was often speculated upon. Mrs Thackeray
had promised her friend to say nothing of its shameful source so
she just sat quietly listening. All sorts of weird and wild guesses
as to how it had happened spun around the lounge, each suggestion more outlandish than the last.

'If she were a man, I'd say it was a duelling scar,' Mrs
Hughes offered.

'Perhaps she had a lump removed from her face.' Jeremy Cross indulged in a little wishful thinking. For a lump was a word of deadly implication and full of promise for his own and further survival. You never knew with a lump. It could grow back, and often did. He would keep a wary eye on that scar of hers: it could well be Mrs Green's undoing.

But none of the residents had any real interest in its cause. Indeed they would not have wished to know, for it would have ceased to be yet another subject for their speculation. Mrs Green's scar was a fertile source of such creative energy, of such imaginative story-telling, that were the truth known, it would not have been believed. Whatever the facts of the case their fiction was far more exciting.

When the scar was exhausted, the conversation turned to the outing that Matron had promised them, a picnic on the Thames. She had first proposed the Tower of London, or a tour of Hampton Court, but these had been voted down as being too tiring. A picnic was a sitting pleasure, and called for less energy. Besides, most of them had been to the Tower and Hampton Court and forgotten every word of the tour guide's lecture. But there were no facts or dates to a picnic. A picnic was not an exam to be passed or failed. You just had to enjoy it, and chalk it up as yet another topic of conversation in the lounge.

That evening, Matron was not to be seen. This was unusual, for every night she managed to drop by to enquire after everyone's wellbeing. Though they wondered where she was, no one would hazard a guess. They were all subdued that evening, and one by one they retired early. Jeremy Cross saw them all out, timed each one to their rooms and slow retirement, then, assured of his own continuance, he took his leisured leave.

Three

After breakfast on the following morning, Jeremy Cross rushed back to his room at an indecent but unwitnessed pace. Once inside, he opened his wardrobe door. Slowly he read his survival list, out loud, to make it more real. He stared at the space below Cissie Thompson, the latest deceased at The Hollyhocks. Then he took a pen and very neatly inscribed the name of Elizabeth Webber, aged ninety-five, and after it, 'natural causes'. He read it aloud, smiling the while, then he closed the wardrobe door, assumed a doleful air and returned to the common lounge to mourn.

Mrs Webber had died in her sleep, the untouched tray at her side. This explained Matron's absence in the dining room the night before. She had gone to Mrs Webber's room to ascertain that she had eaten and had found her way beyond appetite for earthly food. She had cleaned her up and laid her out, an essential part of her Hollyhocks duties. Then she had returned to her office and stayed up for the rest of the night considering her waiting list.

Heading the column was a princess who had registered almost two years before. But meanwhile others had jumped the queue. Matron had seen to that, for when the princess had first appeared to inspect the home, she could not hide her colour from Matron. She was from Africa, she needlessly explained, and the daughter of a chief. With as much courtesy as she could muster, Matron had shown her around the Home, and promised to advise her when there was a vacancy. But though she inscribed her name at the head of the list, she had no intention of admitting her. She was not seduced by the title. Princesses, she had heard, were two a penny in Africa or whatever was the appropriate currency on that dark incontinent. Next on the list was a Mr Peabody who had been aged ninety-six on registration four years ago. It was unlikely that he was still in the land of the living. Even if he were, at the age of a hundred, there would be too many 'trays in the room' for Matron's liking. After Mr Peabody came a Mrs Miriam Feinberg, seventy-three on registration two years ago. Matron remembered her distinctly. She had known from the first moment that the woman was Jewish. Her name and her looks confirmed it, and it was clear that she would go the same way as the princess. But Matron had smelt class on her and she'd not forgotten. Mrs Feinberg was after all, continental, having been born in Vienna, and that, to Matron, signified a class of a kind. Moreover she had heard rumours of racial bias at The Hollyhocks, which, if proved, could lose her her licence. Her choice of Mrs Feinberg would certainly scotch them. There was no harm in having a token Jew. But she would draw a colour line. One token was more than enough. Straightaway she wrote to Mrs Feinberg, advising her that a vacancy had occurred and requesting a reply as to her current interest.

It was already eight o'clock by the time she had finished her office business and she had to supervise breakfast and gently break the news of Mrs Webber's death to her residents. She waited until they were all assembled in the dining room. She herself had earlier removed Mrs Webber's customary chair, in the hope that her absence would be less blatant, but as she entered the dining room, she knew that the missing chair had only served to draw attention to its missing occupant, for the residents were unusually silent, and with little obvious appetite.

'I have sad news for you all,' Matron said. 'Our dear Mrs Webber passed on last evening.' She was wont to use a special vocabulary when dealing with that grey area of death. Each word was laundered, rinsed in respect, and called for mourning and silence. In any case there was little to say. Nobody would enquire as to the cause of Mrs Webber's polite passing. In an establishment where most of the residents were close enough to the Queen's birthday message, it would have been a fatuous if not a dangerous question, designed to inspire fear in them all. So they whispered to themselves that each one of them was available to 'natural causes', each one that is except their very selves. For until the last second of life, death was still something that happened to other people.

'I hope to arrange the funeral for next Thursday,' Matron said. 'Mrs Webber had no relatives, so it will be a quiet burial. Those of you who feel inclined to attend will be welcomed at St Catherine's Church, where our dear Mrs Webber used to worship.'

Matron went back to her office. She was very tired after her all-night exertions, and would have liked an hour or so's rest.

But she had too much to do. There was the church to be con-
tacted, the undertakers, and the general paraphernalia of burial
to be attended to. On registering at the Home some years ago,
Mrs Webber had deposited funds earmarked for her funeral and
they were generous enough to allow for a small party-wake
after the burial. She would stock up on her wine supplies,
Matron thought, and put a case or two by for her own personal
cellar. Then there was the envelope, that ever-so-legal-looking
wrapper that Mrs Webber had entrusted into her hands a few
weeks before. It was her will, witnessed, she had told Matron,
by her solicitor and his clerk who had recently paid her a visit.
The envelope was stamped with the solicitor's franking, and on
it, Mrs Webber had written in a hand quivering with a 'natural
causes' fear, 'to be opened after my funeral'. For many weeks
that letter had lain on Matron's desk. Occasionally, when temptation threatened, she would hurriedly stuff it into a drawer.
That morning it lay on her desk again and she picked it up,
sorely tempted, and held it to the light attempting an optical X-
ray. But the envelope was thick, and concealed its contents.
Only another few days or so, she said to herself. Matron had
great expectations of that will. She knew that Mrs Webber was
a woman of boundless means. Her late husband had been a
banker. She herself was an only child, and she had had no children. There was no obvious legatee. Matron had put herself out
to be especially kind to Mrs Webber during her four-year stay
at The Hollyhocks. She was due for some recompense, she
thought, but she must try to stop thinking about how she would
spend her inheritance. She stuffed the envelope back into the
drawer and tried to forget about it.

For Matron, the days passed slowly. Every evening before
retiring she would finger that envelope so full of promise, so
that by Thursday, the burial day, the wrapping was sweating
with her greedy fingerprints.

Those residents who were going to the funeral, and most of

them had wished to go, were assembled in reception. The hall
looked like a rookery, each black bird purring for take-off.
Dressed in solemn black, the mourners were attired for all
other funerals except their own. Mr Cross looked very dapper
in his morning dress, with a barely concealed dapper smile to go
with it, and if one should look very closely at his left cuff, it was
possible to discern several neatly incised notches, each one
marking the quietus of yet another soul that he had survived.

Matron propped Mrs Webber's will against the ink-stand on
her desk. Beside it she laid a ready paperknife so that there
would be no post-funeral delay in perusing its contents. She
smiled, anticipating that pleasure.

When Matron had first been appointed to The Hollyhocks
home, some fifteen years before, she had invested in a black
funeral suit, knowing that such an outfit would be regularly
called upon. She was still wearing it. It creased slightly around
the hips and it shone somewhat, as black suiting, after many
outings, is offensively wont to do. She put on her mournful
smile and glided into reception.

With a portion of Mrs Webber's funeral expenses, she had
ordered a minibus to ferry the mourners to the church. They
boarded slowly, as befitted their frailty and the occasion, but in
their hearts they were embarking on an outing, a pleasant ride
through the country lanes and a booze-up party to follow, with
only a dull duty to be done in between.

The forecourt of the church was deserted as the bus tried
respectfully to tiptoe across the gravel. The verger came out of
the church and stood waiting on the forecourt; his lone presence
seemed only to emphasise the hollow emptiness all around, and
his shifting feet on the stones pealed like thunder. He greeted
the small party one by one as they disembarked. Then he led
them over the gravel into the church. And on their entry, as if
on cue, the sound of singing rippled through the nave. Matron
was bewildered. St Catherine's Church had no regular choir and

Mrs Webber's wishes had not called for one. But it was not only the singing that disturbed her. It was the colour of the sound. For even without looking, it was undeniably black, a fact confirmed when she dared look at its source and found a group of a dozen or so black men and women, dressed national, and singing likewise. Poor Matron shuddered with horror. She would have a word with the verger after the ceremony. The residents of The Hollyhocks were likewise surprised, and in varying degrees offended. But they did not shudder. Rather they giggled behind their handkerchiefs, for the sight and the sound of the black hallelujahs were so at odds with the demure ever-so-white little Mrs Webber whom they had come to mourn.

'We've come to the wrong funeral,' Mrs Green whispered to Mrs Thackeray, and they giggled further.

Matron was of the same opinion and she couldn't understand how such a mistake had been made. She stared at the coffin and recognised the wreath that The Hollyhocks had donated out of Mrs Webber's leaving purse. But behind that wreath was another, one of many colours and draped across with a wide pink satin ribbon. On it some words were written, and Matron fumbled in her bag for her glasses, her hands trembling. She leaned forward, peering, and was able to decipher the legend, 'To Our Beloved Sister Elizabeth'. Then she was convinced they had come to a stranger's burial, for although Mrs Webber was called Elizabeth, she knew for a fact that she had no siblings and that she never was, and never had been a sister to anybody. She began to fear for her little envelope propped up on her desk ready for opening. She was confused, as were the others, some of whom had read the satin ribbon, and wondered. She decided that she would wait until the preacher confirmed that some black Elizabeth lay in that box and she would then shepherd her flock into the courtyard and make arrangements with the verger to redeem their wreath.

The preacher entered the pulpit and his first words caused Matron's knees to tremble.

'We are come here,' he thundered, 'to celebrate the life of Elizabeth Webber, who, all of that life, gave unstinted and generous service to the oppressed and the deprived.'

'Rubbish,' Matron muttered under her breath. What nonsense was the man talking? Did Mrs Webber have a secret life, hidden from The Hollyhocks, in which she disposed this so-called service of hers? She felt a rage seethe inside her, not only out of fear of the envelope, but because she'd been hoodwinked by Mrs Webber's seeming indifference to anything that occurred outside The Hollyhocks. It's true she went out occasionally, to a church meeting, she always said, or to see an old friend. The preacher was droning on about Mrs Webber's good works and virtuous being, and Matron began to dislike her. By the time he called upon a Mr Ebenezer Obadiah to sing her praises, she hated Mrs Webber with a passion.

Mr Obadiah peeled himself off from the choir of which he was the obvious leader. He was large of girth, and walked slowly, though as Matron reluctantly admitted to herself, with great dignity. He took his stand in front of the whiter-than-white congregation and gave a loud 'Hallelujah' for starters. 'We come here to mourn the passing of our dear sister Elizabeth,' he said.

At this point, the residents' giggling was more than audible and threatened to erupt into something far less excusable. For a giggle could be construed as an hysterical outburst of grief, whereas out-and-out laughter was attributable to nothing except comedy and delight. Matron willed them to control themselves and to save their laughter for the wake.

Mr Obadiah was slowly itemising the good works that his sister Elizabeth had performed and they consisted mainly of donations of large sums of money to the Society for the Advancement of Coloured Peoples. Matron thought of the envelope and her stomach curdled.

When the praises were over, Mr Obadiah rejoined his choir
and together they jazzed the coffin into the dust. The residents
were anxious to leave the church, to find some quiet open-air
corner to give vent to their suppressed laughter, but on re-
entering the courtyard, they found nothing funny any more.
Their laughter had soured into fury that for so many years they
had all been taken for a ride. And there was none more furious
than Matron.

'She was a dark horse all right,' Mrs Green said to Mrs
Thackeray, while she trembled at the thought that there was no
darker horse than she herself.

'Let's go home and have a party,' Matron said, not caring to
lower her voice, and she shepherded her flock on to the bus.

On the way back to The Hollyhocks, the residents began to
hum softly to themselves, but as the bus gathered speed the
humming shamelessly crescendoed into a rowdy sing-song. 'Ten
Green Bottles', led by Jeremy Cross, the doyen of survivors,
and who would be, God willing, the very last bottle to fall.

They went straight into the dining room where the fake-wake
had been prepared. All except Matron, who hurried to her
office. The funeral was over, thus legalising the opening of the
envelope. But her hopes and expectations had dimmed, and she
tore it open with little loving and less anticipation. There were
two sheets of paper, one appearing to be a document, and the
other a covering letter.

She read the letter first.

'Dear Matron,' it said. 'Out of courtesy I am sending you a
copy of my will which is lodged with my solicitor. I want to
take this opportunity to thank you for the wonderful care you
have given me in the last few years of my life. I cannot praise
you highly enough. My heartfelt gratitude and kindest regards,'
[signed] Elizabeth Webber.

The letter had been typed, and signed in Mrs Webber's spi-
dery hand. After all that gratitude, Matron's hopes rose once

more, and she allowed a pause before turning to the document. She skipped the paragraphs of legal jargon that introduced the core of Mrs Webber's last will and testament. There was only one legatee. The Society for the Advancement of Coloured Peoples. Matron spat on the paper. 'You little nigger-loving pig,' she whispered, as her eyes watered over the name of Mr Ebenezer Obadiah. 'My good friend and Chairman of the Socicty will administer the funds according to his great wisdom.'

Matron's hands were trembling as she crunched the papers into a furious ball and threw them into the wastepaper basket. 'I'll tell on her,' was her first reaction. 'I'll tell everybody how ungrateful she was.' But she realised that there was no one to tell, else it would reveal her greedy expectations. May she rot in hell, she prayed. I shall drink to that. And drink my fill.

She joined the revellers in the dining room and took no offence at their ill-timed partying. For partying they were, having already drunk more than would prove good for them. At least the singing had stopped; Jeremy Cross himself had put an end to it. As the minibus had driven up The Hollyhocks' drive-way, there was still one bottle hanging on the wall, and Jeremy, seeing himself in that bottle, made it his business to keep it there.

Instead of singing, there was gossip. Unashamed, wine-fed tittle-tattle. Mr Obadiah was its subject, and speculation as to how Mrs Webber had met the big black man and what was the nature of their friendship. Matron caught up with their drinking and gossip, and in time thought to add to its spice by revealing the contents of Mrs Webber's will. Its telling dropped like a bombshell into the dining room. A silence followed, broken by Lady Celia with a great upper-class hiccup, for even she had drunk too much.

'What monstrous ingratitude,' she managed to say. 'After all you had done for her.'

Matron was delighted to have found an ally. Moreover the others chorused their inebriated agreement.

'Oh, I didn't expect anything,' Matron lied.

'If she had to leave her money to a good cause,' Mrs Green chipped in, 'she could at least have left it to our own people.' Then she took another drink to toast her own wisdom. And the others drank too, sharing her bigoted sentiments.

Matron warmed to them all. She raised her glass. 'Well, I shan't drink to Mrs Webber,' she said. 'Let Mr Obadiah make his own toast. I'm going to drink to us, to all of us in The Hollyhocks.'

There was a great cheer in the dining room and a clinking of glasses, and refill after refill to drown the spirit of the departed ingrate. When all the wine was imbibed, the residents tottered to their rooms, and their whirling beds, though it was not yet lunchtime. Matron too retired. As she weaved through reception, she bellowed into the empty hall, 'We're closed.' Then she giggled her way to her own quarters.

Lunch was not served that day at The Hollyhocks, and though dinner was prepared, few residents made the tables. It was not until breakfast on the following morning that they reassembled, all of them with a monumental thirst and looking very much the worse for wear. And though it was on account of Elizabeth Webber that they had so splendidly partied, it was her name that they now cursed for their hangover, and what little conversation there was at breakfast centred solely on the selfishness and ingratitude of their late resident. But the subject would quickly exhaust itself, and by dinnertime Mrs Webber had been truly buried and forgotten. It was time to enquire of Matron whether she had chosen the Hollyhock who would replace her.

Matron was glad of this opportunity to introduce the name of her choice. She would make no apology for it, but at the same time, if called upon, she would validate it.

'Her name is Mrs Miriam Feinberg,' she began. Here Matron paused. She had said enough, she thought, to elicit some reaction. The name, after all, was hardly white Anglo-Saxon Protestant. No one spoke, but most eyebrows were raised. Surprise was a reaction of sorts, and a silent one at that, which did not necessarily entail racial overtones. The silence was followed by a general sigh as all residential hangovers evaporated at the sound of a name which had such a sobering effect.

'Where is she from?' Lady Celia asked when she had recovered her breath.

'Vienna,' Matron practically sang. 'The city of the waltz,' she continued. 'She's continental,' she insisted, omitting to mention that Mrs Feinberg was a naturalised British citizen and had been for nigh on fifty years. But for Matron, she had to remain 'continental'; such a provenance had a louder and clearer ring of class than 'naturalised'.

'How old is she?' Jeremy Cross asked hopefully.

'That is not a question you ask of a lady,' Mrs Thackeray silenced him.

'We'll be having Mr Obadiah next,' Mrs Green whispered, and the two ladies giggled behind their hands.

'I want you all to make her welcome,' Matron said, and added, 'As you always do of course,' not wishing to single out Mrs Feinberg for any special attention.

After dinner that evening, most of the residents withdrew to the lounge for coffee. Mrs Thackeray and Mrs Green nestled in the corner, and between them they picked at the bones of all blacks and continentals. The two women were delighted to bask in each other's prejudices.

'Was it in Edinburgh you said you were born?' Mrs Thackeray asked, wishing to broaden the limits of their talk.

'Yes,' Mrs Green said, and with such little hesitation and so loudly that Mrs Thackeray suddenly didn't believe her.

'I've never been there myself,' she said, and Mrs Green was

relieved that she would be excused from sharing an Edinburgh experience.

'And you?' she asked, happy to change the location.

Mrs Thackeray had been born in Croydon, but she chose Hampstead in London for her birthplace since nowhere in Croydon was a single street that could lay any claim to class. In any case, Hampstead she thought, was as fictitious as Edinburgh and if Mrs Green wished to play a lying game, it would be discourteous to deny her a partner. After those first patent lies, the relationship between the two women moved into a very different orbit: that of fantasy. Each woman had high hopes of the other, for each would provide a willing ear to the other's invention. Thus Mrs Thackeray would recall a wonderfully happy marriage, and Mrs Green, her spotless young womanhood. In time they might even come to believe in their fables themselves.

It was past midnight when they bid each other good night and risked a peck on each cheek as token of their unspoken conspiracy.

Four

It was mid-morning. A quiet time in The Hollyhocks, and Matron was waiting in reception to welcome her token Jew. She was determined to make a fuss of Mrs Feinberg, to show her all manner of kindnesses and resist the temptation to pat her on the head. She heard the taxi draw up on the driveway and she went on to the porch to begin her welcome. She watched as Mrs Feinberg climbed down from the cab; she noted her attire. A neat tweed suit and a string of pearls around her neck as her only ornament. Her shoes were sensible brogues. She looked 'expensive', but less 'continental' than Matron would have

wished though she was not sure in her own mind what 'continental' meant in matters of style. The woman looked one
hundred per cent English and less 'token' than Matron had
intended, but she was relieved when Mrs Feinberg spoke, for
her accent was undeniably foreign. Her grammar was perfect
and she was not short of vocabulary, yet both were alien to her
mother tongue and country.

'You must be tired,' Matron said, taking one of her bags,
though Mrs Feinberg had travelled only the fifty or so miles
from London. But it seemed the right thing to say. It was
always the right thing to say to an ageing person, Matron
thought. They *ought* to be tired. 'I'll show you to your room,'
she said.

As they crossed the reception area, Jeremy Cross came out of
the lounge. He threw a deeply disappointed glance at Mrs
Feinberg, finding her far too healthy-looking for his liking, but
through that look, he managed to filter a smile. He took the case
from her hand.

'Let me help you,' he said.

'This is Mr Cross,' Matron offered.

'How do you do?' Mrs Feinberg put out her hand. Mr Cross
took it and put it to his lips. He thought that the gesture was
Viennese and would remind the good lady of home. But
unknown to Mr Cross, Vienna was the very last place on earth
that Mrs Feinberg wished to be reminded of. For her part, she
wished the entire city bombed into oblivion together with its
Sachertorte inhabitants, and that its devastation would be orchestrated to the sickly music of a Strauss waltz. She hoped that Mr
Cross would not kiss her hand at their every meeting. They
trundled to her room, Matron leading the way. She had placed
an elaborate flower arrangement on Mrs Feinberg's table. Mrs
Feinberg remarked on it and expressed her gratitude. So had
that dreadful Mrs Webber when she had first arrived, Matron
recalled bitterly. Gratitude was not in the least dependable.

'I'll leave you to unpack,' Matron said. 'If you need help, just press that bell. We lunch at twelve-thirty.' She took Mrs Feinberg's hand. 'I hope you'll be very happy here,' she said.

'I'm sure I will.' Mrs Feinberg turned to open her cases. It was a signal for Matron and Mr Cross to leave the room. Unpacking was a strictly private pursuit. Matron always honoured that privacy until later, when the field was clear, and she could freely pry into Mrs Feinberg's belongings.

'Seems charming,' Mr Cross said on their way back to reception.

'The continentals have something. No doubt about it. Jewish?' he asked in a whisper.

'With a name like Feinberg?' Matron laughed.

'Well there's good and bad,' Mr Cross offered generously.

At twelve-thirty Matron knocked on Mrs Feinberg's door. 'Lunch is ready,' she called. She waited for Mrs Feinberg to emerge. She noted the cashmere twinset she was wearing, and the same string of pearls that she had already coveted on her arrival. Despite her get-up, Matron had no fear that the other residents would think she was English born and bred. Mrs Feinberg had only to open her mouth to declare her continental roots.

She led her into the dining room. All the residents were already seated and there was a sudden silence when they entered.

'This is our new resident,' Matron said. 'Mrs Feinberg.'

A murmured 'how d'you do?' waffled across the tables. The gentlemen residents half-rose from their chairs. All except Mr Cross who felt that, as a bag-carrier, he had already declared his courtesy. Matron sat Mrs Feinberg in Mrs Webber's now-vacant place. Next to her was Mrs Alison Hughes who could be relied upon to talk about her great-grandchild in the nursery down the road. A benign, uncontroversial topic.

As Mrs Feinberg sat down, Matron listed her residents by

name, going around the tables with a hand on each named shoulder. Mrs Feinberg nodded to each one, knowing that it would take time to equate name with shoulder.

'My name is Alison,' Mrs Hughes said. 'It's lovely here. You'll be very happy.'

'I hope so,' Mrs Feinberg told her. 'At the moment it's all a bit strange.'

'You'll get to know us.' Mrs Hughes was confident. 'In no time you'll feel at home.'

Mrs Feinberg scanned the tables. They looked a happy enough ensemble. She registered no particular face, but there was a common denominator to them all. That ripe, if not willing, availability to the scythe. As they were eating the hors d'oeuvre, Mrs Hughes launched into stories of her great-grandchild. In return, Mrs Feinberg offered her Miriam, only daughter of her only son, Mark. Matron noted their together-ness with pleasure. She expected no problems with her newest resident.

Over on Mrs Thackeray's table, the fantasy parade was well under way. It was Mrs Thackeray herself who was holding the stage with a monologue on the subject of her late husband. Suppressed were the whips and the smiles and the stains, and in their stead was a kindly caring of such magnitude that even Mrs Green suspected it was over the top. But as she listened, she smelt the odour of fantasy, and she was forgiving, for she knew that when her turn came, that same smell would flavour her own story-telling.

'He was a wonderful man. I do miss him so,' Mrs Thackeray was saying. 'He never missed a Friday without bringing me a bunch of roses.' A rose would do as a whip, she thought, and their smell would do for his sickly smile. 'And I've never known a *cleaner* man,' she reminisced, as she rinsed his trouser stains with disgust. 'He was so mindful of his appearance. Never a hair on his head out of place. I do miss him so,' she said once more, while in her heart she rejoiced that she would never have to set eyes on him again.

The look on Mrs Green's face was certainly an attentive one, but in her mind she was already fashioning her own fantasies and hoped that they would better Mrs Thackeray's in invention and plausibility.

'What about your late husband?' Mrs Thackeray was saying. She needed a rest from her fabrications. Lying could be a wearying pursuit, she thought, and required above all a good memory. She wondered how long she could sustain her falsehoods. But she was determined to persevere, for the truth was untellable.

'My husband was a very ordinary man,' Mrs Green began. She had never intended her spouse to be a subject of her fantasies. Her marriage contained nothing to hide, which accounted for the interminable dullness of their partnership. There had been nothing wrong with Mr Green. She did not dislike him. She was simply sorry for him and when he left her, she found it a relief that she no longer had to pity him.

'But what about *before* you were married?' Mrs Green asked, hoping in time to bring that same question around to herself.

This was truth ground for Mrs Thackeray and it was a relief to be released from invention. She recalled that she had lived in Hampstead, and thus she set her schooling there. In this subject, the location was her only invention. Then truth was allowed free rein and as truth, it was easily related. It took little time; in essence, it was faintly dull.

'I was at school in Hampstead,' she began. Then in her mind she settled on her real school in Croydon and found she could recall it in surprising if monotonous detail. 'I left school as soon as it was legal,' she said, 'and I didn't do anything until I got married. What about you?'

It was the question Mrs Green had been waiting for. 'Well after school in Edinburgh, I went to a finishing school in

Switzerland.' She paused to allow Mrs Thackeray a moment of envy, but also to cobble together a few details to ornament her invention. 'It was a lovely school. Just girls you know, and I made some good friends there.'

Mrs Thackeray listened as Mrs Green itemised the school's curriculum and elaborated on the joy and excitement of social events. And as she droned on, she heard it all and listened less, as she began to equate her friend's Switzerland with her own Hampstead, each place located in never-never land. Still, she understood Mrs Green's ploy as Mrs Green must surely understand hers. As long as neither verbally rumbled the other, it was a game that could go on for ever.

Over on Lady Celia's table, there was a silence. No one would engage in conversation as long as the Lady held her tongue, but she, poor soul, was still too ashamed of her fake-wake hiccup to favour discourse. There was quiet too on Mrs Hughes' table. It seemed that she and Mrs Feinberg had exhausted great-grandchildren talk. As the dessert was served, 'We take coffee in the lounge,' Mrs Hughes broke the silence, hoping that a change in location would engender conversation.

But if not conversation, the lounge did indeed bring a change. Mrs Feinberg sat on the armchair that Mrs Hughes indicated at her side, from which vantage point the new resident could have a more comprehensive view of the company she would keep for the rest of her life. For the first time she could see their legs, which hitherto had been hidden by tablecloths. Many were elasticated-bandaged and some tailed into slippers. 'I'm in an old people's home,' she suddenly realised and it saddened her. But there was something else. Something indefinable but very disturbing. As she looked around the room, a feeling of unease overcame her. She drank her coffee quickly, then excused herself, pleading fatigue after her journey. When she reached her room, she lay on her bed hoping to sleep, unwilling to examine the nature of her distress. She'd had moments like this before, usually in crowded places, a shopping mall, a theatre or concert hall; she'd ascribed them to an allergy to crowds. But there was nothing crowded about The Hollyhocks. She could not understand her unease; rather than deal with it, she lay on her bed and switched on the television and found a nature programme that mercifully took her mind off the problem she had no idea of how to solve.

Downstairs in the lounge, Mrs Hughes had suddenly become very popular. On the whole, the other residents avoided her. They were irritated by her supreme contentment, by her endless and repeated stories of her boring great-grandchild and the love and loyalty of her whole family. Avoiding her was one way of getting to grips with their own envy. Now they drew their chairs around her, anxious for her Mrs Feinberg titbits, since she was the only one who had gathered information. But Mrs Hughes could tell them little, apart from one son and one granddaughter. She had forgotten their names, so she quickly took the opportunity to remember the name of her own great-grandchild and she embarked on yet another already-told story of the child's nursery wisdom, as slowly the chairs were drawn back to where they had come from. She prattled on alone, while others watched her. She's senile, they chose to think, which thought took the edge off their envy. But Jeremy Cross watched her with no envy at all. Rather with hope, as he envisaged her name on the back of his wardrobe door.

Matron appeared in the doorway. 'A visitor for Lady Celia,' she said.

Lady Celia half rose to greet her guest, but Matron would save her the trouble, because she wanted to announce the visitor by name, so that all Hollyhocks residents would note that their home was a place to be reckoned with.

'Lady Priscilla Waterson,' she announced, as a major domo might call out a name across a crowded ballroom. Nevertheless, Lady Celia did rise to greet her friend and quickly ushered her out of the lounge to curtail her obvious embarrassment. But Matron had made her point. She had proved beyond a shadow of doubt that The Hollyhocks had class.

Once settled in her room, Lady Celia was full of apologies.

'I'm so sorry you were embarrassed,' she said. 'She had no right to land you amongst total strangers. But why have you come, my dear? We agreed long ago that we should not be seen together.'

'I had to come,' Lady Priscilla said. 'I couldn't tell you on the phone. I don't trust that Matron of yours, despite our code. And we're not due to meet for almost a month.' She paused. 'We're in trouble my dear,' she said.

With Lady Priscilla, Lady Celia could let her guard down, as both could in their secret monthly meetings in London. Though their titles were genuine enough, they had no need to live up to them, and they could behave like the pair of full-time and incorrigible crooks that they were.

'What trouble?' Lady Celia asked. She was not over-worried. Their little business was practically foolproof. In any case, since her retirement to Hollyhocks, she was but a sleeping partner, going up to London only once a month to check on the books. If there were problems, she could always plead a coma of total ignorance.

It had all started some years before, when Lord Suckling was still alive. She knew that now. But it was not until he died that she found out. He'd been buried for less than a week when she had received a visit from one Mr Swinton who, with little ceremony, informed her that she was in his debt, and at her own peril should she refuse to settle. With even less ceremony, he detailed the nature of that debt. The late Lord Suckling, he told her – my heartfelt sympathy, my lady – had enjoyed a long and somewhat kinky relationship – that was a word that Lady Celia would have to look up in the dictionary when he was gone – a very kinky relationship, he repeated with a sly smile, with a lady of dubious repute, and even more dubious colour, who lived in Streatham. He, Mr Swinton, had discovered this relationship, and had duly reported it to his boss, who, as guardian of public morals, felt it his bounden duty to profit by it. It was part of his business to do so. A blackmailing business, Mr Swinton had added without shame. And if she, Lady Celia, wished to protect her late husband's name, which as a dutiful widow he was sure she would most eagerly, then the payments were weekly, without leeway. Lady Celia had paid up, week after week after week. She was mindful of her reputation in society and that of her late adultering husband. Then mercifully Mr Swinton's boss died and the business died with him. Lady Celia was now freed from her reluctant obligations. But over the weeks, she had nurtured an amicable acquaintance with Mr Swinton, debt-collector, who, as it turned out, was the ferret in the business. And indispensable. It was he who nosed the fringes of high society social gatherings, who licked steam off double-glazed windows, who followed his prey through London streets, who draped lampposts the night long, his telephoto lens at the ready. 'We're only interested in those who have too much to lose,' he had said, 'career, marriage, business, repute, preferably all of them. Every high-flying gent has a skeleton in his cupboard. It's a good business,' he had added.

Lady Celia thought so too. The business needed no premises. It could be run from her own home; it required no great investment. But best of all, she had the ferret. And he had the nose and the contacts. She offered him a generous cut of the profits. They shook hands on the agreement, and over a sweet sherry, the Suckling blackmailing business was launched. She considered it a fitting monument to her husband as well as a kind of revenge.

Lady Priscilla was also a widow and a close friend of long standing. As such she was privy to Lady Celia's new vocation and when, through frailty, Lady Celia was obliged to enrol at

Hollyhocks, she had, in return for a considerable contribution, invited Lady Priscilla into partnership, though she herself could no longer be active. The arrangement worked well, and in the last three years of her sojourn at Hollyhocks the business had thrived, and all three participants had made their little pile. From time to time, the ferret took a sweet sherry in Lady Priscilla's drawing room.

'What is so terrible that you had to come and see me?' Lady Celia asked again.

'The ferret was mugged,' Lady Priscilla said.

'Oh how terrible,' Lady Celia sighed, though she could see no reason why a mugging should disturb their commerce, unless of course he was seriously injured in the attack. 'Is he all right?' she asked.

'Oh yes, he's fine. Just a bit shaky. But they took his camera.'

'Was it loaded?'

'I'm afraid it was. With Lord Popple.'

'That's trouble,' Lady Celia said. 'You were right to come. But let's not panic. What photos had he taken?'

'He actually had him in bed. Face up. Full frontal. With the girl's head buried in his nether parts. The ferret said the look on Lord Popple's face left one in no doubt as to what the girl was doing.' Lady Priscilla could not suppress a giggle, and Lady Celia joined her.

'So he is recognisable,' Lady Celia said.

'It could be no one else, I'm afraid. So the ferret said.'

Lord Popple was a new blackmailee. On the basis of reliable hearsay, the ferret had been shadowing him for weeks. He was a government spokesman in the House of Lords, a virtuous chairman of sundry charities, a pillar of the Establishment; Lord Popple had a great deal to lose. So he was fair game, and those photographs were the first hard evidence that would entail the weekly payment of hush-money. It was a great loss.

'Let's not panic,' Lady Celia said. 'What is the worst that

can happen? The muggers can get the film developed. They could go into the blackmailing business themselves. But that would be risky. They would have exposed themselves to whoever developed the film. It would be more likely that they would throw away the film and keep the camera. We're not in trouble at all,' Lady Celia concluded. 'Nobody can trace anything to us. Nor even to the ferret. And he wouldn't squeal anyway. We're in the clear, my dear. At worst we've lost a client. And we must now lay off Lord Popple. Leave him alone. Absolutely alone. We can't afford a possible competitor.'

'Oh I feel so much better now,' Lady Priscilla said. 'But you know what a worrier I am.'

'We have to replace his camera of course. We have to be grateful that he wasn't injured,' Lady Celia said. 'We couldn't do any business without him.' Then as an afterthought, 'He didn't report it to the police, did he?'

'No,' Lady Priscilla said. 'Of course not. We can't afford to involve the law.'

'Well done,' her friend said. 'Now we'll drink to our luck. Because luck it is.'

She went to her private cabinet and brought out a bottle of whisky. 'Here's to all skeletons in all cupboards,' she laughed, raising her glass, and the two friends drank to their future profits.

Downstairs in the lounge, Mrs Green was wallowing in the social whirl of her Swiss finishing school and Mrs Hughes was whispering to her great-grandchild in the nursery down the road. Up in her room, Mrs Feinberg could not concentrate on the nature programme. Her sense of unease frightened her, and she wondered whether her mind was on the turn.

Five

It was close to Christmas. Of all the residents, only Mrs Hughes was offered an alternative to The Hollyhocks for the celebrations. As always, she would spend the time with her daughter and sundry offspring, and return in the new year with new Minnie stories whether the residents liked it or not. But this year Mrs Feinberg too would go on leave. Being Jewish, she was not too concerned with the birthday of the Saviour, and though she liked the tunes of most of the carols, she was uneasy with their lyrics. Matron fully understood. In fact she over-understood with an understanding that bordered on racism.

'Of course it's not meant for your kind,' she said and she all but patted Mrs Feinberg on the head. The other residents did not take Mrs Feinberg's leave as kindly. They were used to Mrs Hughes' absence each Christmas. In any case it was a relief to be rid of her for a while. Now their envy spread to Mrs Feinberg who not only had a family to go to, but one that wanted her.

'I do think it shows a lack of respect,' Mrs Green said, 'to ignore one of our most holy festivals.' And she spoke for them all.

'Well at least that saves us a present,' Lady Celia said.

They set about decorating the Christmas tree. There were already many wrapped gifts on the floor and one could tell without looking inside them that they were a warehouse of bedsocks and jackets. These seemed to be the standard Christmas gifts in old people's homes, and the residents would have to live many ageing lifetimes to wear them out. Most long-term residents had a special chest for those things that they would never wear again, those that reminded them of happier and younger days that they could not bear to discard. And on top of that pile lay the bedsocks and jackets, some only half-opened and many no doubt by now moth-eaten. But there was something different this Christmas. Underneath the tree lay a pile of unexpected parcels, clearly from one source for they were wrapped in identical silver paper. Mr Cross was the first to notice them, and boldly sifted them, seeking the name of the donor.

'They're all from Mrs Feinberg,' he said.

There was a shamed silence in the room and a general look of disgust was turned on Mrs Green who had spoken so ill of their surprising benefactor. In silence they hung the remaining lights on the tree, a silence which was not broken until Mrs Green expressed remorse.

'I was hasty,' she said, 'and I'm very sorry.'

Then the odd compliment was insincerely paid to their newest resident and speculation began as to what the parcels could contain. No one hoped aloud that they were not bedsocks, since those had been their personal contribution to the tree, but all hoped that Mrs Feinberg had been original. From the look of the parcels, and the feel of them – only Mr Cross dared the latter – the gifts were certainly harder than bedsocks and they were identical. At least she had shown no favouritism.

'I can't wait to open mine,' Mrs Primple said. 'Perhaps I'll sneak a little peep.'

Mrs Primple was the longest-stay resident at The Hollyhocks. This was her seventh Christmas there. She was very much an outsider in the home, keeping herself to herself. She rarely opened her mouth or mixed with the other residents. She even kept her own single table in the dining room. Over the years she had been accepted as the silent one, so it was surprising that she offered speech at all, much less such a risqué declaration. It pointed to Primple depths that no one had ever dreamed of. Suddenly there was a curiosity about Mrs Primple about whom, over the years, the residents had gleaned nothing. By wishing to open her present before Christmas, and possibly going as far as to do it, she had revealed herself as 'naughty' and they began to wonder what little tricks she was up to within her intense privacy. For the first time, Mrs Primple became a target for silent speculation. They would wait for her to retire to her room before voicing their surprise at this sudden window on a hidden character. They didn't have to wait long for Mrs Primple spent most of her days in her own quarters, a room which no one had ever visited. They wondered what she was up to. But they could wonder away. For nobody knew. Not even Matron. Mrs Primple had made sure of that. On entering the home, she had insisted on her own telephone, that is, on her own private line, for she wanted no eavesdropping on her hobby. That was how she liked to think about it. And a hobby it certainly was in her pre-Hollyhocks days. But now, and over the last seven years, that one-time pastime of hers had become an obsession. For Mrs Primple was hooked on chat lines. When she was not eating in the dining room, or taking an obligatory after-dinner coffee in the lounge, she was cosily ensconced at the desk in her room cradling the telephone receiver in her hot little hand communing over the wires with exciting anonymity. Sometimes, depending on the nature of the callee, she would lie on her bed, stretching the phone cord to its generous limit. Over the years she had tasted the flavours of various numbers. She knew exactly what number to dial if she wanted a good, honest and straightforward friendly chat. But if she wanted innuendo or *double entendre*, there were other numbers she could dial, and these calls she would make while lying in bed. Mrs Primple enjoyed her life immensely. With her little hobby she had no need of fleshly company. No need of the tedious and repetitive talk of the old codgers in the downstairs lounge. No need to listen to their groans and their moans, their ill-concealed malice and bigotry. For in their dull company, she had to be the woman they took her for; eighty-six years old, and like themselves a candidate for the scythe. Whereas in her room, at the end of her phone, she could be anybody. And since she could disguise her voice – she had been active in amateur dramatics as a young woman – she could be of any age, and sometimes even of either gender. She could have fun playing a young boy to an older woman on the end of the line, and occasionally a young girl, hoping for a young man's favour. There was no end to the roles she could play and indeed no time limit, as her quarterly telephone bill testified. It was astronomical. But Mrs Primple was not short of money, and she knew that to spend it in this fashion served sensibly to enhance the life-quality of her remaining years.

Sometimes it was a risky business. But the risk sharpened her pleasure. Once, while lying on her bed, she had been explicitly propositioned by the gentleman on the other end of the line. He had wanted her address so that he could call on her and make good his telephonic promises. Mrs Primple had flushed deeply and hastily replaced the receiver, and as quickly made a note never to call that number again.

Downstairs in the common lounge, they had soon run out of Mrs Primple guesswork. No one of them could come up with any suggestion of Primple tricks so they became cross, first with each other, and then with Mrs Primple herself because over all the years she had not given them a single clue. Then their irritation spread to cover Christmas in general, for despite the promise of tinsel and holly, and drinks and turkey, and especially the bread sauce of which all of them were inordinately fond, despite all the trimmings, they had finally to accept that Christmas was a bloody miserable time with its annual talent to evoke the past, and better and younger days. In desultory fashion, they continued to tinsel-drape the tree, until one of them, Miss Bellamy, who had never in her life had family, and who knew nothing of her own siring, the gentle Miss Jennifer Bellamy, eighty years old, who all her life had given no one any trouble, chose that very moment to blow her top. She was seen to clutch at the organised tinsel at the top of the tree, and its red needles pierced her hands and fingers, and she thrust herself bodily into the tree itself so that it toppled a little with astonishment. Her nose landed on a plastic figure of a manger Saviour and she plucked it from its fir sheathing and held it before her as her eyes gathered venomous tears.

'Fuck you,' she screamed at the plastic. Then turning to her astonished audience, 'And fuck you too. All of you. Fuck, fuck, fuck,' and a rogue tone of joy crept into her voice as she cursed them with a word, repeated over and over again, a word which she had never in her life used before, and of whose meaning she certainly had never had experience. Perhaps she was now bent on making up for lost time, if not with the thing itself then with the terrible word that hallowed it, and as her screams faded she whispered the word, over and over again, that gentle mono-syllable that slowly climaxed into silence. Then she fell exhausted and weeping on to the floor.

The other residents stared at her for a while, all tingling with survivors' relish, and they thought that what with Mrs Feinberg's unexpected presents, and the even more unexpected Mrs Primple give-away, and now the Bellamy bedlam, it promised to be a merry Christmas after all.

'I'll call Matron,' Jeremy Cross said after a while.

They all knew that something had to be done, and that only Matron could do it. The situation called for some figure in authority, and when Matron rushed into the room carrying a blanket, a general sigh was heard in the lounge, a sigh that was a mixture of relief that poor Miss Bellamy was to be seen to, and a sadness that the show was undeniably over.

Matron knelt down beside Miss Bellamy and covered her with a blanket.

'I'd like you all to go to your rooms,' she said. 'Wait for a moment while I ring the doctor.'

When she had gone, they circled the sobbing blanketed figure on the floor, like a school of vultures awaiting the moment of truth. All except Jeremy Cross who stood to one side, and sadly too. He knew that one didn't necessarily die of lunacy. He had known mad people in his time. Indeed, such a condition seemed to favour longevity, as if its sufferer had opened new windows on to his own soul, and entered new dimensions of thought, for which regions time would be given to accommo-date. Contrary to his usual habit, he was the first to leave the lounge, and the others slowly followed. Mrs Thackeray was the last to leave. She was troubled. She hadn't liked what she had seen, much less what she had heard, for she had to acknowledge that that terrible Bellamy word was the very same which thun-dered across her own nocturnal dreams. Indeed she had occasionally woken with the word on her loose and watering lips, and its sound promoted neither shame nor joy. Simply terror. She hurried to her room, wanting to escape into sleep, but she feared the dreams that would itch her slumber. She wondered if Mrs Green had dreams like hers, and whether all old people, unshackled from convention, were finally granted the freedom of filth, and whether that dire monosyllable was their own farewell to a life underlived.

When she reached the landing she heard the doctor's car in the driveway and she paused to watch his arrival. Matron greeted him in the hall, and led him straightaway into the lounge. She heard the door close and after that there was silence. She shuffled to her own room and sat on her bed, and then, astonishing herself, she began to cry.

They gathered once more at supper. They noted that Miss Bellamy's chair was empty and they were relieved that at least it had not been removed. The sight of it encouraged Mrs Thackeray to ask after Miss Bellamy's wellbeing. Matron assured them all that Miss Bellamy would be her usual self in the morning and she urged them to make no further reference to what she called Miss Bellamy's 'little turn'.

'It's not uncommon, such a breakdown,' Matron said, who had heard it chapter and verse from Mr Cross when he had fetched her. 'It passes,' she went on, 'and usually the sufferer has no memory of it. So let's all forget about it, shall we, and get on with our soup.'

The residents were surprised at their own appetites. But Matron had expected it and had ordered extra portions for their supper. Whenever there was a crisis in the home, those residents unaffected usually developed a craving hunger as a defying clutch after life. All of them had second soup helpings and had no problems putting away the meat course and dessert. After supper in the common lounge, Matron served their night drinks, and as a small reassuring bonus there was a glass of port for each of them. Then she played a record of gentle carols. It was only two days to Christmas, and time to get into the spirit of things. But despite the port and the carols, they each retired early to their rooms, with a slight envy of Miss Bellamy who was far more likely to forget her 'little turn' than they themselves.

As Matron had promised, Miss Bellamy showed up for breakfast as if nothing untoward had happened, and though there was a great temptation around the tables to jog her memory of the day before, they all held their tongues. They noticed that Matron had tidied up the tree, that the loose tinsel had been replaced and the debris swept away. And the offending infant Jesus had gone back to sleep in his plastic crib. With the lack of a shred of evidence of yesterday's turning, and the silence that now attended it, Mrs Thackeray began to suspect that she had imagined the whole episode, and that thought depressed her even further. She had little taste for breakfast, but Mrs Green at her side showed no loss of appetite. Mrs Thackeray gave her a sideways glance and was faintly appalled by the manner in which the woman was stuffing her mouth with such greed and relish. Within an instant their former intimacy curdled. She wondered whether the woman ever gave a thought to another than herself. From that moment she had begun to dislike her, and wondered how she had ever expected a friendship from such a cold uncaring creature. She recalled her marriage fantasies that she had offered her. That grand upstanding gentleman whom she had called husband. And she was ashamed. She wanted to tell Mrs Green to her face that all was lies. But she would not tell her the truth of the stains and whips and smiles. Mrs Green was not worthy of truth; she was even less worthy of invention and fantasy. And as far as her own fables were concerned, Mrs Green's that is, they showed little inventive skill, and her Swiss finishing school was clearly a dull daydream. She would drop her, she decided, in so far as it was possible to drop someone who slept and ate under the same roof. She stared at her chumping non-stop jaws, which ugly sight confirmed her decision.

'Brazen, I call it,' Mrs Green whispered, not even bothering to empty her mouth, and Mrs Thackeray winced at the sight of the mashed egg and toast below the gums. 'Sits there and behaves as if nothing has happened.'

'We're not supposed to talk about it,' Mrs Thackeray said.

'No one can hear,' Mrs Green whispered, her mouth still full.

'That doesn't matter,' Mrs Thackeray said firmly. 'I don't want to talk about it.'

Mrs Green went on chewing. She didn't seem to hear the finality of her neighbour's remark and if she did, she certainly didn't take it seriously. All that she cared about at that moment was her breakfast and perhaps that extra half of grapefruit that her neighbour didn't seem to be in need of. She fondled the fruit's yellowish-pink peel. 'D'you want this?' she said.

Mrs Thackeray roughly shoved her plate towards her, and swallowed her anger in a gulp of coffee.

That evening, for Christmas Eve, Matron had promised them a little carol concert. She asked the residents to dress in festive fashion to give dignity and honour to the occasion.

'I myself shall be wearing evening dress.'

Matron had never made such a suggestion before. She knew from inspections of her residents' luggage that each of them had packed a festive garment, packed carelessly in most cases, probably with little hope of wearing it ever again.

'Mary, our new kitchen maid, has kindly offered to do any ironing that you may wish.'

They dispersed shortly after breakfast. Mrs Thackeray declined Mrs Green's invitation to her room, possibly, unwhispered, to pursue the Bellamy affair. But Mrs Thackeray claimed she had letters to write. She could not yet bring herself to tell the woman that suddenly she could not bear the sight of her.

Mary was dispatched to each room in turn to collect the
dresses and shirts for ironing, and she returned to the kitchen,
only her legs visible. The rest of her was masked in a mountain
of lace and coloured taffeta that reeked of camphor.

The house was unusually silent that day. Few residents
appeared for lunch and none of them were women. Most of the
ladies had put their hair in curlers and did not wish to take
them out until the last moment, so they rang for trays in their
rooms without fear of the dire innuendo. But most of the men
took lunch in the dining room. They had no hair to curl and
little to do by way of preparation, except to wait for the return
of their ruffled shirts from the kitchen. Major William Carson,
usually a quiet-spoken man, with little to say for himself, and at
seventy-four the baby of The Hollyhocks, was suddenly talkative and jovial. He was deeply uneasy in the company of
women, preferring that of men whose presence could loosen his
tongue.

'Are we all ready then for tonight's festivities?' he boomed
across the table.

Some of the other men jumped at the sound and were
annoyed. They were too old to be startled. But Major Carson
was back at his beloved mess-table, an opportunity too rarely
offered to be missed.

'Are all the medals spat and polished?' he insisted.

Jeremy Cross spoke for them all. 'With respect, dear Major,
we're trying to eat our lunch,' he said.

But the Major chose not to hear. At the mess-table there was
always talk. Too much of it sometimes and the food was of sec-
ondary importance. 'I'm all for formal dress,' he said. 'It adds
tone, whatever the occasion.'

'I hope I'll still be able to get into mine. It's many years since
I wore it.' This from Eric Thurlow, a relatively new resident at
Hollyhocks and the most smartly dressed both at breakfast and
dinnertime. Little was known about him. His closest companion

at the home had been Mrs Elizabeth Webber and she had taken
his secrets to her grave along with those other dark secrets of
her own. It is possible that, in exchange for his confidences,
Mrs Webber had given him Mr Ebenezer Obadiah and all that
he stood for, but Mr Thurlow had kept his mouth firmly shut
since that farcical funeral. 'Ought to fit me still,' he was saying.
'I don't think my weight has changed that much.'

'I shall be wearing my kilt.' Coming from Jock MacPherson,
this was no surprise. Mr MacPherson was aggressively nation-
alist, and what he missed most at The Hollyhocks was
somebody to argue with. For not one of them could give a
damn whether Scotland had home rule or not and they couldn't
understand why he was so obsessed with it. He was not unlike
Mrs Hughes and her endless Minnie stories. Both residents
were supremely avoidable. 'Best thing about a kilt,' he droned
on, 'a pound or two here or there, won't make any difference to
the fit. A good fold-over and a generous choice of slots to
buckle in.'

'Well that's all of us fitted out,' Jeremy Cross said. 'Now
perhaps we can get on with our lunch.'

'You're not showing a great deal of Christmas spirit I fear,'
the Major said. 'Half the fun of dressing-up is talking about it.'
He gave a loud laugh, his idea of Christmas spirit. Mr Thurlow
echoed with a giggle in the name of comradeship. So did Mr
MacPherson, for the same reason, since he did not consider that
a show of Christmas cheer could diminish the cause of Scottish
home rule. Jeremy Cross, fearful of ostracism, was bound to join
in, and there followed a sustained if uneven laughter across the
tables. Then the Major, who saw no reason to follow Matron's
advice, took the plunge. 'Well I do hope that Bellamy woman
behaves herself this evening.' It was a signal to spill all the
tittle-tattle that had festered since Matron's injunction.

'A bit much, all that, I thought,' the Major went on. 'Didn't
you think so?' He invited their ready opinions.

'Such language from a woman,' Mr Cross said.

'From a man too,' the Major added. 'I would never have heard it round a mess-table.'

'You know what her problem is, don't you,' Mr MacPherson offered, all-knowing.

They all knew what poor Miss Bellamy's problem was, and again a giggle spread around the table. But someone had to spell it out. It was Mr Thurlow who put it into good and honest words. 'Never had one, you see. Never had a fuck in her life.' Mr Thurlow's articulation of the word gave licence of its use to anyone who wanted it. And each of the men wanted a turn and could not wait to put their filthy oars in. It didn't have to relate to poor Miss Bellamy. Mr Thurlow had uttered the word and they didn't need her as reference any more. The action of fucking had moved from the particular to the general. Its target was now irrelevant.

'That's the trouble with women.' Mr Cross's donation was the first. 'Especially this lot here. What they all need is you know what, and probably never had it.'

'A good fuck you mean,' Mr Thurlow said. He was afraid lest the good word slip away.

'A good fuck,' Mr MacPherson thundered with the enthusiasm he was wont to donate to a good home rule.

'And all those dykes out there.' Mr Cross broadened the discussion. 'What d'you think the matter is with them, for God's sake? It's a good fuck they need. Should be compulsory. But who'd want to give it to them?' he joked. 'I wouldn't touch one of them with a barge-pole.'

Mr Cross wasn't in a position to touch anyone, barge-pole or not. It had been many years since his stubborn member had performed. And the same could be said of the others around the table who were venting their spleen in exactly the same way as poor Miss Bellamy had done; all of them were simply shrieking the word as a sad alternative to its practice.

There was a silence then around the table as each of them realised how limited was the subject for discussion. Only the word itself mattered. Only the word could help.

'Fuck fuck fuck fuck,' said Mr MacPherson at last achieving as much orgasm as his age would allow, and all the others round the table echoed his pathetic coming. Then, breathless, they returned to their lunch. Not one of them would look at the other. It was Mr Cross who eventually broke the silence.

'Isn't it *nice* without the ladies,' he said. He spoke for them all.

Six

They gathered in the common lounge before supper. It was
the champagne hour, as befitted the occasion and the style that
dressed it. For it was certainly dressed, and immaculately.
The ladies with their ball gowns and hairdos were faintly
unrecognisable. The cardigans and slippers had been discarded. Bare shoulders were seen for the first time, and here
and there an unsteady high heel. And the jewellery blinded the
eye, and revealed secrets of wealth that were unknown before.
The belle of the ball was undoubtedly Lady Celia. She had
kept a slim figure, a talent reserved for a lady of the English

upper class, and she wore her long silk gown with the dignity
that the material and cut demanded. Around her neck hung a
cluster of diamonds matched by a bracelet that drooped over
her wrist.

A close second to Lady Celia was none other than she who
yesterday was known as 'poor Miss Bellamy'. Without her
habitual shawls and cardigans, she looked half her size, and
revealed a figure that equalled Lady Celia's. And possibly for
the same reason, for it was rumoured that, though labelled an
orphan, she was begotten in a grand house below stairs. She was
wearing black, but it was the black of elegance rather than
mourning. The absence of any jewellery only served to confirm
that elegance, but she wore a single red silk rose on her wrist.
The others stared at her. She was an enigma, that one. They
couldn't make her out. And the men were flummoxed. Her
appearance entirely negated their lunchtime assessments.
Contrary to all that they had assumed, Miss Bellamy looked as
if she'd spent all her life doing nothing else but fucking, and
enjoying every minute of it. They were very cross indeed.

There was no one among the ladies who took third place. It
seemed that all fell into that category; though far behind the
looks of Lady Celia and Miss Bellamy, it was still a fair placing.
They had concentrated on jewellery rather than frocks, for jewellery always fitted, indifferent to the ravages of time. On the
whole they wore taffeta and tulle, of a quality and making that
was never nowadays seen. Private-seamstress-made and many
many years ago, with the promise that the frock would last a
lifetime. As it had.

Matron too had dressed in her finery, though her jewels
were not of her character. They had clearly been left to her in
acts of resident-gratitude, or quite simply she had knocked
them off. She filled their glasses and they all stood for the toast.

'A happy Christmas to us all,' she said.

They drank, sipping at first at the unaccustomed beverage,

then with courage and enjoyment, draining the glass. A refill was required to toast to a good new year. Then Matron sat down giving the signal to all of them to seat themselves, which they were glad of, especially the ladies, whose heels were not made for standing.

'Now I shall ask the gentlemen to circulate a little,' Matron said after a while. Usually the men kept themselves to themselves, and the ladies likewise. But Matron thought that Christmas called for a change in the normal routine. As the gentlemen rose she placed their chairs between the ladies. She would have wished for a boy/girl, boy/girl circle but the shortage of men did not allow for that symmetry. Matron found herself together with three other ladies who had between them to share Mr Cross who had barely enough for one of them. He was not happy with his placing. He would have preferred to be next to Miss Bellamy, and have her all to himself, as would the other gentlemen, who that lunchtime had been so wide of the mark. But Miss Bellamy was saddled with Lady Celia with whom the only thing she had in common was haute couture.

After the second glass of champagne, Mary was called in from the kitchen. Matron had provided her with a special Christmas apron. She was thus festively dressed according to her standing. Matron handed her a glass.

'A merry Christmas to you Mary,' she said, singling her out, to the poor girl's deep embarrassment. She would much rather have had a straight gin in the kitchen. A general thanks was given to her for her careful ironing. Most had already pressed a mean coin into her hand on her delivery of their goods. In all she had made a mere six pounds for her labours, which she considered a poor acknowledgement of a hard day's work. Her mother, who had been in service all her life, had always told her that there was none more mean than the rich. She should not have expected more. She sipped at her champagne wondering what people saw in it, then she handed round the dish of canapés she had made after her ironing.

'She's a treasure that girl,' Matron whispered to Mrs Thackeray at her side.

'I hope she'll stay,' Mrs Thackeray said, but with little conviction. The turnover of kitchen maids at The Hollyhocks was rapid and regular. Matron could not have been easy to work for. Mrs Green came over to join them. She had not as yet noticed the sudden cooling-off of Mrs Thackeray's friendship, though to anyone even slightly more sensitive, it would have been very plain.

'How lovely everybody looks this evening,' she said. No one had as yet complimented her on her appearance, and she hoped that her general remark might elicit a more particular reference. But Matron simply agreed with her generality. 'You're right Mrs Green, everybody looks lovely.'

Mrs Green tried again. A direct hit at Mrs Thackeray. 'And you're looking absolutely beautiful,' she said.

Mrs Thackeray ignored her. 'We've run out of champagne I think,' she said.

'Then it's certainly time for supper,' Matron announced to the company. 'Take your partners into the dining room.' She took Mrs Thackeray's arm, and Mrs Green was obliged to take Matron's other, rather than be left on her own. 'There are place names tonight,' Matron said as they trooped down the corridor. 'Will you all look out for your own?'

There was a great 'Ah' as they entered the dining room. There was just one long table and a silver candelabra had been placed at each end. In the middle was a floral decoration of holly, ivy and mistletoe. There was a silver paper cracker at each setting, supporting a floral place-card. The residents stood at the door for a moment marvelling at the sight. Matron always went to town on Christmas celebrations. Starting in January, she put a little money by each month. Funding for the home was more than adequate and with creative accounting she could legitimately save for Christmas as well as, slightly less legitimately, creaming off something for herself.

Matron helped them to their placings. Mrs Thackeray was nervous that she might be seated next to Mrs Green, because Matron was under the impression that they were still close friends. But for Matron, this night was going to be different. Residents who rarely exchanged a single word were seated next to each other and by this token Mrs Thackeray found herself seated next to Miss Bellamy. She was mindful of Matron's injunction of the day before, and she scratched in her mind for some unloaded topic of conversation. 'The table looks beautiful,' she said. She hoped that such an observation would lead to an itemised catalogue of its beauty, which talk might keep them going for a while. But Miss Bellamy was not interested in the beauty of the table. Her elegant attire had tuned her into far less mundane topics. She turned and looked Mrs Thackeray straight in the eye. 'I gather I flipped yesterday,' she said.

'Flipped?' Mrs Thackeray played for time. It was a word she didn't know, but she could guess at its meaning. She feared that Miss Bellamy was about to undergo yet another 'little turn', that would release a lexicon of words unknown and rarely used. And all of them dangerous. 'Flipped' was a modern word, which would never have escaped Miss Bellamy's mouth while she was grey-cardiganed and slippered. Mrs Thackeray scrambled for safe ground. So she quoted Matron.

'You had a little turn,' she said.

'Is that what they called it?' Miss Bellamy laughed. 'Well it *was* a turn in a way. But a very *big* turn. I turned into my true self.'

Poor Mrs Thackeray didn't know how to respond. She should have enquired as to the nature of the 'true' Miss Bellamy, but she had gathered that from her language of the day before.

'D'you feel better today?' she asked timidly, though she knew that there was nothing better than the declaration of one's true self.

'I was never poorly,' Miss Bellamy said. Then mercifully she changed the subject. 'You're right,' she said. 'The table does look beautiful.'

Mrs Thackeray heaved a sigh of relief and began to itemise. The crackers, the linen napkins, the silverware and the pink candles. The list was short, and silence followed, a silence that had already settled on the table, prompted no doubt by the unusual seating arrangements. The women wanted to get back to the women, and the men to the men. Both were more comfortable with their own kind.

Supper was eaten in comparative silence. Remarks were passed on the fine quality of the food. Glasses were raised to no one in particular but as a simple gesture of good cheer.

'I'm looking forward to the carol concert,' Miss Bellamy suddenly broke the silence. Having made her declaration of truth, she was content to sink back into the mundane exchange of everyday Hollyhocks. The others offered their excited anticipation of the singing and the subject was quickly exhausted. The dessert was served and silently consumed.

'We'll take coffee in the lounge,' Matron said at last, and they followed her down the corridor, regrouping as they went, so that when they settled in their usual chairs, they were happily ensconced with their own kind and conversation got under way.

The carol singers arrived shortly after coffee. There were eight of them, equally gender-divided, from which ensemble the audience could expect descant and harmony. They were soberly dressed in what was clearly a professional uniform, the women in black skirts and white blouses and the same colours were translated into the men's attire. One of the women handed round copies of a small booklet containing the words of the carols they would be treated to.

'We hope you'll join in with some of the choruses,' one of the black and white women said, though she knew there would be little hope of that. She'd sung before in old people's homes and they didn't make the greatest of choruses. For the singing-tone was a reliable giveaway of age, which awareness held their crooning tongues.

They started with 'Away in the Manger'. The residents gave a sideways glance at Miss Bellamy for whom surely it must have been a painful reminder of her little turn. But Miss Bellamy was actually heard to hum along with the song, smiling a little, as if she had been vindicated. The sight of her gave the others courage to hum too. Humming was safer than singing and in any case it was by way of polite appreciation. Best of all, it was invisible. Neither was it audible enough to distort the harmonies of the professional group who seemed indifferent to the questionable counterpoint from the floor. But during the course of the next few carols, the audience became more daring, and by the time of 'We Three Kings', the humming had filtered nervously into song. It was clear they were all beginning to enjoy themselves.

After the 'Three Kings', Matron called for an interval. She didn't want things to get out of hand. In time her residents might drown out the choir entirely. She served a further round of coffee and invited the choir to join them. They accepted but kept themselves to themselves. Fraternisation was not part of their deal. The residents felt snubbed and resentful and perhaps it was this indignation that fired a belligerence and a determination to sing their hearts out after the interval.

But the second part of the concert began with a little-known carol, and though they had the words in their hands, they could not partake of the tune. Thus even humming was out of the question. Another little-known carol followed which sobered up the audience a little, though they had not entirely lost their appetite for a grand sing-song. With the third carol, the choir took a risk and launched into 'We Wish You a Merry Christmas'. The risk was ill-taken. The residents lost no time in joining in raucously and unharmoniously, so that by the end of the carol they were singing alone, the choir having earlier retired from what they accepted as a losing battle.

Here Matron stepped in. She was paying good money for this choir, and opposition or not, they were here to do a job. She tried to make light of it all, ascribing the jollity to the festive season – Christmas could be useful sometimes – then she had a quiet word with the residents, a word that could be seen but not heard. They started to clap which might or might not have signalled surrender, but either way it displayed a wish for the concert to continue. The choir broke into song and 'Once in Royal David's City' pealed through the common lounge. The residents, though familiar with the tune, and even the words, for they were schoolday words and thus most easily recalled, held their tongues even from humming, even when the temptation to give way to some kind of voice was unbearable. The choir smiled after their rendition, acknowledging the audience's decorum, and more carols were sung to a similar itching silence. Then came the final number and the choir-leader actually invited the residents to join in. 'Silent Night', the annual number one in the pop charts, would round off the evening. The residents braced themselves. They had no need to read from the booklet. Those words too echoed from school halls, not to mention the countless times they had heard it on celluloid, for there were few war films that did not include that carol of oddly German origin in times of Christmas truce. And then, as soon as the *heilige* or holy night was over, and the *stille* or silent night had passed, they could go back to beating the shit out of one another until the next Christmas.

There were tears in the Major's eyes as the song dribbled from his mouth in remembrance. Jeremy Cross, too, was tearstained, clearly dwelling in regions of survival. Lady Celia paid polite homage to World Wars One and Two, but beyond that it seemed none of her business. Jock MacPherson did not sing at all. His mouth might well have been clamped. He possibly thought that holy and silent nights did not bode well for Scottish home rule. But most vocal of all was Mrs Green, who not only joined in heartily, but did it in German. Her face was suffused with joyful memory. *Heilige Nacht* followed *stille Nacht* in holy pursuit and the other residents thought she was simply showing off. Mrs Thackeray was disturbed. She now thought it possible that Mrs Green *had* attended a Swiss finishing school after all, and the thought came close to spoiling her evening. She had to set her mind at rest, and when the concert was over she turned to Mrs Green whose reminiscent joy still glowed on her cheeks.

'I didn't know you spoke German,' Mrs Thackeray said.

Mrs Green's cheeks reddened even more. It could have shown guilt, Mrs Thackeray thought, or a deepening of joy.

'I learned it at finishing school,' Mrs Green said. 'I thought I told you.'

'You did,' Mrs Thackeray said. 'I must have forgotten.' Then she moved away to deal with her disappointment.

The choir took a glass of port before retiring and Matron was seen to press an envelope into the leader's hand.

When they had gone, conversation was lively once more.

'Tomorrow is the big day,' Matron said. 'In the morning we shall have breakfast and then we shall open our presents. Dinner will be at five o'clock so there will be plenty of time for a siesta.' Matron fancied a foreign expression from time to time. Café au lait was another of her favourites and haute couture another, though there was rarely a call for the latter. She laughed at her little joke and the others joined her.

'For a siesta I shall need a hammock,' Mr Thurlow said. Apart from a smattering of carol, those were the only words he had uttered the whole evening.

'I'll see what I can do for you,' Matron said. Then she bade them all good night. It had been a good evening, she thought to herself as she made for her quarters. She had already managed to make quite a sizeable profit on her Christmas funding.

The residents retired shortly afterwards, Mr Cross as usual bringing up the rear.

Seven

It was cardigan and slipper attire for breakfast the next morning, with conversation to match, though there was little of it, for they were anxious to open their presents and especially to discover what Mrs Feinberg had been generous enough to offer. When the meal was over, they waited for Matron to lead them into the common lounge. Her presence was necessary, for out of the funds she had given gifts to everybody, and she hoped to receive as many herself. When they were all settled, she stood beside the tree and picking up the parcels, she read out the name on each label. She had decided to save Mrs Feinberg's packages till last. Even she did not know what they contained. But she knew that each resident had received one, including herself. Thus she knew that they were not bedsocks for she was not yet ready for such a gift. She left the pile at the side of the tree while the residents were opening their other presents. A chorus of 'Oh how lovely, thank you very much, very kind, just what I wanted,' wafted across the lounge as bedsock followed bedsock out of its wrapping and slipper after slipper. All were promptly rewrapped for consignment to that might-come-in-handy drawer. When they were done, they eyed the remaining packages under the tree, and Matron stepped forward to do her duty. She handed them out one by one, but no one started to unwrap. It would have looked like stealing a march on a communal surprise. When everybody was in receipt of their present, they looked at each other, knowing that the unwrapping would be a slow process, and none of them wishing to take the responsibility for the very first discovery. But by some miracle all contents were revealed at the same time. A white square box was the first to show itself, a box that was opened simultaneously around the circle. Inside was a wodge of addressed white postcards of the finest paper. At the head, the address of The Hollyhocks was given, together with the telephone number. But above all that was inscribed the name of the sender. A personalised present for each one of them.

The discovery was greeted in silence. Their feelings were confusedly mixed, ranging from pure delight, through bewilderment to bitter resentment. So wide a range that only silence could cover it. There were those who were in awe of the sheer expense of the gift, and for the moment that awe precluded any other reaction. But there were those who bypassed the awe, unimpressed by the cost, and who found the gift faintly offensive. For what purpose could it be used? To whom could they write, 'How are you?' or 'Thank you for your visit', or 'How kind of you to remember my birthday' or 'Many thanks for your invitation'. To whom could they write anything at all? The wounds of loneliness and isolation were painful enough without Mrs Feinberg's sprinkling of a pinch of salt. Nobody said anything, but all of them slowly rewrapped the gift knowing that of all the contents of their might-come-in-handy drawers, Mrs Feinberg's gift was the most improbable.

Not so Miss Jennifer Bellamy, who did not rewrap at all. She stroked the package on her lap and was seen to smile. She would put at least one of the cards to good use. Shortly afterwards she slipped out of the room unseen and, cardiganed and slippered, she shuffled her way to her own quarters. Once inside, she sat at her desk and extracted a white vellum envelope from underneath the printed cards. In the desk drawer, she found a book of stamps, untouched since her arrival at Hollyhocks in the less hopeless days of five years before. She did not know whether those old stamps were still valid, so to cover herself she stuck three of them on to the envelope, which she then proceeded, in her best writing, to address.

'TO WHOM (IF ANYBODY) IT MAY CONCERN', she wrote. Then she took one of the cards and proudly read her name aloud above the address. She used a different pen for her message, a red-inked biro. And on the card, in capital letters, she wrote 'HELP'. Then she slotted the card into the envelope and sealed it with a certain satisfaction. She did not bother to change her slippers, but walked in them to the post-box on the corner of The Hollyhocks' drive. With no hesitation, she dropped the letter into the box.

When she returned to her rooms she sat calmly on her bed. In her mind, she saw the little envelope nestling in the box. On top of it would fall less urgent messages, messages of thanks, of joy, and expressions of hope, all of them too light to outweigh the urgency of her own. She was satisfied. Miss Jennifer Bellamy would not bother to wait for a reply.

Eight

What a mess she had made. Matron was furious. Who would have thought that the frail Miss Bellamy would have had so much blood in her? The bedding was blood-soaked, as was the mattress, and the carpet would never see Axminster again. It was Mary, the new kitchen maid, who had found her. Miss Bellamy had not appeared for Christmas dinner and Matron had sent Mary to fetch her. They were taking their seats around the table when the screaming was heard. A curdling cry that stopped them in their tracks, as if the music had suddenly cut out in a game of musical chairs.

'What's that?' they said in chorus.

'I'll see to it,' Matron said. 'Now sit down all of you. Major, will you pour the wine? I'm sure it's nothing to worry about.' She hurried from the room.

She knew it was not nothing. Far from it. Mary was not an hysterical girl. There must have been good reason for that horrendous cry. She hurried to Miss Bellamy's room. The door was open and Mary was crouched on the floor outside, shivering. Matron did not need to ask what was the matter. She saw the whole matter, or what was left of it, from the threshold.

'Jesus,' she cried in unconsciously seasonal fashion. Then, 'Get up girl,' she said roughly. She didn't mean to be cruel to Mary but Mary was the nearest target for her sublime rage. For sublime it was. Miss Bellamy had no right to do what she had done. And if she had to do it, she could have done it elsewhere. But not at Hollyhocks. Nothing could give an old people's home a worse name than a suicide on its premises. Whatever could she tell the governing board? She looked at what was left of Miss Bellamy. 'I'll kill you,' she muttered under her breath. Then to Mary, 'Not a word of this Mary. We'll say she had a little turn. And a tray in her room. Then she can die of natural causes. Tomorrow perhaps, or best, in her sleep.' She hoped that a 'little turn', and a 'tray in her room', would explain Mary's screaming. She closed the door on Miss Bellamy's selfish hara-kiri. 'We'll lay her out and clean her up later,' she said. Then she straightened herself, stiffened her gait and returned to the dining room. 'Another little turn I'm afraid,' she announced, and she heard the quiver in her voice. 'She'll have a tray in her room. Mary was obviously frightened,' she offered lamely, hoping that that would adequately explain the curdled scream.

'Poor Miss Bellamy,' was whispered around the table.

In Matron's absence the Major had allowed the wine to flow into every glass, and the phrase 'poor Miss Bellamy' was about as much caring as they were disposed to show. They were anxious to get on with their Christmas dinner, and Matron was glad to serve it. Perhaps it might take her mind off the horror above stairs, and the worry as to how she could deal with it. She was relieved that the residents seemed to have bought her story and as long as Mary kept her mouth shut, Miss Bellamy would have gone as gently into that good night as Mrs Elizabeth Webber had done, 'tray in her room' untouched at her side. She tucked into the turkey and wondered at her own appetite.

When the course was finished, Mary came in to clear away the plates. Matron looked at her carefully. She seemed composed enough and as she turned to leave the room, Matron dared to wink at her.

'We need a little rest before the pudding, Mary,' she said. 'So take your time. And check that Miss Bellamy has eaten her dinner.' It was more likely, she knew, that the dinner had eaten Miss Bellamy and she shuddered as she recalled the horrendous mess she had left behind. She would not study her waiting list, she decided. It would take some time to refurbish that room. It would need a total repaint, for the walls were spattered with blood. A new carpet was called for and furniture too, for there was not a square inch of habitation that did not smell or show signs of poor Miss Bellamy's despair.

Matron refilled the glasses and raising hers, she said, 'A Merry Christmas to you all.'

It was at this juncture that Jeremy Cross chose to excuse himself. After all that drinking he badly needed to empty his bladder. He did not think he could make the upstairs toilet, so he chose the one off the reception which was hard by the dining room. After his relief, he emerged in time to see a street-dressed Mary, looking distraught, with suitcase in hand, hurrying towards the front door. He rushed after her, intending to carry her case, and he asked her where and why she was going.

'Can't stand it here one minute longer,' she said. 'Miss

Bellamy cut her throat, whatever Matron told you. Little turn, my arse. She's going to say she died in her sleep, of natural causes, but Miss Bellamy's already good and dead and there's blood all over the place. I'm not staying to clear up the mess. Nor lay her out. That's not my job at all.' And with that she was gone, scurrying down the driveway, fleeing from ghosts.

Mr Cross was stunned. He dared not believe what Mary had said, yet it was too detailed a story to have been invented. As quickly as he could, he climbed the stairway to Miss Bellamy's room, and silently turned the knob. He needed only a crack in the door to confirm with horror that Mary's report was true.

Mr Cross didn't know what to do. Mary would be missed soon enough and reasons would have to be given. There was no way Matron could continue to dissemble. He walked slowly back to the dining room. He would hold his tongue, he decided, until Matron could hold hers no longer.

As he took his seat at the table, the Major remarked that he was looking rather pale.

'I've eaten too much,' Mr Cross said lamely, and he looked across at Matron and wondered how she could keep her colour. Conversation around the table was unusually animated, fuelled as it was by the Major's endless top-up of glasses. Even Matron was in lively conversation with Eric Thurlow who sat by her side, and though contributing little himself, seemed in a state of acute listening. The time passed; during a rare silence, Matron began to wonder where the pudding was and Mary was called.

'We're ready, Mary.' She braced herself for the entry of the brandy flames, and the sparklers that she had instructed Mary to light before leaving the kitchen. But there was silence from the kitchen quarters that now infected the whole dining room. 'Mary!' Matron called again, and receiving no answer, she rose from her chair.

She might as well be calling Miss Bellamy, Jeremy Cross thought. 'She's gone, Matron,' he said, saving her a journey. 'I saw her leaving. With her suitcase and all.' He wanted nobody to hope that Mary had slipped out for a simple breath of fresh air. Mary was not coming back and the mention of the suitcase confirmed a single ticket.

'But why?' came the chorus from the table.

Mr Cross looked at Matron, and Matron stared back at him, knowing that he knew exactly why Mary had left and willing him to keep his mouth shut.

'I'll go and see to the pudding,' she said.

When she had left the room they all turned to Mr Cross, sensing that he knew more than he was giving away.

'Why did she go?' the Major asked speaking for them all.

'She didn't want to clear up the mess,' Mr Cross teased them.

'But that's her job, clearing up the mess,' Lady Celia chirped indignantly.

'Not *that* kind of mess,' Mr Cross teased further.

'What kind then?' Mrs Thackeray asked.

Mr Cross looked in the direction of the kitchen to make sure that Matron was not in sight. Then he leaned over the table and whispered, 'Blood. Blood. That kind of mess.'

'Whose blood?' It was Mrs Green who wanted the particulars.

'Miss Bellamy's,' Mr Cross said. 'Little turn. Tray in her room, my arse,' he said, quoting Mary. 'She cut her throat. That's what she did. This morning. After breakfast.'

Mrs Primple gave a little cry and tears were seen to flow down her cheeks. 'Poor dear Miss Bellamy,' she said, and of all the company she was the only one who would have no appetite for pudding. And the flames of it were just entering the dining room.

Matron set it down on the table and looked around at her residents. She had deliberately taken a long time in the kitchen half hoping that Mr Cross would spill the beans and thus save her from spilling them herself. But there was no indication on their faces as to their knowledge or their ignorance of the reasons for Mary's sudden departure. She waited for the flames of the pudding to subside, then she started its serving. When that was done, she passed around the cream and brandy butter.

'How wonderful it smells,' Mrs Thackeray said, feeling that somebody had to say something that had nothing to do with the subject of Mary's departure.

But Mrs Green was not prepared to let it lie, for she, like Mr Cross, revelled in a spot of *Schadenfreude*.

'Has poor Miss Bellamy had her pudding?' she asked with a feigned innocent concern.

There was a pause before Matron replied. 'I'll take it up shortly,' she said. Whether they knew the truth or not, she was giving them instructions that lips were to be sealed, that no further Bellamy reference must be made, and that they must believe what she herself chose to tell them in her own time, and that Mr Cross, if he had heard anything at all, was sorely mistaken.

The residents were confused and they cast a glance at Mr Cross who shrugged in reply. He thought Matron very stupid. Sooner or later, the truth would out. But Matron stuck to her unreliable guns and that evening, when the festivities were done, she solemnly entered the now cardiganed common room, and announced that poor Miss Bellamy had passed away peacefully in her sleep. Quietly she told Mr Cross that she would like to talk to him in her office.

But first he had work to do. Now that poor Miss Bellamy's demise was in the public domain, he had to bring his list up to date. He hurried to his room and gently inscribed the name of Miss Jennifer Bellamy on the back of his wardrobe door. After her name, whatever cock and bull story Matron chose to tell, he wrote its cause. 'A deeply cut throat'. Then he went to Matron's office.

She was sitting sternly at her desk. 'I don't know what you've heard,' she said, 'but it's all lies. Mary left because she found the work too heavy for her. I think it was all that ironing she had to do that was the last straw. Poor Miss Bellamy was able to eat and enjoy her Christmas pudding and she passed on quite some hours after Mary had left.'

She told her story with such authority that she almost believed it herself. When, some weeks later, Miss Bellamy's sad postcard was returned to sender since the address and whereabouts of 'To whom (if anybody) it may concern', were unknown, she read the monosyllabic message with a tinge of sadness, but destroyed it quickly for it was a marginal proof of what she was trying to hide.

She had actually succeeded in so doing, for the doctor had been persuaded to 'natural causes' though there was nothing natural about the deep gash on the neck that no nature, however cruel, could have inflicted. But the doctor was sorry for Matron; he knew that that gash severely threatened her livelihood. They would keep it to themselves, they decided. They would have to, for each had a living to lose. He had helped her clean her up, and Miss Bellamy was quickly shrouded, her neck concealed in a ruff of winding-sheet. She was buried quietly on New Year's Day. There was a short, sparsely attended service in a neighbouring church and it was as if poor Miss Bellamy had never lived at all.

It was a sour start to the new year. The residents were uneasy. They weren't entirely sold on Matron's story of natural causes, nor on her reasons for Mary's swift leavetaking. Mr Cross's tale disturbed them. It was not the kind of story one could make up on the spot. And for what reason anyway? Of them all, Lady Celia was the most uneasy. In her business over the years she had been trained to smell a rat, and although it was the ferret who ran it to ground she knew when a rat was abroad. Now she smelt one in The Hollyhocks.

Shortly after Miss Bellamy's funeral, she had found herself alone in the common lounge when Jeremy Cross joined her. He had picked up a newspaper to read and Lady Celia had taken the plunge. She asked him outright what had really happened to Jennifer Bellamy. 'I've already told you,' he said coldly. 'She committed suicide. She cut her throat. Matron hushed it up. Not good for Hollyhocks. Mary told me and I believe her. And I'll tell you something else,' he said. 'Doctor Leigh's in it too. I was waiting for Matron in her office. There was a copy of the death certificate on her desk. "Natural causes", it said. The whole business is a cover-up.'

'How d'you know Mary was telling the truth?'

'Because before I came back to the dining room, I nipped up to Miss Bellamy's room. No natural causes there, I can tell you. Unless mother nature cut Miss Bellamy's throat and spattered the walls with blood.'

Lady Celia shivered. She excused herself quickly, claiming a sudden headache due to shock. But she'd never felt finer. On reaching her room she dialled Lady Priscilla's number and informed her that she was taking the next train up to town. They had urgent business to discuss.

Ensconced in Lady Priscilla's drawing room, Lady Celia gave her details of their new client. Or rather clients, for she had landed an opportunity to kill two birds with one stone. Matron had passed off a suicide as natural causes and Dr Leigh had falsified the death certificate. The ferret must be informed. When all was settled, the two ladies celebrated their finds with a glass of sherry. Then Lady Celia returned to The Hollyhocks to await developments.

Nine

Mrs Feinberg returned to The Hollyhocks on the thirteenth day of Christmas, that day when all the paraphernalia of holiday had been removed. Mrs Hughes also returned on that day, having exploited the holiday season to its full, and as she entered the common lounge, a ready Minnie-story on her lips, with promise of many more to come, the room slowly and fitfully emptied until only Jeremy Cross remained in her company. Quickly he took up his newspaper as a signal that his ears were closed. But later on that day, when Mrs Feinberg returned, she was greeted with polite, if guarded, thanks for her presents, which they said were just what they wanted. They remarked on how well she was looking, and indeed Mrs Feinberg looked a lot better than she had on leaving The Hollyhocks before the holidays. She felt much better too. The moment she had settled in her son's house, that Hollyhocks feeling of unease had lifted. She had slept and eaten well, and for most of the time she had even been happy. She had said nothing to Mark about her Hollyhocks discomfort. She did not want to worry him. She began to think that in any case it was a trivial matter and that the unease was due to the radical change in her life, that surrender of her independence, and that in time she would grow accustomed to Hollyhocks care. She decided she would make the best of it. She would spend less time in her room and she would mix more sociably with the other residents.

With this resolve, she joined them in the common room before dinner. There was a great deal of chatter and Mrs Feinberg sat herself next to Mrs Thackeray, because there was an empty chair beside her. Mrs Thackeray was glad to be granted a virgin ear for the Miss Bellamy story and there and then she treated Mrs Feinberg to both versions, the authorised and the otherwise. Mrs Feinberg felt as if she were being asked to make a choice, but Mrs Thackeray saved her the trouble.

'Of course,' she said, 'there's no doubt in anyone's mind that Miss Bellamy did herself in. Matron's version is a simple cover-up.'

'I wouldn't be so hasty,' Lady Celia interrupted. 'I'm inclined to Matron's version, whatever anyone thinks.' She was glad of an opportunity to put herself on the legal side, and she made sure that she was overheard by Mr Cross. She wanted it thought that she was in no way connected with the visit of the ferret to The Hollyhocks which he had arranged for the following Monday.

'What does it matter?' Mrs Feinberg said softly. 'She's gone, poor Miss Bellamy, and there doesn't seem to be anyone to mourn her.'

'Oh we miss her all right, don't we?' Mrs Green turned to the other residents for support.

'Of course we do,' they muttered and wondered how they could miss a person whose presence over the years they had barely noticed.

'Did you have a good holiday?' Mrs Hughes asked, hoping for a valid opening for a Minnie story.

'Very pleasant thank you,' Mrs Feinberg said. 'It was quiet. We don't celebrate of course, but my son wasn't working and we were able to spend time together.'

'Mine was anything but quiet,' Mrs Hughes said and the residents, sniffing the entrance of Minnie, slowly withdrew, all except for Mrs Feinberg who was obliged to listen to a story that she was sure she had heard before. And even as she listened, she was appalled by the threat of that old feeling of Hollyhocks unease, as it crept into her bones. She would ignore it, she decided. She would have to. She could not spend the rest of her life hiding in her own quarters. Yet there was no way she could pinpoint its source. Was it the Hollyhocks food, the people, or the sheer ozone of the place? Or was it perhaps something within herself, something that had always been there, and had sprouted under conditions unknown? She made herself listen to Mrs Hughes and stayed in her company until dinner. Even after dinner, she joined the residents for a nightcap and forced herself to stay in the lounge until only Jeremy Cross remained. Then she saw fit to retire, with a certain satisfaction that she had steeled herself against surrender.

At breakfast the following morning, she found herself sitting next to Mrs Green. Polite greetings passed between them but Mrs Green was too intent on her food to offer further conversation. It was at breakfast time that Matron gave out the post. There was always very little, and most mornings nothing at all.

But that morning Matron handed a letter to Mrs Green. Not one of them had ever known Mrs Green to receive post and all eyes eagerly awaited its opening. Mrs Feinberg had a good view of the envelope. It was brown and oblong and announced in black capitals that it was On Her Majesty's Service. She could not quite read the letters of the particular department underneath. Mrs Green was seen to pale and it was clear that she was not about to open the envelope in the presence of witnesses. She put it beside her plate and made to get on with her breakfast. But she had lost her appetite, it seemed. For a while she played with the egg and toast on her plate and then abandoned it. She picked up the envelope and put it in her bag and those who watched her saw that her hands were shaking. She did not excuse herself, but rose, pushing the chair behind her and she was gone from the room with a speed that spoke of terror in her heels.

'On Her Majesty's Service,' Mrs Thackeray said who, sitting opposite Mrs Green, had read the envelope upside down.

'On Her Majesty's Service,' Mrs Hughes echoed as if that explained the mystery of Mrs Green's hasty departure. She was running off to see Her Majesty and to be at her service.

Word of Mrs Green's unaccustomed letter and the nature of its sender quickly spread throughout the dining room and speculation as to the contents of that letter and the reason for her departure kept them all gossiping throughout breakfast. They hoped that they would pick up a clue at the lunch table. But Mrs Green didn't appear for lunch, nor even dinner that evening, and when Mr Cross asked after her, Matron told them that she'd been called to London on urgent business.

'When will she be back?' Mrs Hughes asked.

'She wasn't able to tell me. It was a private business,' Matron said.

Mrs Thackeray was intrigued. An old age pensioner, as all of them were at The Hollyhocks, was too old for private business.

Everything by that time had usually been settled. But one couldn't rely on Mrs Green to tell the truth when she returned. There was more to Mrs Green than met the eye. Or less perhaps, but either way lay deception.

That morning, shortly after Mrs Green had left for London, Mrs Thackeray received a telephone call from her estate agent. After six months on the market, an offer had finally been made on the Seven Pillars. It was only a few thousand short of the asking price, and the agent advised Mrs Thackeray to accept. The buyers, he said, had expressed a wish to meet her. They had some questions concerning the history of the house. But this request Mrs Thackeray swiftly refused. On no account did she wish to meet the incoming owners. She was deeply sorry for them. They were buying a property peopled by malign ghosts, ghosts of greed, lechery and self-righteousness. Now she was no longer a woman of property, and that, considering the nature of the property, should have afforded her a great measure of relief. But as she sat in her room after the agent's telephone call, she felt bereaved. An overwhelming sense of loss suffused her. It was not the loss of bricks and mortar, nor of deeds, nor of furniture nor monogrammed plate. The loss of all those things she regarded as a positive gain. What she mourned was the loss of her battlefield, a pitch, an arena in which to place her enemy, the target for her hatred, her bitterness and her consummate lament. Now she could not inhabit such a place any more. That arena was now alien-tenanted, all boundaries shifted, the rage transplanted, the rot translated, and the sick memories buried for ever. Now she would have to imagine such an arena, and she knew that, rootless, her rage would fade, her bitterness would shrivel, and in time, the greatest danger of all, she would forget every single event of her Seven Pillars nightmare. In such oblivion, what was left of her life would be meaningless. But there was still the vault, she remembered, the Thackeray family vault, where the whole rotten tribe of them, at this very moment of sale, were turning in their graves. That vault would be her arena, she decided, a fixture in her imagination around which would circle the ghosts of her past, which would, with their evocations, nourish the remainder of her days. One could live on love she thought, and its memories. But by the same token one could live on hate, which was equally energising. This thought gave her a certain pleasure and she settled down to dwell on it, knowing that, however long she lived, she would never exhaust the bitter contemplation of her past.

Over the next week workmen were seen to come and go in the direction of poor Miss Bellamy's rooms. There was no way Matron could hide its spring-clean. But there was no comment on it. Poor Miss Bellamy seemed to have been entirely forgotten, together with the stories that surrounded her sudden demise. In time the bedroom was utterly transformed, newly painted, newly furnished and carpeted and if not exorcised, then thoroughly fumigated. It was ready for a new occupant. But Matron was in no hurry. There was no name on her waiting list that seemed to be suitable. Moreover she was short of staff. Mary's replacement was only temporary, and unsatisfactory to boot. She would wait until adequate staff was found. Nevertheless she would keep up her waiting list, indeed that very afternoon she was expecting a visit from a Mr Venables, who wrote from a Hall in Hampshire, enquiring after the possibility of registering his ageing mother at The Hollyhocks. It was a good address, Matron thought, and she'd given him an appointment for four o'clock.

At precisely that time, Lady Celia was watching from her window that overlooked The Hollyhocks' drive and, as she expected, she saw a confident Mr Venables, swinging his cane along the gravel. The clock in reception struck four as he pulled on the bell. She smiled. The ferret could be relied upon. He was always on time. Lady Celia would have given much to be a fly on the wall in Matron's office during the interview, but she would have to wait for its report until her regular London meeting.

Matron welcomed Mr Venables in reception and led him into her office. She liked the look of him. He was smartly dressed as befitted a gentleman who came out of a Hall in Hampshire, though Matron could never have located such a Hall, because it simply wasn't there. She offered Mr Venables a cup of coffee, then settled down to enquire as to his particulars. She passed him a biscuit, a special one from her private supply, and she took one herself, a gesture that pleased Mr Venables for he knew she would need a certain strength to accommodate what she called his particulars.

'How old is your dear mother?' Matron began.

The ferret was not one to mince words and he came straight to the point.

'I have no mother,' he said. 'She died twenty years ago.'

Matron was perplexed. Automatically she responded with sympathy, though she couldn't help feeling that a score of years was long enough to get over a bereavement.

'I thought you were enquiring on behalf of your mother,' she said lamely. 'According to your letter,' she added.

'The letter was a mere ruse to get an appointment,' the ferret said. 'I have come on an entirely different matter.'

Matron was angry that she was so deceived. And fearful too, having heard a tone of threat in the man's voice.

'I'm very busy,' she said. 'Perhaps you will come to the point straight away.'

'Gladly,' the ferret said. He leaned towards her. 'I have come regarding the matter of Miss Jennifer Bellamy.' He gave pause to let the name sink in, and he noted her sudden pallor with pleasure.

'Poor Miss Bellamy,' Matron managed to say. 'Are you a relation?' She asked with a certain confidence, for she knew absolutely that Miss Bellamy had no family and had been kinless most of her life.

'I'm no relation,' the ferret said. 'I simply want to see justice done.'

'Justice?' Matron whispered.

'I have it on good authority,' he said, 'and I'm not prepared to give my sources,' he pre-empted any enquiry into that matter, 'I have it on good authority,' he repeated, 'that Miss Bellamy did not die of natural causes as you and Dr Leigh proclaimed. She cut her throat, poor soul. In other words, she committed suicide.' He was careful not to pause to allow her a denial and almost in the same breath he continued, 'You covered it up Matron, because a suicide is not good for the reputation of an old people's home, and it is possible you would have lost your job on account of it. Moreover,' he went on, 'Dr Leigh, though knowing the cause of the death, for it was clearly visible, colluded with your deception and falsified the death certificate. I have all this on good authority,' he repeated. It was then, and only then, when his story was out, that he paused for breath. And watched her as she tried to still her trembling.

'Poor Miss Bellamy died of natural causes,' she said and in her mind she cursed Mary, who could have been his only source.

'D'you insist on that?' he threatened her.

'It's the truth,' she said. A deep red flushed the pallor on her face and spread to her neck and God knows where else, the ferret dared to think as he viewed her discomfort with intense pleasure.

'If you insist on that kind of truth, then I shall have to take my proof to the board of trustees. And in the case of Dr Leigh, to the British Medical Association.'

It was a small comfort to Matron that she was not alone in her predicament, but a partnership in a cover-up did not lessen her culpability.

'Oh yes,' the ferret went on. 'Dr Leigh is my next port of call.' Matron sensed an avenue of postponement. 'Then I shall wait to see what he says,' she said hopefully.

'What he says will make absolutely no difference to your involvement,' the ferret told her.

There was a silence then between them.

'What are you suggesting?' she said.

Though short of utterance, everything but the word 'blackmail' and all its terrible letters silently throbbed between them.

'I think two hundred pounds a week will let you off very lightly,' he said. 'In cash of course,' he added with a smile. 'I shall ask the same of Dr Leigh. I don't need to remind either of you of what you have to lose if you do not comply.'

'She died of natural causes.' Matron made a last pathetic stand.

'As natural as a deeply cut throat,' the ferret said.

Again there was a silence. The ferret allowed it for a while.

'I'm a busy man,' he said, making to rise from his chair, 'and I would like to take your first instalment right away.' He waited, staring at her.

'Two hundred pounds,' she stammered.

'Every Monday,' he said. 'I shall call for it myself. At the same time.'

'I'll tell on you,' she screamed at him. 'I'll tell the police.'

The ferret settled once more into his chair and laughed in her face. 'Phone them,' he said. 'I'll wait.'

And then Matron began to cry. 'I've worked hard all my life,' she sobbed.

'So have we all,' the ferret said unmoved. 'Two hundred pounds, Matron. I'm waiting.'

'How long will this go on?' she whispered.

'Until you die,' the ferret said. 'Of natural causes of course,' he added. 'And may your life be long and merry.'

She fumbled with her bunch of keys, her first gesture of surrender. Then with one of them she opened a desk drawer and drew out a wad of notes. She had difficulty in counting out the two hundred pounds he demanded, for her fingers were trembling beyond control. The ferret waited patiently and when the counting was done, he took the pile and checked it himself.

'Very good,' he said, a remark that could have applied to her obedience or to her arithmetic. Either way it was insulting.

'I shall leave you now,' he said, pocketing the money. 'I can see myself out. I look forward to seeing you again. And often. Till this time next week then.'

He took his time across the reception area, then, twirling his cane, he practically skipped down the gravelled driveway. At her window, Lady Celia noted the triumph in his stride and she sighed with pleasure.

When the supper bell rang, she walked breezily into the dining room and noted without surprise that Matron did not make an appearance. The kitchen maids managed the servings. Neither did Matron enter the common lounge to bid her residents good night, as was her wont. But as Lady Celia returned to her own quarters, she caught a glimpse of Matron on the stairs. And it seemed to her right and proper that Matron's face had taken on a distinctly yellowish hue.

At breakfast next morning Matron managed an appearance but she looked far from well. The residents remarked on her pallor. She protested a headache coming on, one that she knew would assail her for the rest of her natural life. And Dr Leigh as well. She had delayed phoning him, but he had lost no time in phoning her as soon as the ferret had left his consulting rooms. He was distraught. Yes, he had paid, as she had paid. Two hundred pounds as the first of ever-weekly instalments. 'What choice do we have?' he had whispered. Then quickly, 'I'd rather not talk on the phone. I'll come over tonight after surgery.'

His implied suggestion that their telephones might be bugged in no way eased Matron's peace of mind. She now felt wholly invaded, the property no longer of herself, but of other forces.

That evening after supper, Lady Celia heard a car draw up on the driveway. From her window, she saw Dr Leigh running up the steps. She was not surprised to notice that he was not carrying his usual black bag. She knew that his visit had nothing to do with medicine. She dropped the net curtain smiling. All was going according to plan.

Over the next few days, Matron looked more and more peaky, peaky enough to merit speculation in the common lounge.

'Perhaps she's sickening for something,' Mrs Hughes said.

Jeremy Cross said nothing, but he wondered how soon Matron would be a candidate for a tray in her room, and who would take it to her when the time came.

'She's overworked,' the Major offered his conclusions. 'She's short of staff, and there are too many demands on her.'

Certainly the latter, Lady Celia thought, and looked forward to the following Monday and every Monday thereafter, when Matron would look more peaky than ever.

'She needs a holiday,' Mrs Thackeray said. 'When did she last have one?' She turned to the longer-stay residents.

'Not in my time,' Mrs Primple said. 'And that's seven years.'

It was a rare common-lounge offering from Mrs Primple who, for some reason, had taken a break from her anonymous congress at the end of a telephone line.

'D'you think we dare suggest it?' Major asked.

'I don't think so,' Mrs Thackeray said. 'She might think we were criticising her.'

'I'll suggest it if you like.' This from Mrs Feinberg who over the past week or so had slowly become a contributing member of the Hollyhocks band. She had changed. One could say that she was almost happy. Gone were all the traces of discomfort and unease that had plagued her in her early Hollyhocks days. She attributed the change to her own stamina, to her unwillingness to surrender to those feelings. Nowadays she spent little time in her own quarters, her erstwhile disturbing retreat. She mixed happily with the other residents, and seemed to have won the respect of all of them, especially the Major who, despite his fear and mistrust of women in general, seemed to have made an exception in Mrs Feinberg's case.

'Jolly decent of you,' the Major said. 'And I wish you luck. And we at headquarters will look forward to your report.' He gave a slight giggle after this last remark as if in apology for being unable to shed his military uniform.

'Yes sir,' Mrs Feinberg said, entering his game. It was a public flirtation between them and the other residents looked at each other, all of them getting the same message at the same time, and all of them with a mixture of envy, surprise and delight.

'When will you do it?' Mr Cross asked.

'I shall wait for a convenient moment,' Mrs Feinberg said. 'In private of course. I'll think of some excuse to go to her office.'

'Today?' one of them persisted.

'I'll try,' Mrs Feinberg said.

Matron kept a supply of stamps in her office for the use of those few residents who still communicated with the outside world, and before supper that evening Mrs Feinberg knocked on Matron's door. An order to enter was loud and abrupt and signalled an ill temper. But Mrs Feinberg was not intimidated. Her newfound feeling of wellbeing gave her courage.

'I've come for a couple of stamps,' she said as she entered.

Matron fumbled in her desk drawer. 'Are you settling in nicely?' Matron asked without looking at her.

Mrs Feinberg picked up her cue. 'Much better now,' she said. 'I think the break did me a lot of good. We should all take a holiday occasionally.'

Matron did not respond. But Mrs Feinberg persisted.

'Do you ever take a holiday, Matron?' she asked.

For the first time Matron looked at her. 'And who would look after The Hollyhocks?' she said.

'You could find someone temporarily,' Mrs Feinberg suggested.

'I suppose so,' Matron said with little enthusiasm.

Mrs Feinberg allowed a pause. 'If you don't mind my saying so,' she said, 'you look as if you could do with a break yourself. Some sun perhaps. A rest somewhere.'

Matron was indignant. 'I'm perfectly well thank you,' she said. 'I don't need a holiday.' What she needed was a hit man for Mr Venables and she was not likely to find one on holiday. The thought of a hit man had certainly crossed her mind. She had even dared to share it with Dr Leigh. She had disguised it as a joke, but even as a joke, Dr Leigh did not find it very funny.

'Will that be all Mrs Feinberg?' she asked, handing over the stamps.

'That's all,' Mrs Feinberg said, disappointed that she would have little of worth to report back to headquarters.

Matron watched her leave. Those bloody Jews, she thought. Always interfering in business not their own. She might well put up Mrs Feinberg's fees – she could find some grounds for doing so – and the surplus could go towards her weekly hush money. In fact she might do exactly that with all her residents. She would take the suggestion to the board pleading the rising costs. Her creative accounting could do the rest. This thought gave her a little comfort. She would mind it less if the bribe came out of pockets other than her own. And when at the following board meeting her request was granted, and her residents informed, it was only Lady Celia who knew that 'rising costs' had nothing to do with anything except lining the ferret's pockets and ultimately her own. Certainly Matron looked less peaky as time went by though every Monday at four o'clock through her net curtains, Lady Celia checked on the ferret's prompt calling.

On hearing of the rising fees at The Hollyhocks, the ferret had wished to up the payments accordingly. This he did, with Ladies Celia and Priscilla's approval, to two hundred and fifty pounds, and Matron's peakiness returned with a vengeance. Once again she cursed that kitchen maid of hers and in her fantasies she added Mary to the hit man's list.

It was around this time, after almost three weeks' absence, that Mrs Green returned to The Hollyhocks. No one had particularly missed her, and it was only when she showed up in the common lounge that the residents realised she had not been amongst them for some time.

'Where have you been?' they asked.

'I had business to attend to,' she said, quickly, as if she had rehearsed the line over and over again. 'It took longer than I thought, but it's all settled now.'

'Satisfactorily, I hope?' Mrs Thackeray said, who was disappointed that Mrs Green had returned at all.

'Very,' Mrs Green said, and smiled to herself, and Mrs Thackeray thought that whatever business she had been about, even if it was in Her Majesty's Service, it was certainly shady.

At supper Mrs Green was silent. She did not wish to encourage any discussion as to her doings in London. And she was grateful that in any case, nobody seemed to be interested. She noticed that the Major had changed his dinner sitting and was now happily ensconced at Mrs Feinberg's side – that Jew lady, Mrs Green thought, wanting to be at the centre of things, like all of her kind.

Their seeming partnership offended her, and she decided to make an early night and hope that by the morning the Major would have come to his senses.

But at breakfast they were still together, though she was pleased to notice that Mrs Feinberg looked distinctly unwell. And unwell she was indeed, with a raging headache that made her leave her breakfast untouched. When the Major suggested a short walk, she was happy to oblige, for whatever was disturbing her was certainly within the confines of The Hollyhocks. She began to feel a little better as they walked together down the driveway, but still with some aftertaste of the Home. But as she distanced herself from The Hollyhocks that taste faded, and by the time they reached the village, she felt her true contented self. The Major took her arm, squeezing it a little, and she returned that gesture of affection with gratitude. She wondered at their friendship. It gave her pleasure, though the Major was not her type at all. Her husband had been a musician, a cellist in one of London's leading orchestras. It was more than possible that the Major was tone-deaf. She had never known a military man. Such species had not moved in her circle of friends. They were all artists of a kind. Writers, painters, composers. It was possible that the Major had never read a book. Yet he had a quality that she found enchanting. It was his courtesy and chivalry, and above all his self-assurance. He felt safe with himself, and she felt safe in his company. In the light of events of Mrs Feinberg's girlhood, safety was the most precious commodity. She had yearned for it daily, prayed for it, and lived in terror of its departure. Even when safety was finally assured, having failed all those she had loved, even then she did not trust it to stay by her side. Her husband in his boyhood had lived within that same daily terror and he too never ceased to look over his shoulder. Together they had turned their backs on past shadows but could never resist the temptation to steal a glance behind. When he died, it was their loving she had missed and their shared history. Not his cover, not his protection, for he had had none to give. But safety was the Major's constant companion, both inside and out. His very presence was an all-embracing protection. Which was why she had squeezed his arm in gratitude.

Throughout their growing friendship, the Major had never asked her about herself. And she was grateful for that for she was loth to talk about her past. She was happy to listen to the Major's military stories and he was more than happy to find a willing ear. But that morning he was silent for he sensed that she was troubled. He thought perhaps she would confide in him and he suggested a coffee in the village teashop, a suitable venue, he thought, for a more intimate exchange.

They were the only clients in the café, so they could not be overheard, and once settled he said, 'You're troubled my dear. I can see it. Would you like to tell me about it? In confidence of course. I would be honoured to share your trouble with you.'

She smiled at him. 'You're a good kind man,' she said. 'I *am* troubled. You are right. And I would share it with you if I could. But I don't know what it is. I simply don't know,' she said helplessly.

That seemed to put an end to the conversation that the Major had hoped for. 'Ought you to see a doctor?' he asked after a while.

'It's not that,' Mrs Feinberg said. 'Physically I'm in good health.'

The Major did not wish to suggest an alternative avenue of help, so he said nothing.

'It will pass,' she said after a while. 'I've had times when I've not been troubled at all.'

The poor Major was at a loss to advise her. But rather than prolong the silence between them, he suggested she tell him a little about herself, about her life before she came to The Hollyhocks. It would make conversation, he thought, with little inkling of where it would all lead. Mrs Feinberg who, like the Major, did not wish the conversation to flag, was happy to oblige him, and she talked about her years in England, that comparatively safe time, her marriage and her husband's death. She worked backwards, from the day of his funeral. And she took it slowly so that its telling would last many tearoom meetings.

Almost every day they took their walk after breakfast and in the tearoom, with undisturbed spirit, she unfolded her married life. The Major was a good listener and he marvelled at a style of living so very different from his own. And one morning, having worked backwards on her story, she reached the point of her arrival in England. And then she brought her story to an end.

'And before that?' the Major asked.

'I don't remember,' Mrs Feinberg said quickly and with a finality that implied that she had no intention of jogging her memory. The Major let it lie. There would be other meetings and further cups of tea. He took her arm and they walked slowly back to The Hollyhocks. She always dreaded their return, and once there, apart from mealtimes, she kept to her own quarters. In the subsequent tearoom meetings, they talked of other things. The Major reverted to his wartime stories; occasionally he probed her regarding her pre-England life. But it was clear that she did not want to talk about it.

So their one-sided teabreaks continued, as did Mrs Feinberg's unease, as she kept to her quarters burdened with her unspeakable untellable past. One day, the Major risked broaching the subject yet again. His growing attachment to Mrs Feinberg had somehow or other diminished his joy in military recall. The telling of his wartime stories gave him less pleasure as his concern increased regarding his companion's malaise. They were the only clients in the tearoom that day, and it seemed to the Major that in such silence and privacy Mrs Feinberg could be persuaded to confide in him. He waited for the tea to be served, then when the waitress withdrew, he dared to take her hand. 'Miriam,' he said, leaning slightly towards her, 'it upsets me, these unhappy feelings of yours. And I can't help thinking that somehow they are connected with what happened to you before you came to England. Those stories that you can't share with me.' He tightened his grip. 'I'm not very intelligent,' he said. 'I'm only a military man, my dear, but something tells me that they are connected.'

She was surprised at his insight, and astonished too. It was a link that she herself had never considered. That pre-England experience of hers had been so tragic, so studded with loss, that she could never connect it with anything else. Yet she knew it could not help but colour her everyday life, her every moment of survival, her every pang of guilt that that survival entailed.

She had learned later on that she had survived six million, a figure too large to be meaningful. For her, the figure was a manageable and catastrophic five, as she had stood alone and watched her father, her mother and three younger sisters as they were shunted into the wrong line and never seen again. Only five people. But they were the population of her whole world. She looked into the Major's eyes and felt she owed him something for his concern, yet she could find no words for him. So she rolled up her sleeve of her right arm and showed him her numbers. Five of them in all. One for each of those she had lost, those deemed too useless to merit a tattoo at all.

The Major looked at the figures. And he understood all the words she had not been able to tell him. He did not scrutinise the numbers, but he saw that there were five of them and proclaimed at least ten thousand before her. And that was only in one camp. He caressed the tattoo with the tips of his fingers.

'Where were you?' he asked. He regretted the question as soon as it was out. What did it matter where she was? One gas chamber was very like another. Unserved by architecture or design, they were simply functional. And they functioned with evil efficiency. He had seen them, smelt their lingering odour.

'Auschwitz,' she whispered.

It was there that he had been, attached temporarily to a Russian unit, struck dumb in that landscape of horror. And amongst those barely breathing skeletons, too weak to give thanks, was it possible that Miriam stood, doubting, mistrustful, assailed for one brief moment by a stabbing and reluctant belief in God? He would not tell her he was there. Auschwitz was Miriam's place, a private place. An eyewitness, even as rescuer, would simply be an invader. So he said nothing. And he asked no more questions. She had told him of everything that had soured her soul. They sat there in silence for a while and on their way back to The Hollyhocks, he put his arm around her shoulder.

'I'll keep you safe,' he said.

Ten

The minutes and hours crept oh so slowly at The Hollyhocks, but time flew. In no time at all, the Monday dinner of meatloaf appeared on the table almost as soon as it was eaten, even though Tuesday's liver, Wednesday's lamb, Thursday's chicken, Friday's fish, Saturday and Sunday roasts, had come routinely in between. The residents measured their days according to their favourite dish. Mrs Primple lived from one Thursday to another because she was partial to chicken, and since many of the residents favoured fish, it was Friday that was their measuring calendar. But for Lady Celia, it was Monday, when through her net curtains she watched the ferret twirling his cane up The Hollyhocks' drive. You could set your watch by him. And promptly at four-ten, he would twirl his return journey and Lady Celia would drop her net curtains on a share of two hundred and fifty pounds. And in another hour, a share of five hundred pounds which would have given time for Dr Leigh's contribution.

Two chicken dinners later, Mrs Primple complained of a sore throat, and she could scarcely speak above a whisper. This debility put paid to her little hobby for a while and she was at a loss as to how to spend her time. Matron insisted on calling the doctor, and behind her net curtain, Lady Celia watched out for his arrival. She wished to view his peakiness. But it wasn't Dr Leigh who carried the black bag up The Hollyhocks' steps. It was a stranger, an older man whom she had never seen before. She was puzzled and it was not until her monthly meeting in London two weeks later that she learned the cause of Dr Leigh's replacement. The good Dr Leigh, Lady Priscilla informed her, had simply died. The ferret had reported a heart attack, no doubt occasioned by stress. Neither woman felt any pang of guilt. Dr Leigh's untimely demise simply meant the loss of a client. But his death did not let Matron off the hook. She had made no mention of it to her residents. It was as if she pretended that nothing had changed, but in truth his death had left her isolated, had left her to carry the can alone. Nowadays she looked more peaky than ever before.

In time Mrs Primple recovered under the new doctor's care, and in full voice, she went happily back to her chat lines. The Major and Mrs Feinberg took their daily tearoom round and Jeremy Cross continued the nightly reading of his survival list. Mrs Hughes continued to prattle her Minnie-stories to unwilling if not deaf ears, and Jock MacPherson did not cease to dream of Scottish home rule. The penny had not yet dropped for Mrs Green who wondered why Mrs Thackeray kept avoiding her.

But Mrs Thackeray was otherwise engaged. She was about another business altogether. And though she was not sure of what kind of business it was, she was aware of a constant occupation.

It had started unknowingly some months before, at the Christmas Eve celebrations. That was the night when Matron had made changes in the normal seating routine. It was during that evening that Mrs Thackeray found herself seated opposite Eric Thurlow. They had looked at each other and smiled but not a single word had passed between them. Subsequently they had found themselves side by side in the common lounge and occasional comments on the weather broke the silence between them. But they were joined in mutual smiles, smiles that suggested that a special relationship was incumbent upon them. Such a relationship did indeed develop almost unknown to either of them. Yet it seemed the most natural thing in the world, the obvious corollary of all that smiling. One day Eric Thurlow, catching Mrs Thackeray alone in The Hollyhocks' gardens, approached her and without preamble asked her to marry him. Apart from a few comments on the climate, they were the first real words he had spoken to her. She was smelling the roses at the time, small buds of early spring. She heard his request and found it totally unsurprising. She turned to face him; for the first time, neither of them smiled. Both knew that for some months the smiling had been mere foreplay and that now a serious engagement was entailed, one that called for an expression more concrete than a smile. And because she had expected such a proposal, she gave him a simple 'Yes', for she required no consideration and he, unsurprised at her acceptance, said, 'Shall we walk awhile and make our arrangements?' He took her arm, the first time he had actually touched her. As they walked between the flowerbeds Mrs Thackeray wondered who he was, where he came from, had he been married before, did he have children? In all, what was the man *about*? And Eric Thurlow wondered likewise about Mrs Thackeray but for neither of them did the answers matter. They were embarking on an unknown journey and the prospect excited them. Even the likely possibility of disaster seduced them both, and they gave each other a conspiratorial smile like two naughty children who were about to disobey their parents on a very grand scale indeed.

That evening Mr Thurlow asked Mrs Thackeray to call him Eric and in her turn Mrs Thackeray gave him Mildred as her Christian name. Using her name for the first time, Eric placed a ring on her engagement finger and pronounced himself betrothed. When later on in her room she examined the ring very closely, she found it faintly distasteful. It was clearly a piece of green glass barely passing for emerald.

Over the next few days, Eric was sparing with his stories of his pre-Hollyhocks life, as was Mildred. Close as they both were to the end of their days, they felt they had all the time in the world to get to know each other, for there was nothing else to do. And it didn't really matter if they didn't. In any case, to tell the tale of the late Mr Thackeray, a minute was too long and a decade not long enough, so his name was never mentioned. But she gathered that Eric had never been married and that he was a man of considerable means. That he had inherited his wealth from his father who, in his turn, had inherited it from his own. Eric Thurlow came from a long and undistinguished line of unearned income, accrued initially from the exploitation of native labour in the diamond mines of South Africa. It had been many generations since any one of the Thurlow clan had done an honest day's work.

In return for this scant biography, Mrs Thackeray had given him a dreary but honest account of her childhood in Croydon and her childless marriage in Seven Pillars. She tried to spin out her stories, but in both locations she was short of presentable ornamentation. She did not want to lie to Eric as she had done to Mrs Green. But lying by omission she thought permissible.

They decided to keep their engagement a secret from the residents until such time as their marriage had been arranged. They agreed that they should stay at The Hollyhocks, and blushingly suggested they be given an adjacent suite of rooms. Each of them would marry the boy/girl next door and that boy/girl would stay next door to give the marriage a chance to endure. Eric took it upon himself to have a confidential word with Matron. He would also make arrangements at the registrar's office and for the reception to follow. They reckoned that three weeks would be an adequate time to make their preparations and by that token they fixed the date of their wedding. The question of a honeymoon was discussed and Mrs Thackeray offered to call in at the travel agency to collect brochures.

That night, she retired early to her rooms and wondered what she had let herself in for, and how she was going to cope with it all. So did Eric Thurlow. Both were green to such an event, and for many long years, unpractised. And both, after such long celibacy, were now, as it were, of repaired virginity, and each one was nervous of losing it once more.

It had been many years since Mrs Thackeray had looked at her naked body. Seriously looked, that is, assessing it as if it belonged to some stranger. In her daily baths she kept her eyes tightly shut, and not for any fear of getting soap in them. She did not know what would be expected of her in a marriage and she tried not to imagine it but she felt obliged to evaluate whatever she had to offer, should it be called upon. She dared not risk an overall view. Each day she would inspect by instalments and later on, if she could gather the courage, she would risk a full-frontal. That night she started with her feet, her ankles and calves. She knew these were safe areas. Through luck she had avoided varicose veins, and bypassed corns and bunions. She took off her shoes and stockings and tucked her skirt up to her knee. At first she viewed them through the mirror, but she

knew that reflection as only partially reliable. It was the direct
eye on the flesh that mattered and Eric Thurlow's eye at that.
So she viewed them through her own spectacles so that nothing
could be missed. And she found them entirely satisfactory. She
decided to give them a mark and to apply such ratings to all her
other parts and knowing that her feet and calves were the best
part of her, she gave them ten out of ten. She reckoned she had
done enough for one session. Tomorrow she would examine her
face and dare her neckline.

In his room down the corridor, Eric Thurlow was under-
going a similar self-examination. He too had asked of himself
what would be expected. But not in terms of his appearance. He
considered that all men were entitled to look their age, to be as
fat or as thin as their nature dictated and likewise to look as old
or young. It was women who had to keep up their appearances.
He knew that his father had felt this way, and his mother had
accepted it. He assumed that Mildred Thackeray would feel the
same. His concern and self-examination dwelt in a different
area. His libido. Or what was left of it. In short, he was not
entirely confident that he could still perform. Oh it worked well
enough on his own, a lone congress with imagined anonymity.
A pigtailed schoolgirl was the most effective companion and
sometimes a black and servile whore served him well, and occasionally a nubile schoolboy, the most effective of all, he had to
admit, but he used the child rarely because his ensuing climax
riddled him with guilt. But Mildred Thackeray, he thought. As
an imagined partner in his solitary nights, she would never
never do, and he wondered whether his regular mates would be
as effective if Mrs Thackeray lay by his side.

Mrs Thackeray had no such fears. She had never knowingly
had an orgasm; she didn't know what it was. But like many of
her gender she knew how to fake it, and had done so throughout that early period of her marriage when it was called upon.
She marvelled that her husband had never seemed to notice. On

the contrary, he considered himself a great lover in being able to satisfy her so thoroughly. Her loud breathing and shouting confirmed it. Mrs Thackeray had no doubt that she would fake it with Eric Thurlow whatever the 'it' was. It was her body that concerned her and over the next few evenings she continued to examine her body giving marks to each part; each part rated lower than the last. She scrutinised her stomach and in all honesty she could not award it a single tick. All her life, as a girl, as a bride, and later on as a widow, night and day she had kept her knickers on. She saw no reason why, in the autumn of her days, she should break the habit of a lifetime. Especially now, when they were needed as much for concealment as for modesty. To take her mind off her body she set about thinking of a new dress for the wedding.

Eric had broken the news to Matron. He had expected a measure of joy from her. Instead she coldly offered her bewildered congratulations. In return she gave him the news of Dr Leigh's 'untimely passing', as she put it, as if a piece of good news was invalid without its opposite. Mr Thurlow thought her words were as peaky as her looks, for they were mean and sickly, but he simply didn't care. He put forward the suggestion of an adjacent suite of rooms, and without hesitation Matron said that such an arrangement would be impossible.

'It would unsettle the residents to have to change their quarters and I don't see any need for it,' she said sharply.

'I didn't expect you would,' Mr Thurlow told her with equal coolness. 'But no doubt we shall manage.'

'Do you want me to arrange the reception?' Matron asked. She would not want to miss out on an opportunity to make a little profit even if that profit went straight into the greedy pockets of Mr Venables.

'Thank you but no,' Mr Thurlow said. 'We shall make our own arrangements.'

'As you wish,' Matron said.

As he reached the door, she wished him well and grudgingly admitted that she was happy for them both.

Later he made arrangements at the registrar's office and reserved a reception hall with its catering facilities. Then he invested in a summer wardrobe for the honeymoon. For out of the sundry brochures that his bride-to-be had gathered together, they had chosen a week on the island of Barbados. It was an extravagant choice but Mr Thurlow was anxious to show his generous spirit. At least to start with.

He was still in a state of surprise that he was getting married at all. At times he had come close to such a commitment but his mother had strongly disapproved of his choices. So did he, in his own way, but he needed occasionally to take a stand. His mother would have disapproved of any prospective daughter-in-law. Eric was her only child and she was determined to keep him by her. Especially after she was widowed, when her resolve was tyrannical. He was in his late fifties when she died, and by that time, though he needed no one's approval, he simply couldn't be bothered. So he had continued his bachelor days, with regular forays to clubs of dubious repute. His continuous appetite surprised him and he ascribed it to his uncommitting promiscuity. It was not until he registered himself into The Hollyhocks that he began to think seriously of marriage simply on the basis of the fact that after a lifetime of idleness, it was something to *do*. On his first evening in the common lounge, he had viewed the ladies with dismay. Mrs Hughes had appealed for a while, but it was clear that in taking her to his bosom he would have to marry Minnie as well, and that was too great a burden. Mrs Thackeray had become a Hollyhock some time later and he had considered her as a serious proposition from the very beginning. At her every entrance he had mentally stripped her. He had eavesdropped on her chatter. He had monitored her appetite and noted her manners. In all he found her a very *proper* woman, with no obvious defects. He was glad that she was not clever for he couldn't abide clever women. In his terms a woman ought to know her place. Above all, he noted that she was meek and obedient. She did whatever Matron told her and without question. She lived by the rules, no matter how irrational those rules might be. His proposal had not been a spontaneous one as Mrs Thackeray firmly believed. Over months he had studied it, its manner and execution. He never had the slightest doubt that he would be accepted and for months before, he had decided on Barbados for their honeymoon. When Mrs Thackeray had suggested that island, it was as if she were picking a card from a conjuror's pack. A card that the conjuror had forced on her.

Mrs Thackeray took herself to London on a shopping spree. It was a sunny spring day and she decided to drive. On her way to the main London road, she made a detour to pass Seven Pillars. At first she passed the house by, not recognising it. She did a U-turn, tried the street once more and stopped at the large clusters of hydrangeas, familiar landmarks. But the only one. For the pillars had gone: all seven of them. Clearly if there were any pretensions to wisdom in the new occupiers, they were at pains not to advertise them. Without the columns, the house looked very different, in that it was the same as any other house in the street. She was glad of it, for it seemed that with the pillars' removal, all the ghosts had been exorcised and she could now drive past it without a sickening flutter in her heart.

She parked her car close to Debenhams, then decided against it. Debenhams was where she had shopped as a Thackeray, as had all the Thackerays before her. That chapter of her life was over, gone with the pillars. With much daring she took herself off to Liberty's. Much of the time she spent in the swimwear department. The ultimate giveaway. She dared not risk the mirror for any of the try-ons. She kept her eyes firmly shut all the while, and felt herself for the fit. She restricted herself to black, a sensible colour for her age, and she found one that pleated itself over the stomach area so that any bulge could be ascribed to the folds in the material. She bought sandals, underwear and a pretty white nightdress. She was entitled to a little white, she thought, and what better department than her nightwear. She blushed as she handed it over to the assistant for wrapping. She left the bridal dress till last, and allowed the help of an assistant to choose. She was happy to confide to her the nature of the occasion and the assistant entered into the celebration with enthusiasm. Between them they chose a mushroom silk dress and coat which would double for dinner evenings in Barbados. As she drove back to The Hollyhocks, Mrs Thackeray thought that with her wedding dress in the bag, she was entitled to rehearse her new baptism. Mildred Thurlow, she said to herself over and over again, sometimes putting the words to melody, so that by the time she reached The Hollyhocks she couldn't imagine that she'd ever answered to another name.

Eric had had cards printed announcing the date, time and place of the wedding reception, and these they addressed to The Hollyhocks' residents, not excluding Matron, though Eric hesitated on her name. Neither bride nor groom had friends outside The Hollyhocks so it would be a small gathering with not a strange face amongst them.

A few days before the wedding, after supper had been served, they slipped the invitations under each resident's door. They did not think a longer notice was necessary, for appointment books at The Hollyhocks were not overfull. For all the residents, the discovery was a surprise and their reactions varied. Mrs Green was furious. She would lose a friend, she thought, still ignorant of having lost her already. But why Mrs Thackeray? Why not her good self, younger, prettier, and altogether a better catch? She cursed them both, long and loud, and not even under her breath.

Mrs Hughes on the other hand, was delighted, and looked forward to telling her family. Mrs Primple was mildly indifferent.

As long as there was a telephone, she couldn't understand why anybody needed anybody. Mrs Feinberg's reaction was mixed. She was happy for the couple, but she sensed that with their joining together, the whole notion of marriage might well be in the air. Contagiously. And she wondered how she would react to the Major, should he be thus infected. Lady Celia simply laughed. At *their* age, she thought to herself. It was plainly rude.

On the whole, the men's reaction was one of indifference. Jeremy Cross nourished a faint hope that their coupling would wear one of them out. Or with luck, both, and thus lengthen the list on his wardrobe door. Jock MacPherson showed a distinct lack of interest since the nuptials could have no effect on Scottish home rule. Only the Major affected some kind of reaction, one rather similar to that of Mrs Feinberg, a sense that marriage was in the air and its breeze was inviting. But all the residents, whether indifferent or not, male or female, had one thought in common. After the couple were married, would they, or would they not, *do* it? This thought could not of course be shared, and certainly not discussed, and at breakfast the following morning there was no speculation, but there were congratulations, sincere and otherwise, all around. When Eric divulged the location of the honeymoon, some openly confessed to envy. But not Mrs Green, the most envious of all, who said she was most happy for them. Then she took a gulp of coffee to swallow her bile.

At supper that evening Matron reluctantly offered champagne to drink a toast to the bridal couple. After her refusal of a marriage suite, she had not expected to be invited to the wedding. The champagne was her lukewarm gratitude.

On her pre-nuptial night, Mrs Thackeray was overtaken by an acute attack of nerves. Since Eric's proposal she had basked in happiness and had enjoyed every single day of preparation. But now in the morning she would be called upon to justify all her shopping, all her honeymoon research, and most of all, all her expectations. She tossed and turned in her bed, and it was not until dawn that she managed to fall asleep. Matron's waking knock on her door sounded like thunder, and when she rose from her bed every bone in her body protested in pain. She knew that they were telling her that she was about to make a terrible mistake, but there was nothing she could do about it. She decided to pull herself together and to concentrate her thoughts on her new wardrobe and the prospect of sea and sun that waited her. But she would think of them well outside their context, stripped of association, as if they arose from no cause and would manifest no effect. Clothes, sun and sea, she said to herself. Over and over again and as she relaxed in her bath, the pains ceased but she knew she would ever be conscious of their warning.

Eric Thurlow on the other hand had risen long before Matron's call. He had showered and dressed himself in his wedding attire. He was lacing his shoes when Matron knocked on his door.

'Are you up, Mr Thurlow?' she called.

'I'm up and ready,' he said.

'Could I have a word then?' she asked.

He opened the door.

'Your big day,' Matron said entering the room.

'Indeed it is,' he said. He was about to offer her a chair but she had already taken one.

'You wanted to talk to me?' he said.

'I was wondering,' Matron came to the point, 'whether from now on you would want a double bill for your stay and whether I should put it all on your account.'

He stared at her.

'In other words,' she went on, in case she hadn't made herself quite clear, 'will you now be footing Mrs Thackeray's bill?'

Such a thought had never crossed Mr Thurlow's mind. Not for one moment. This was no regular marriage. His wife would not have to cook for him, clean for him, do his laundry, iron his shirts, the sort of things regular wives did in return for their keep. Footing Mrs Thackeray's bill – and he would never think of her as Mrs Thurlow – was a ridiculous suggestion. He was doing more than enough, he thought, in paying for the honeymoon.

'I don't think that will be necessary Matron,' he said. 'We shall both go on as before.'

'As you wish,' Matron said, rising. 'Now I must go and wake the others.' And lose no time in telling them all, she thought to herself as she knocked them awake on their doors. She had been surprised at Mr Thurlow's reaction, and faintly disgusted. Yet she was pleased and she allowed herself a rare smile. The Thurlows were off to a very bad start indeed. No good would come of it, which for Matron was right and proper. In her terms, since her encounter with Mr Venables, no one in the whole wide world was entitled to be happy.

But she had the decency to bring Mrs Thackeray's breakfast to her room, for she had heard that a groom should not see his bride before the ceremony, although she herself had ordered a car to take them both to the registrar's office. The breakfast was received with tears of gratitude, not all of which were for thanks. She had dressed herself with all but her dress and shoes. She wore her old dressing gown over her new underwear and a pair of slippers over her silk stockings. She had little appetite for the food on the tray, but she knew that she must eat something else she would faint with hunger as well as with her other anxieties. She took a sip of coffee and nibbled at the toast. The grapefruit was more than she could handle. She concentrated on thinking of her new clothes and the sun and the sea that awaited her. But no longer could they be viewed without that compulsory accessory. She hoped it would not take

long. Twenty minutes at the most, she hoped, and then she
could enjoy the sun and the sea for their own sakes. She did
not consider that she would have to do it more than once.
Then she would have done her duty, paid his conjugal rights
and they could spend the rest of the time in the sun and sea.
This thought gave her appetite, and but for the grapefruit, she
cleared her tray.

Eric Thurlow, on the other hand, was obliged to breakfast in
the dining room. He expected to be the target of some teasing,
but none of them referred to his nuptials, as if it was not a
matter to be taken seriously. He was content with their indifference, for he himself didn't take it very seriously either. It was
simply something to do. There would be sun and sea, and who
knew what else? Unlike his prospective bride, that was a region
in which he was unafraid to dwell. Indeed the thought of it gave
him pleasurable expectation, and he had no doubt his expectations would be fulfilled. As he left the dining room, the others
wished him good luck, their first reference to the event of the
day. 'See you all later,' he said. Then he went to his room to
don his gold cuff-links.

At ten-thirty he knocked on Mrs Thackeray's door. The car
was waiting in the driveway. She had been standing by the
door for some ten minutes, waiting for his summons, unwilling to sit down for fear of creasing her dress. She wondered if
she could stand up in the taxi. He told her that she looked
beautiful, not because he thought so, but because he knew it
was the right thing to say. But on second thoughts he considered that she looked more than presentable, and he commented
on the elegance of her dress, her shoes, itemising, so that she
would appreciate his eye for detail. He took her arm and led
her down the stairs into reception. There was not a soul about,
as if all the residents were hiding away with their embarrassment or envy. Mrs Thackeray was relieved. She was too
embarrassed herself to face anybody. They're all dressing, she

decided. She would have to confront them at the reception. As they made their way to the car Matron, already dressed for the occasion, appeared on the steps to wave them goodbye. She was clearly doing her matronly duty, for her face was without expression. They could have been going to a funeral. And in a way, they were. Both of them. To the registrar's office to bury their pasts, his of indiscriminate bachelorhood, and hers of too many unmentionables.

The registrar had provided two witnesses from off the street whose anonymity seemed appropriate. When the formalities were done with, the registrar gave Mr Thurlow permission to kiss his bride. Mrs Thackeray gave an involuntary shudder. That accessory to the sea and sand was making its first claim on her. She had never kissed Mr Thurlow and she hoped he wasn't going to make a production of it. Mercifully he gave her a mere peck on the cheek, and for that she could have kissed him.

On the way to the reception he took her hand and called her Mrs Thurlow. But in truth he was addressing his mother, who in his mind was the sole claimant to that title.

The residents had already arrived and were assembled on the steps of the hall. Matron had provided a mean sprinkling of confetti to be shared between all the Hollyhocks, barely a fistful each but adequate, she thought, for a gesture of good luck. Mrs Green aimed hers at the pavement, and it fell, polka-dotted, into a puddle.

The reception was a lavish one. Though privately mean, Mr Thurlow courted a reputation of public generosity so there was champagne that preceded a sit-down luncheon. Mr Thurlow placed Matron at the head of the table in an attempt to wipe the sour smirk off her face. He and his bride sat side by side in the centre of the long table, while the others took their places at random. The meal was served and eaten in an uncanny silence. In the light of the event there seemed nothing sensible to say.

Jeremy Cross attempted a rundown on the island of Barbados. He had never been there, but he had read about it in a geographical magazine. But there were no takers for his dissertation, and there was silence once more. The end of the meal undoubtedly signalled speech time but not one of them was willing to take the responsibility of a toast. They all looked at Matron. She in her turn looked at the Major, and went further, calling upon him to toast the bride and groom. The Major was not by nature given to speech-making and it was with great reluctance that he rose to his feet. He had no idea of what he should say. He looked across at Mrs Feinberg; she seemed to him to be the natural target of any toast he had to offer. And looking at her, words came into his mind, appropriate words, that he would address to her, so that they would be meaningful. For he hardly knew Eric Thurlow and had even less acquaintance with Mrs Thackeray. He wished them both well, but those few words hardly made a speech. He smiled across at Mrs Feinberg and he began. 'The autumn of our lives is an appropriate time for marriage,' he said. 'for it is then more than at any other time that we feel the need for companionship and for sharing our past lives.' He looked again at Mrs Feinberg and kept his eyes on her as he gave the toast to the newlyweds. 'I ask you to raise your glasses to the health and happiness of the new Mr and Mrs Thurlow.'

Mrs Feinberg raised her glass with the rest of them, but it was to the Major that she pointed it, as he did in her direction. He felt with that gesture that he had proposed to her and that she, with hers, had accepted him.

They drank the toast, then it was Eric Thurlow's turn to reply. 'Thank you for wishing us well,' he said. 'I know we'll be very happy. And let us drink a toast to your good selves.'

The newly married pair raised their glasses and as the new Mrs Thurlow drank, Mrs Green caught her eye and sincerely hoped it would choke her. After the toast, Eric gave his wife a public peck on the cheek and again she was grateful that he had not gone further.

The new Mrs Thurlow need not have worried. In that department, a peck was the most she would get, and only a meagre few of those. But there would be no kisses. Kisses were for a relationship, and Eric Thurlow had no concern with that. His primary interest was *connection*, a pursuit in which kissing would have been rudely out of place.

He took his wife's arm. 'We'll be off then,' he said to the assembled company. 'But please stay, all of you, and drink to our bon voyage.' Which the guests did as soon as the coast was clear. It was Matron who poured herself the first extra glass. And refilled it again and again. Lady Celia watched the poor woman's desperate chase after oblivion. For a moment she pitied her.

They stayed around the table until Eric Thurlow's largesse was exhausted. Then slowly they staggered to their feet, cursing their frailty.

'D'you think it will last?' Mrs Green was heard to say.

But no one was sober enough to bet on it. In any case, they didn't care. They all wanted their beds and didn't quite know how they would reach them. In the absence of Matron's capabilities, for she was as drunk as a snake, it was Lady Celia who took charge. She went to the phone and ordered a number of taxis to take them home. Then she took Matron's arm and helped her into the vestibule. The pity still lingered and it irritated her. It threatened to shake her resolve, and to make her contact Lady Priscilla and decide to let Matron off the hook. But she would leave it till the morning. By then perhaps, her pity would have evaporated.

Which it had. There was a hangover breakfast on the following day and a whispered buzz of Barbados speculation. Otherwise the Hollyhocks had returned to what the outsider would see as normal.

Lady Celia raised her net curtains on Mr Venables' Monday arrival, the Major and Mrs Feinberg took tea, Mrs Primple chatted over the hot and lukewarm wires, Mrs Hughes Minnied away, Mrs Green sulked, Jock MacPherson loyally bagpiped, and Jeremy Cross viewed his wardrobe list and wondered how soon it would lengthen.

Eleven

After the scheduled week, the honeymooners returned. Mrs Thackeray, as she still considered her title – not a happy name, but certainly happier than Mrs Thurlow – went straight to her room, unwilling to show herself. Jeremy Cross caught sight of her on the landing and was appalled by her appearance. Her face was sheet-white and she was limping painfully. He hid himself, sensing that she did not wish to be seen, but he was possessed of a story that he could gladly transfer to the common lounge, one that he could embroider with the dishonesty of a eyewitness. But Mr Thurlow was already there, brazenly displaying his tan, clearly not one that had come out of a bottle. Suddenly the man looked very much out of place in an old-age home. Rather like a bouncing visitor who had dropped in to call on an ageing relative. Mrs Thurlow had clearly done him a lot more good than he had done for her, and Jeremy Cross wondered how soon she would show her face to prove it.

They had had a wonderful time, he was telling the gathered residents. Swimming, sunbathing and eating the wonderful island food. He must have relished all those pleasures alone, for his poor wife showed no signs of sun, exercise or nutrition.

'And how is your good wife?' Jeremy Cross dared to ask.

'More to the point, *where* is she?' Jock MacPherson said. 'Is she playing the blushing bride?'

'I think she's jet-lagged,' Eric Thurlow said. 'Wants to catch up on her sleep.'

A likely story, Jeremy Cross thought. For no amount of jet-lag could account for Mrs Thurlow's pallor and limp. The other residents wondered why Mr Thurlow didn't join his wife, and Mrs Green had high hopes that the honeymoon was over.

It was lunchtime and there was a general move towards the dining room. Mr Thurlow moved along with them, and the others wondered why he didn't at least check on his new bride to see if she was hungry. But from the look that he had caught of her, Jeremy Cross could see that she had no appetite at all and at best, she would ultimately qualify for a 'tray in her room'. He felt sorry for her, and equally resentful of Mr Thurlow with his tan and his bonhomie, and he was glad that there were no willing ears for his Barbados adventure.

Lunch as usual was silent, and even after it, Mr Thurlow still hung around for coffee in the lounge. When that was done, he went as far as to announce that he was going for a walk and without ado, made straight for the garden and The Hollyhocks' drive. The residents looked at each other.

'Funny?' Jock MacPherson queried. He asked for them all.

Upstairs in her own quarters, Mrs Thackeray sat trembling on the edge of her bed. She was fatigued beyond measure but she didn't think she could ever sleep again. Indeed for every night of the last week she had hardly slept at all. Barbados had been an horrendous nightmare. The location was irrelevant. She had seen nothing of it at all. She had not felt the sun, nor tasted the sea, not indeed ventured once outdoors, whatever scenery that held. What little food she had managed to eat was brought on a tray to her room and the only gentle words she heard during her sojourn came from the chambermaid who served her. Now she trembled on the edge of her bed, trying to have a very serious board meeting with herself. She had decisions to make, and in order to make them, she had to review the past terrible week and wonder why it had happened at all.

It all began on their arrival at the hotel. She was excited by the luxury of it all; the chandeliered foyer, the liveried footmen, the exotic flower arrangements and the distinct smell of wealth. The plane journey had been smooth and pleasant enough and she was less fearful of what might be expected of her. She remembered waiting for the elevator to take them to their suite and looking back on the luxuriant foyer, deciding that she had made a very sensible marriage. When they had been installed in their suite, and the page boy suitably tipped, she had offered to unpack his clothes for him. She could not now think of him by name. She did not consider him worthy of any human title. So it was 'his' suitcase she'd offered to unpack because she thought that was a wifely duty. He had refused her offer, rather crossly, she thought, then he had turned his back on her to start unpacking. As the case was opened, she caught a glimpse of its contents. Ordinary enough, she thought, for anyone's viewing. Until he unravelled a towel, and a length of rope revealed itself. She thought perhaps he was fond of skipping, but she intuitively knew that she should not comment on it. They took showers in their separate bathrooms and dressed for dinner. By the time they were seated in the marble-encrusted dining room, with champagne as a wedding gift from the hotel management, she had put the rope out of her mind and confirmed once more to herself that remarriage had been a worthwhile decision. After dinner, while waiting for the lift, she recalled the rope once more and to comfort herself she looked back on the foyer, the lusciousness of the flora, the brilliance of the crystal. But apart from her limping return to the airport one week later, it was the last time she would view that oh so promising grandeur.

Their suite was on the thirty-fifth floor and though direct, the ascent took a little time. She remembered that as the lift doors opened on their suite, her trembling had begun.

At this point of her recall, Mrs Thackeray found herself trembling once more. She felt cold, and she wrapped the eider-down around her shoulders, but very gently, for they were sore and throbbing. She closed her eyes. She earnestly wished that she could sleep, but her longstanding insomnia seemed to have taken over and become her norm. She screwed her eyes tight, hoping to blind herself to memory, but she knew that the one sense had nothing to do with the other, and that recall, however discouraged, would finally conquer. She drew the eiderdown around her as snugly as she could bear, then she took herself back into their suite and shyly undressed according to her many pre-nuptial rehearsals. He had done likewise, though she sus-pected that his overweening self-confidence had never suggested rehearsal. First-night silk-nightied, she had slipped into bed, and he too beside her. But he was not alone. He had brought the rope with him.

At this point in her recall, Mrs Thackeray cried out, as per-haps she should have done between those nuptial sheets. But she had not even whimpered. Her astonishment and fear had been sublime, and for a nightmare moment she thought she lay again at the late and unlamented Mr Thackeray's side. And she had wondered what it was about herself that invited such a scenario. Did she ask for it? Was the sub-text of everything she said and did an invitation to cruelty? Did she, by her own nature, gravitate towards those who would punish her? And had he, that one she couldn't name, had he smelt the victim on her and pounced on his prey? He said it was a game he wanted to play. Only a game, he had insisted. They could both have fun together. He hadn't asked her if she'd wanted to play. He must have assumed she wouldn't refuse him. He'd turned her over then, like a piece of meat, and had tied her ankles and wrists to the brass bedposts. She had said nothing, too mortified to protest. Out of the corner of her eye, she had seen him reach for another rope and he was ready to play. She had lain there, suffering his sportsmanship, and she knew that there was a smirk on his face and that in time his pyjamas would be stained. It was Seven Pillars all over again, and she wasn't even poking the fire. But unlike Seven Pillars, this so-called game was far more hurtful. The force of his lashing increased and she marvelled that such an old man retained such strength. When he was done, he had had the temerity to ask if she had enjoyed it, and she had been too polite to tell him the truth. In any case, she did not wish him to think badly of her. Which was why she hated him beyond measure. She had wanted very much to go home.

When morning came, after a sleepless night, while he had snored beside her, the bright sunlight cheered her a little, but she found it painful to rise. She noticed that there was a spotting of blood on the sheet, and she knew how misleading such a stain could be. She stood by the bedside, supporting herself on the rail, and every bone in her body protested. She caught sight of herself in the mirror and was appalled by the reflection. Overnight she had aged a hundred years. She would not go downstairs, she decided. She would stay in the room and hope to heal. Six more nights to go, she said to herself, and she had staggered to the bathroom to cry.

And she was crying now, wrapped in her eiderdown, finding the recall too painful. Not so much for the matter of it, but for the shame that she had allowed it to happen. She could well have packed her bags and moved into another hotel. She could, with some dignity, have stepped out of the line of fire. But she had stayed. Not from any deliberate choice, but because she was afraid of what he might think of her. She shuddered at the thought of her offensive meekness, her bleak self-contempt, and she gripped her shoulders, pressing on her wounds, by way of punishing herself. To extend that punishment, she returned to her recall.

She had stayed in the room for the whole of that day. And for the next. Trolleys of food arrived, but she'd had little appetite. She saw nothing of him during the day, but at night he returned, bronzing, to their room, and without words between them, he had set about his 'game'. On the fourth night, he had abandoned the ropes, except those he used to tie her with. Instead, for the beatings, he used his hand. Although she could not see it, she had sensed that it was sheathed in a rubber glove. Halfway through the game he had taken it off and she felt the slimy flesh of it; although the flesh was less painful than the rope, it was somehow more disgusting. And more frightening, for she feared that it would lead to a different kind of flesh, to something worse than a hand.

And it did. It was their last night together, and when she thought of it now, the very worst. It was the most painful part of her recall and she decided to get it over and done with. Straight away.

He had used more than his hand. In his end game, he had simply buggered her.

Mrs Thackeray shivered. She knew that as long as she remained meek, subservient, indecisive, she would never get over it. In time the wounds would heal and the limp would mend but the scars would itch for ever. She straightened herself, letting the eiderdown slip, and she called herself to attention. A decision had to be made. Not as to the future of the marriage. That was over. There was no doubt of that. It was a question of how to engineer the separation. She had two choices. She could either pack her bags and leave herself, find another home, in London perhaps, and try to put the past behind her. Or she could insist that he left. He would refuse of course, on the grounds of inconvenience. She could insist and even threaten him. Threaten him with exposure. Exposure to all the residents. But would they believe her? Or would it be easier to assume that she, like poor Miss Bellamy, had suffered a little turn? It was a difficult decision but she knew she had to make it, and quickly. She favoured the second alternative, that of staying, whatever the consequences. She was the victim after all, so why should she inconvenience herself? Moreover, if she left, she would appear the guilty one and God knows what stories he would weave on her departure. No. Come what may, she would stay. She would tell him to go. Today. And if he refused, she would tell on him. And if he should say that no one would believe her, she would threaten to show her wounds.

She rose painfully from her bed. She would shower gently with lukewarm water. Then she would dress, not too smartly, she decided, and make an appearance at dinner. But before that, she hoped for an encounter with him, a meeting at which she could lay down her terms. She did not expect him to come to her rooms, so she would go to his. Before dinner.

During his walk, Eric Thurlow was having a similar board meeting with himself. He suffered no pain that would interrupt his recall, and few scruples to interfere with its flow. He reckoned he had had a pretty good holiday. He had his tan to show for it and a new spring in his step. He had eaten and slept well, and his carnal cravings had been more than satisfied. It was those that he would dwell on, the highlight of his honeymoon. Never in his life had he had such a compliant partner. She had been obedient, uncomplaining, and best of all, silent. She had been as mute as an inanimate object, which was exactly as he viewed her, a mere recipient of his scourge, a trite receptacle of his lust. Wonderful. He'd always considered that he adored women. But they had to be Madonnas. Figures made of plaster, with fake diamanté tears falling over rouged cheeks. A baby in her arms heightened the adoration, and the pedestal on which she stood humbled him into ecstasy. Clothe that figure in flesh, no matter how rouged, how weeping, and the passion soured into apathy, the adoration into hatred. But Mrs Thackeray, as he still considered her, sensing her unworthy of the Thurlow pedigree, Mrs Thackeray hadn't moved. She'd been *done* to, manoeuvred with, manipulated at his will. She had fulfilled every condition of his sick passion. Could it continue? Could he count on her silence? And if not, what was his next move? If by her choice the alliance was over, how could the separation be accomplished? He could ask her to leave. She might refuse, and even threaten him. Or he could leave The Hollyhocks himself, a move that would be deeply inconvenient. There was a bench at the end of the road; he made to sit on it, but hesitated for he considered it was placed there for the benefit of the elderly and in his present state of fitness it seemed to him inappropriate. But he could not deny that he was weary. He had walked a long way and the matter of his thought was in itself fatiguing. He made for a front garden wall, one of comfortable height, to rest himself upon. It was decision time. To go or to stay. But that was only on the assumption that the marriage was over. He did not think that likely. The woman was far too lethargic to alter the status quo. Besides, she would be too ashamed to admit that their nuptials had been a mistake. But he had to be prepared for such an eventuality. First he weighed up the pros and cons of staying. She would not speak to him, thus neither could he to her. They would seek to avoid each other, an uneasy undertaking at The Hollyhocks. The other residents would take notice and begin to talk. And to speculate. He would be loth to turn his back on the common lounge. To stay was not a happy prospect. He then considered the possibility of leaving. It did not occur to him that his departure would imply guilt. On the contrary, the guilt would stick to the one who stayed. He had gone, they would assume, because in all conscience he could stand her no longer. And like the gentleman he was known to be, he had done the decent thing.

He rose from the wall, his decision made. He would go to her rooms before dinner. He did not suppose she would come to his.

It was thus that they met, as Mrs Thackeray was going to his rooms and he to hers, in the corridor, midway between their separate quarters. They stared at each other for a while. It was Mrs Thackeray, in her new mood of resolve, who spoke first.

'I would like to talk to you,' she said. 'Would you come to my room?' She turned and led the way, relieved that the show-down would take place on her own territory.

For a moment he could not move. The woman had changed. The inanimate object had given voice. The plaster had fallen away and turned to flesh. The marriage was over. He found it difficult to move from his spot, and it was only his growing bile and loathing that fuelled his feet to her door.

She asked him to take a seat, but she did not sit down herself. She preferred to stand and look down on him, translating her seething contempt.

'Our marriage is over,' she said. 'And I want you to leave. I want you to leave The Hollyhocks,' she added in case she hadn't made herself clear.

He said nothing. It was the decision he had already made for himself and he was damned if she was going to assume that she'd made it for him. At last he found his voice, and it was one of rage.

'How dare you tell me what I should do. *I* am the one who

makes decisions. And in any case, I had already decided to leave this place. D'you think I could stand to look at your miserable face any longer? D'you think I'm prepared to spend one more penny on your measly ingratitude? I would be ashamed to be seen with you. Even in the dark.' With her decision, the wind had been taken out of his sails and he salivated with rage. In place of the bronze which had kindled his skin there spread a flush of crimson, and for a moment she thought he might detonate. She could not help but smile, a smile that slowly broke into laughter.

'If I weren't such a gentleman,' he said, 'I would hit you.'

'And what in the name of God have you been doing to me this past week?' she said.

That had had nothing to do with hitting, he thought, and he realised that the stupid woman hadn't understood it at all. He considered himself well rid of her.

'I'll go in my own good time,' he said.

'You'll go now.' Mrs Thackeray surprised herself with her sudden authority.

'How dare you talk to me like that,' he said, his voice trembling with defeat. 'You ugly old scum-bag.' He was almost weeping.

Then Mrs Thackeray blew. 'You're nothing but a pathetic pervert,' she said. 'A filthy sex-mad maniac. You poor little bugger. Maybe it's because you've got such a tiny cock.' She had to sit down then, stunned by the words that fell so naturally from her lips, words that she had never in her life uttered. All those words that she'd never had the courage to give to the deserving Mr Thackeray she uttered now, and despite their long and bitter storage they had lost none of their power. 'You pathetic little man,' she said, 'pack your stinking pyjamas and dirty ropes, and get out of here.'

He stared at her. How could he have been so mistaken? 'I'll go in my own good time,' he said again.

'You'll go now.' Mrs Thackeray rose. 'You'll go now or I'll tell Matron on you. And all the residents too.'

He was beaten and he knew it.

'And you can count yourself lucky,' Mrs Thackeray ploughed on, 'that I won't sue you for grievous bodily harm.' She was now well into her stride. And she was actually enjoying herself. She was back in the Seven Pillars poking the fire, then turning to beat her late husband fair and square with the poker. She knew that she had undergone a radical change, and that the so-called honeymoon, however horrendous, had on the quiet done her a power of good. She opened her door. 'I never want to look upon your rotten face ever again,' she said. She shoved him as he passed through the doorway and he lost his balance. For a moment, the old Mrs Thackeray thought she might help him to his feet. But bugger him, she decided. 'Funny,' she said, 'but you look better on all fours. Much more in character.' She shut the door after him, sweeping away his jacket with her foot as if he were a scoop of rubbish. Then she had to sit down. She was exhausted with shock at the change that had overcome her so suddenly and with utter confidence. She started to giggle and for the first time in many years, she began to feel happy. But a different kind of happiness. One that depended on nobody else but solely on herself. Astonishingly, she felt no more pain. She looked in the mirror of her dressing-table and noticed that her cheeks were glowing pink. Her eyes were bright and she looked as if she'd returned from a wonderful holiday. She would take a bath, she thought, and put on her best dress, and without fear join the other residents for dinner.

As she was undressing, she heard the sound of luggage being dragged outside her door. The enemy, his tail well between his filthy legs, was in retreat. She opened the door slightly and saw the bent back of him and his slow gait. He looked like an injured beetle, and she was delighted that she felt no pity for him.

As she luxuriated in her over-foamed bath, she wondered what cock and bull story he was giving to Matron. But she didn't care. She was not even curious. She preferred to concentrate on how she would spend the rest of her life and to what use she would put her newfound independence. She knew that she could not engineer a radical event, but she was confident that whatever would now happen to her would be viewed in a very different light and through her own vision, unblurred by others' expectations. As she put on her bathrobe she noticed that all her pain was gone. The limp remained, but less acute than before. She had a distinct feeling that she had been reborn.

As she was dressing, there was a knock on her door. She trembled slightly, fearing that he had returned.

'Who is it?' she asked, in a tone of voice which indicated that she was not open to everybody.

'It's Matron,' she heard.

She opened the door. Matron stood there with a suitable expression of sympathy on her face. Mrs Thackeray could guess at the kind of story she had heard.

'I'm so sorry it didn't work out,' Matron said. 'I hope that you will soon get over it. Rejection is a terrible thing for a woman.'

Mrs Thackeray laughed in her face. 'I think the boot was on the other foot, Matron,' she said. 'It was I who told him to go.'

Matron sat down. She was confused. 'He told me a very different story,' she said.

Mrs Thackeray had no wish to ask her what it was. She didn't care whose version Matron believed.

'D'you want to know where he's gone?' Matron asked.

'No,' Mrs Thackeray said firmly. 'I don't want to hear anything about him. Or whose version you care to believe. It's over, Matron, and I've never felt better in my life.'

Well she certainly looks better, Matron thought, better than she'd ever looked since coming to The Hollyhocks. Prettier too. She inclined towards Mrs Thackeray's version. No rejected woman ever looked like her.

'What am I to tell the other residents?' she asked.

'What you wish,' Mrs Thackeray said. 'I shall tell them the truth. That I threw him out.'

'I'm inclined to believe you,' Matron said with half a smile. Though she tended to favour her gentlemen residents, when the chips were down she didn't like them very much. She had only to think of Mr Venables to confirm that loathing. 'I hope to see you at dinner Mrs Thurlow.'

'Mrs Thackeray,' she corrected her, 'and I don't want to hear that name ever again.'

Matron went to the door. 'I didn't like the way he refused to pay for your residence,' she said. Thus she declared herself on Mrs Thackeray's side.

When Mrs Thackeray entered the dining room, they asked her quite naturally where her husband was.

'He's gone,' she announced to the general assembly. 'I threw him out.' Then she took her seat. 'That's all there is to say.' Her voice pierced the stunned silence. It was clear that no questions were to be asked. So dinner was taken in silence all around, a silence which overlapped the night drinks in the lounge. The residents wished Mrs Thurlow, or whatever she now called herself, would retire, so that their tongues were free once more. But she showed no sign of fatigue. Mrs Green could stand the silence no longer and she moved her chair next to that of Mrs Thackeray.

'I'm so sorry,' she whispered. Mrs Thackeray stared at her for a while, long enough to make Mrs Green wish she'd never opened her mouth.

At last Mrs Thackeray spoke and she made no attempt to lower her voice. 'You're not sorry at all, Mrs Green,' she said. 'Not a bit. You're simply delighted. I think you have wished nobody well in all your life.' Then she twisted her chair away and poor Mrs Green was left on stage, spotlit and speechless. It was then that Mrs Thackeray saw fit to retire. She wished everyone good night and she did not linger outside the door to eavesdrop on the astonished buzz inside.

Meanwhile, Matron was once again at her waiting list. She now had two vacancies. Poor Miss Bellamy's rooms were by now sufficiently aired to accommodate a newcomer. And Mr Thurlow's quarters only needed a cleaning. She had hopes of redressing the gender balance of The Hollyhocks but, alas, there were no gentlemen on her list. She herself was in favour of advertising The Hollyhocks, but the board of trustees were opposed to the idea. They felt that advertisement was common and would only serve to diminish The Hollyhocks' reputation if they were seen to be touting for clients. They were in favour of recommendation by word of mouth. Matron had tried to explain to them that the residents received very few visitors from the outside, and that the only reliable word of mouth could hardly come from a mouth already dead. She looked at her list once more, as if by reading it very carefully it might conjure up a name that was suitably masculine. She decided to postpone her decision and at most to fill only one of the vacancies, and hope that, in time, a gentleman would materialise and fill the other. She was tired and she longed for her bed. But it was Sunday, the eve of Venables, and she knew she would have a restless night. She loved her job and the power and authority that it gave her, and her life would have been a contented one if only it did not contain a Mr Venables. She was angry that Dr Leigh had deserted her, though his presence would in no way have reduced her weekly debt. But it had been a comfort to know that she was not the only one in thrall. She opened her drawer and counted out the payment from her petty cash. She put the notes in an envelope so that they were ready. She could not bear to look at him, and the sooner the transaction was over, the better. She dragged herself to her quarters. She thought she might knock on Mrs Thackeray's door to check that all was well. But bugger her, she decided. She had problems of her own.

Downstairs, the lounge had almost emptied. Jeremy Cross, always the last to leave, was still sitting there. But so was Mrs Hughes who usually retired early. Mr Cross couldn't understand what she was waiting for, but he'd be damned if he'd be the first to leave. He would sit her out. She sat there reading a newspaper, or pretending to do so, he was sure. He stared at her in the hope of ousting her with his look, but she deliberately did not look in his direction. If he were to leave before her, he would be breaking the habit of his Hollyhocks sojourn, and the survival that it entailed. Whatever the circumstances, and wherever the place, he would be the last to quit. So he sat there, glowering and trying to keep his tired eyes open.

But Mrs Hughes seemed settled for the night. She even turned the page of the newspaper, as if she had a mind to read every word of it. Mr Cross sat it out for a little while, but when she turned yet another page, he could hold out no longer. He prayed to God, in Whom he had never believed, that He would turn a blind eye to this lapse in his routine and that He wouldn't hold it against him and his chances of survival. And without bothering to say good night, he stalked out of the room.

For the first time that evening, Mrs Hughes raised her eyes from the newspaper, so full of words that she had never read. She gave Mr Cross time to climb the stairs and to reach his own quarters. Then she folded the newspaper, laid it on the table and waited. A hopeless tear fell from one eye, and then from the other. Slowly she rose, and with her two hands held her handbag behind her. She walked awkwardly to the door. She would not turn around. She did not want to see the wet stain she'd left on the armchair behind her. As she climbed the stairs, her handbag bumping rhythmically on her behind, the tears flowed freely and she had no free hand to wipe them away. Tomorrow, Matron would notice the stain and with a little detective work she would discover who had made it. The following night there would be a discreet rubber sheet on her bed. She undressed herself and washed as best she could, crying all the while. Not even the thought of Minnie could console her. Indeed it only served to augment her depression, as she wondered for how much longer she could relate her Minnie tales. The realisation that she would never see Minnie as a grown woman struck her for the first time. Now her tears were unstoppable. Mrs Hughes had never given much thought to death. Her constant contentment had led her to believe herself immortal. Now all that had changed. She was now like the rest of them at The Hollyhocks, playing the waiting game, a game that was no fun at all.

PART TWO

Twelve

Nothing happened at The Hollyhocks except the passing of time. Over the next few weeks a Mrs Scott was settled in poor Miss Bellamy's quarters. Jeremy Cross was often tempted to apprise her of the unsavoury passing of its last tenant in the hope that it would frighten the poor lady to death. But he held his tongue. There would come a time. And an appropriate time too. For Mrs Scott, all seventy-five years of her, was into horoscopes. She was as addicted to her daily clairvoyance as was Mrs Primple to her chat lines. At seventy-five, she still had hopes. Hopes of a lottery win, hopes of a dark and handsome stranger who would ask for her hand in marriage. She ignored all advice to caution, and, in full hearing of the common lounge, she would read those warnings aloud and with disdain. Yes, thought Jeremy Cross, there would certainly come a time.

Mr Thurlow's room was still vacant, awaiting that elusive male applicant. Mrs Primple still prattled along the wires, sitting or lying in various voices. Every Monday Mr Venables made his regular call and Lady Celia raised and lowered her net curtains. Matron looked peakier than ever. The Major and Mrs Feinberg took their morning tea and still Mrs Feinberg kept her unease in her quarters. Jock MacPherson persistently waved his Scottish banner, and uttered 'Scotland the Brave' as a prayer before every meal. Mrs Hughes wet her knickers while, down the road in the nursery, little Minnie did likewise. Both were ashamed. And Mrs Thackeray, because of the victim she had once been, had now quite naturally turned into a bully.

Then one day Mrs Green received another letter from Her Majesty. She covered it hastily with a trembling hand. She was seen to grow threateningly pale, and she swayed slightly, steadying herself with a grip on a neighbouring chair.

'Are you all right, Mrs Green?' Mrs Feinberg asked.

Mrs Green could well have done without their concern, most of all from the Jew-lady's quarter.

'I'm fine,' she said, slowly getting to her feet. She refused help out of the dining room, and walked unsteadily to her rooms. Once there, she sat on her bed and tried to calm herself. Then when her trembling had ceased, she opened the letter.

There was no need of a careful reading of the preamble. She already knew the facts. It was the final paragraph that melted her bowels in fear. In it, she was summoned immediately to London.

She packed a small bag with trembling hands, then straightened herself, and forcing a brave smile she said to herself, 'I've bluffed them before. And I shall bluff them again.' She walked to the station and caught the first available up-train.

This time, Mrs Green was absent only a few days, and she returned with a beaming air, totally satisfied. For those who asked, she gave a garbled report of having had business to attend to. Mrs Thackeray saw fit to ask the nature of that business. Mrs Green had not expected a cross-examination, and she hesitated.

'Private business,' she offered.

'Well I hope Her Majesty was satisfied,' Mrs Thackeray sneered, then she turned to talk to the new Mrs Scott who happened to be sitting beside her.

When Mrs Green had left The Hollyhocks for the second time, Mrs Feinberg felt a surge of relief. And looking back in her diary, which she had kept daily since arriving at The Hollyhocks, she noted that her last period of wellbeing had coincided with Mrs Green's earlier absence. Bewildered, she put two and two together, and took her findings to the teashop the following morning.

'Your ill feelings have something to do with Mrs Green,' the Major concluded. 'There's no doubt about it in my mind. She reminds you of something unpleasant. We'll have to take a jolly good look at her. Not just her face. We know that pretty well by now. But the way she eats, or walks, or even sits. Little things like that. I can't help you in that respect I'm afraid. It's all up to you. You can report your discoveries to me. Don't worry my dear, we'll get to the bottom of it all.'

It had started to rain, so they took an extra pot of tea and Mrs Feinberg was pleased to delay her return to The Hollyhocks. When the rain lifted, they dawdled slowly home, reaching there in time for lunch. Mrs Feinberg, guided by the Major, took her seat opposite Mrs Green and watched her every mouthful. She scrutinised every finger on each hand, as Mrs Green raised the fork to her lips. She brazenly spied on each movement of her jaw as she chewed her food, but no movement rang a bell. After lunch she reported her non-reactions to the Major.

'All is not lost,' he said. 'We shall work by a process of elim-ination. So far we have proved that you have never seen Mrs Green at table. Now you must scrutinise her walk.'

For the next week Mrs Feinberg forbore to return to her quarters and she kept an eye on Mrs Green's every movement. But nothing about the woman jogged her memory. She lost heart.

'Perhaps it was just a coincidence,' she told the Major. 'She simply doesn't remind me of anything. She's just an ordinary woman, living out her days at The Hollyhocks. Like the rest of us.'

'It's happened twice,' the Major persisted. 'It's not a coinci-dence.' But Mrs Feinberg saw no point in further supervision, and once again she took to retiring to her rooms.

Then one day, Mrs Primple asked for a tray in her room. And the next day. And the next. More ominous still, she had a visitor, her first in all of the years she had been at The Hollyhocks. He was her nephew, in for the kill. When the res-idents asked after her welfare, Matron came clean. She'd learned her lessons from Mrs Webber and poor Miss Bellamy. There was no question of Mrs Primple being 'right as rain in the morning'. Mrs Primple was simply never going to come downstairs again.

'I'm afraid she's very poorly indeed,' Matron told them. 'She has pneumonia and she's showing no signs of recovery.' She was quoting directly from the doctor who had only just left Mrs Primple's bedside. 'She's in no pain,' she quoted further. 'Her nephew's with her now.'

'I didn't know she had any family,' Mrs Thackeray said.

Matron explained. 'When she came to The Hollyhocks, she gave her nephew as next of kin. And in the seven years that's she's been here, poor dear, he's never once phoned or visited. I don't call that much of a family.'

The residents agreed with a sigh.

'I'll keep you informed,' Matron said as she left the room.

Lady Celia noticed a spring in her step and she ascribed it to a relief that one of her charges was going to die incontrovertibly of natural causes.

Although Mrs Primple had rarely shown her face in the common lounge, she was suddenly missed by all the residents. Whereas nobody had noticed her absence before, it was now manifest and palpable. It was as if her truancy and its cause had pierced a personal hole in the heart of each resident. A general depression settled over the common lounge, an ominous reminder of the waiting game all of them were playing.

That day, the nephew joined them for lunch, while the tray went upstairs. He seemed particularly jolly, given the circumstances. No doubt he was in premature celebration of the windfall that would come his way, for the almost late Mrs Primple was known to be a very rich woman indeed. The nephew, who never offered his name, was puzzled by the coolness of his lunch companions. But they simply didn't like him. They thought his seven-year neglect of his aunt was unpardonable. It was Mrs Thackeray who broke the silence, and voiced the sentiments of them all.

'You've not visited before,' she accused in her newly acquired barbed tone. 'And your dear aunt has been here for some time.'

'It's not easy to get down from London,' the nephew said belligerently.

'Only London?' Lady Celia sneered. 'Why, I go up to town and back again once a month, with no problem at all.'

'I'm a very busy man,' the nephew said. And knowing that he had no leg to stand on, he became aggressive. 'I travel a great deal,' he said. 'I have a large staff that depends on me. I have a wife and children with whom I already spend little enough time.'

'Oh we do understand,' Mrs Thackeray said with heavy sarcasm. 'It's so good of you to have found time to see your aunt for the last time.' After that there was nothing more to be said, and the nephew left the dining room forgoing his dessert.

The tray in the room routine continued and after the fourth day the nephew tired of cooling his heels. His aunt was taking an indecent time over her demise and he decided to let her get on with it. At the end of the week, he went back to London.

But he was back again on the following day. And Jeremy Cross was at his wardrobe door. He left a large gap under poor Miss Bellamy. Hers had been a cruel death, ungentle, far away from the peaceful, accepting passing of Mrs Primple. So he wrote her name below the respectful gap, and after it, 'natural causes'.

Mrs Primple had waited for her nephew to leave so that she could die in peace. Which she did, serenely in her sleep. Matron broke the news of her sad passing, as she called it, while the residents were at breakfast. She had sent for the nephew, she told them. Mrs Primple's body would be taken to London and buried next to her late husband.

'It had been her last wish,' Matron said. She left the dining room, almost skipping, the residents noticed, and wondered at her sudden show of wellbeing.

Matron did indeed have cause for her cheer. She had sat with Mrs Primple a few hours before she had died and she had held her hand and comforted her.

'I've left you a little something,' Mrs Primple had whispered and had closed her eyes once more. A 'little something' could have meant anything, but in the light of Mrs Primple's wealth it could have meant a great deal. Matron would have to wait until the will was read. No doubt she would be informed and the expectation was exciting enough to buoy her up for a time. But she couldn't help daydreaming of the coming of a time when Mr Venables would be a mere caller to be seen to, as she would see to the laundry.

The residents lined up in reception as Mrs Primple's coffin was manoeuvred down the stairs. The nephew had brought a solemn face from London, as separate as a handkerchief, and he wore it smugly as he led the bearers through reception. He avoided any glance in the residents' direction, keeping his eyes firmly on the ground, a look he hoped would pass for mourning. As the hearse disappeared down the driveway, the residents knew that although they had seen little of Mrs Primple during her Hollyhocks sojourn, and knew her even less, they would miss her terribly. They shuffled back into the common lounge and grew angry. Any reminder of their own mortality roused them to fury. They would find fault with each other, find this one a nag, and the other a bully. It would take a little time until they looked into themselves and once again joined in the waiting game.

The following week, Matron received a letter from Mrs Primple's solicitors. It informed her that she was a beneficiary under the last will and testament of the late Mrs Sarah Primple and she was invited to attend its reading at the lawyer's office. Alas, the meeting would take place on the following Monday at four p.m. Mr Venables' calling hour. She cursed him long and loud. There was no way she could leave The Hollyhocks on a Monday afternoon. There was no one she could depute to hand over the money to her blackmailer. She rang the solicitor immediately, hoping he would grant her a private viewing. He told her his time would not allow it, but he would send her a copy of the will as soon as it was known to the other beneficiaries. So Matron had to wait. She busied herself so that the time would pass more quickly. She saw to it that Mrs Primple's room, the late beloved Mrs Primple as she now thought of her, was made ready for a new occupant. She now had two vacancies, and once again she considered her waiting list. It was exactly the same as it had been when she had last consulted it. She'd had vague hopes that while her back had been turned, a masculine name might have trespassed on that exclusively female territory. But it was as before: women's domain.

In time, the solicitor's letter arrived, and she postponed opening it until her free hour in the afternoon. For the whole
morning she was excessively caring to her residents, smiling all
the while, and Lady Celia wondered whether the ferret had
missed a call or perhaps, God forbid, had faded out of the picture altogether. She would have to wait another week before her
London visit to find out why Matron had suddenly lost her
peaky look. But by the evening, it was back again in spades.

Matron had read Mrs Primple's – no longer beloved – last
will and testament, and it was as disappointing and as shocking
as the late ungrateful Mrs Webber's. She had indeed been left
a legacy. But it was not a personal one. It was a gift of twenty-
five thousand pounds to the Hollyhocks Home, and 'with many
thanks,' she read aloud, 'for Matron's care and attention.'

'Bugger her,' Matron said. Mrs Primple was even more
ungrateful than Mrs Webber. All that legacy would do for her
was to increase her standing with the board of trustees. She
wondered whether they might give her a bonus for enabling
such a generous gift. 'They bloody well ought to,' she shouted
to her desk, and her bile rose and flooded her face with its erstwhile jaundiced hue. With little curiosity, she read the rest of
the ingrate's will, and its matter puzzled her. For apart from a
few minor bequests to odd societies for the prevention of cruelty to children, animals and birds, she had left the bulk of her
estate to three specified chat lines, 'in gratitude for the pleasure
they have given me over the years'. Such a legacy was as surprising and as outlandish as Mrs Webber's gift to Ebenezer
Obadiah. There were no other legatees, and Matron was
cheered in the knowledge that the nephew had been thoroughly
avenged for his long-term neglect. He had not received a single
penny.

She lost no time in apprising the board of trustees of their
unexpected windfall. She heard the surprise and delight at the
end of the line.

'You'll be hearing from us Matron,' the chairman said, and she took it as a hint of a bonus. Within a week, it duly arrived. A cheque for one thousand pounds for her good services. She thought that in view of the sum of the legacy, it was a mean proportion, but she comforted herself with the fact that it would keep Mr Venables quiet for the length of a month. Then she resented the fact that such a bonus would be wasted on such a recipient. But she was happy to share the news of the nephew's disinheritance with her residents, for she knew that they had not warmed to him. They cheered when she announced it in the dining room. She told them too of the recipients of the bulk of her wealth, for she needed to share her own bewilderment.

'So that's what she was doing all the time in her room,' Mrs Thackeray said. 'That's why we only saw her at mealtimes.'

'She was a dark horse, that one,' Mrs Green said, a favourite phrase of hers, which she applied to anybody when she needed to talk to herself.

The topic of the late Mrs Primple's will served them well through the next day, and then she was forgotten, as poor Miss Bellamy was forgotten, and Mrs Webber too, for any reminder of them interrupted their waiting game and brought its inevitable end to their attention.

Then one morning, out of the blue, Matron got a letter. A letter of application. Its sender was one Mr John Rufus.

'A gentleman at last,' Matron sighed, and she read his particulars. Seventy-five years old, and a retired bank manager from Manchester. He would welcome an appointment.

Matron wrote to him straight away and arranged to see him at his convenience. Would he telephone and let her know when he was coming? She had already decided to take him at all costs – she would even waive the class qualification if necessary – and that he would occupy Mr Thurlow's old rooms. She was tempted to tell him to bring his luggage with him to the appointment. But she didn't wish to appear too eager. It was important that outsiders continued to believe that The Hollyhocks Home was very picky with its residential list.

Mr Rufus kept his appointment the following week, and even without his favoured gender, Matron found him more than satisfactory. He was spry and smartly dressed and seemed to know exactly what he wanted. Matron wondered why he felt the need for residential care. He seemed fit enough, with all his senses intact. Mr Rufus had expected such doubts as to his readiness for The Hollyhocks and he gave his assurance that his decision was a sensible one.

'I've always wanted to live in London,' he said, 'and I decided that after retirement I would move to the capital. But I stayed in Manchester because I was offered consultancy work there. Now I feel too old to make two moves. Eventually I will have need of care, and a home near London is like killing two birds with one stone. Made sense to me.'

It made sense to Matron too and she invited him to take up residence as soon as he wished. She gave him a guided tour, first showing him the rooms that he would occupy. She had taken care to set a flower arrangement on the occasional table. Mr Rufus found it to his liking. She showed him the common lounge, but apart from Mrs Hughes who seemed glued to her usual chair, there was no one about.

'They're probably out walking,' Matron explained as if she were running a physical training establishment, 'but you'll meet them all next week. I'm sure you'll be very happy here.'

At dinner that evening, she announced the advent of Mr John Rufus, dressed in all his particulars. Mrs Green automatically primped her hair. She was the only woman in the room who had not given up on conquest. Except perhaps for the new Mrs Horoscope Scott, but she relished the promise more than its fulfilment. Mrs Hughes, glued to her seat, accepted that she no longer qualified. Mrs Thackeray, twice bitten, was quadruply shy. Mrs Feinberg was bespoke, and Lady Celia had better fish to fry. Mrs Green was confident that, with Mr Rufus, there would be no competition.

Indeed he made a beeline for her as soon as he arrived. He was careful to include the other ladies in his interest but it was clear that his focus of attention was Mrs Helen Green. Other gentlemen represented no competition. The Major was bespoke. Jock MacPherson had but one mistress, Scotland, and to her he was eternally faithful. And Jeremy Cross was too engrossed in his pursuit of survival to risk the threat of any relationship. So for Mr John Rufus, the field was clear. But he did not play it continually. Indeed he spent much of his time in his rooms and quite often he went up to London to see friends or to take in a theatre. His absences added spice to what Mrs Green liked to think of as a courtship, and her wardrobe was seen to expand and her *maquillage* thicken. Pathetic, Mrs Thackeray thought, and actually commented on it whether the occasion arose or not. The two women were now openly hostile to each other. With the arrival of Mr Rufus, Mrs Green had dropped any overtures of friendship to Mrs Thackeray. It wasn't that the penny had dropped. She'd never understood the reason for Mrs Thackeray's sudden cooling-off. It was that now she had no need for such a friendship any longer. She was too engrossed in the exciting possibilities of Mr Rufus' coming. Not that Mr Rufus had hinted at any. He simply took her walking from time to time. He talked mainly about himself and Mrs Green was glad of that for she was too confused to know exactly who she was and what she was about. Once when he had told her of a holiday he had taken in Switzerland, she had volunteered her sojourn in a Swiss finishing school, but she was no longer even sure of that. In any case, he seemed uninterested, and had continued with his holiday stories including one about a wine that he had come upon, a Riesling, a very sweet hock. He gave her the name and said how much he would love to come across it again. Mrs Green made a mental note of the name and as soon as she was alone she wrote it down, resolving to find a bottle for his gratification. She did not expect to find it in the local off-licence, since he had given the impression that it was a rare vintage, but there were half a dozen or so lined up on the shelves. She considered buying two of them, but decided against it, since one would be enough to excite his palate and lead to whatever it might lead to. She flushed as she took it from the assistant and carried it back to her rooms, concealed under her overcoat. On her next shopping expedition, she bought a corkscrew and a couple of paper cups and it all reminded her of the dormitory feasts in the Swiss finishing school that she had never attended. She would wait for a propitious moment before issuing her invitation.

That moment came a few days later. That evening, the dessert at dinner had been a crème caramel.

'This reminds me of Switzerland,' he had told her. 'It would be perfect with a glass of hock.'

It seemed that he had invited himself.

'If you'd like to come to my rooms after dinner,' she said, 'I think I may have a surprise for you.'

'I love surprises,' he said. 'And I'd be glad to.'

After dinner they adjourned quite openly to Mrs Green's room. The move passed largely unnoticed. Interest in Mrs Green and Mr Rufus was minimal. But Mrs Thackeray noticed the move and called it to the attention of Mrs Scott because she needed somebody to sneer with.

Upstairs in her rooms, Mrs Green unveiled the bottle. Mr Rufus expressed his delight and cleverly hid his disappointment. His original bottle was a vintage one. This was of the current year's harvest and was likely to taste like saccharine.

'You do the honours,' Mrs Green said, handing him the corkscrew. He opened the bottle and poured the wine into the paper cups thinking them a fitting receptacle. Then they toasted each other. He sipped it and tried not to show his distaste; it was full of acid and sugar at the same time, a sweet-sour wine, suitable for a cheap Chinese takeaway.

'Does it take you back to Switzerland?' she asked him.

'Very much so,' Mr Rufus said, though no wine on earth could have taken him back to Switzerland, for he had never been there in the first place. He stayed awhile, talking of mountains, then, pleading fatigue, he declined a second glass, thanked her and wished her a good night.

Mrs Green viewed the three-quarters full bottle, and had to admit to herself that the evening had not been a roaring success. But she was damned if she was going to waste good money. She refilled her cup again and again and wondered what Mr Rufus was going on about. After the fifth cup, she got used to it and finishing off the bottle was no hardship. She staggered to her bed without the strength to undress, and she awoke the following morning crumpled, headached and with a raging thirst. She kept to her bed that day, but she made sure not to ask for a tray in her room. She knew from experience how such a phrase was tossed around in the common lounge. In any case she had no appetite. She half hoped that Mr Rufus would pay her a visit during the day, concerned as he might be with her wellbeing. But the day passed with no visitor except for Matron who came after dinner with a welcome cup of tea.

The following day, Mrs Green was herself again, and when she went down to breakfast she noticed that Mr Rufus' chair was empty. She discovered that he had gone up to London the previous day and ought to be back by evening. This news pleased her, for it explained his lack of a visit. She looked forward to dinner. But his chair was still vacant, as it was the whole of the following day. And the next. Mrs Green started to become lovesick. She missed him terribly. She had to admit to herself that perhaps she had fallen in love with him. She knew the feeling. She had had it once before. In her twenties, before she had married. She recalled his name but kept it even from herself, because it belonged to the truth of her past, and as such it was unmentionable. But she pictured his blond hair and blue eyes, which could have belonged to anybody and in any place. He too had gone away from time to time, and she had waited for him with longing. And at each reunion they had renewed their love for each other. Then there had come a time when he went away and had never come back. He had run, and she had later heard that he had been cut down in his flight.

She had mourned him long and loud. She recalled her feelings at that loving-time, how everything in the world looked beautiful and how everybody in it was forgivable. And now at this time she was noticing each flower in The Hollyhocks' gardens, marvelling at each sunset and even finding Mrs Thackeray, with all her bullying, fairly tolerable. She hankered after Mr Rufus' return.

She heard a car grinding to a halt on the driveway and she rushed to her window. It was a big black car and it disappointed her for she knew that John Rufus did not drive. She had hoped it would be a station taxi bringing him home. But the door was opened, and one dressed as a chauffeur alighted to open the rear door. And it was indeed Mr Rufus who was the passenger. Mrs Green was mightily impressed. She watched him have a word with the chauffeur and then turn into The Hollyhocks' entrance and disappear under the porch. She sat on her bed and shivered with delight. She would take her time, she thought, before making an appearance downstairs. It was her turn to keep him waiting. She would not mention the chauffeur or the car, she decided. She would not want him to know that she was looking out for him. She thought the appropriate phrase was 'playing it cool'. She had heard it on the television. And that was exactly what she would do, but the waiting was agony. She would go down at suppertime, she decided, a good three hours till then, and she must find some way of occupying her time. She took a key from her bag and opened one of the drawers in her tallboy.

As she did so, she wondered how many other Hollyhocks had secret drawers and what they kept in them. She doubted that any of them had anything to hide though she imagined that poor Miss Bellamy had had secrets in plenty. The Major's drawers were probably unlocked, his military medals available for all to view. And as for that Jew woman – Mrs Green's present good-will did not stretch to Mrs Feinberg – her drawers were probably empty for she had nothing she would wish to recall.

She unlocked the drawer and took out a file of letters. She put the file on top of her desk, then went to lock her door. For the next few hours she would be closed to everybody, even to Mr Rufus should he choose to knock on her door. She sat at her desk and lit a cigarette. Mrs Green smoked rarely. She took a cigarette to celebrate a moment of happiness. Or a treat. And the reading of the file would be a treat of sorts, a recall of past joys, a testimony to her own genius for deception. The time passed quickly and when she heard the supper gong, she noticed that it had grown dark. She opened her window to let out the smell of smoke, then she locked the file away, renewed her make-up, primped her hair, and made her way to the dining room. And there was John Rufus, the target of all her breath-lessness, seated next to Mrs Thackeray and clearly in animated conversation. To be fair, when he saw Mrs Green enter the dining room, he rose from his chair and greeted her with a dis-tant wave of the hand. She had to be satisfied with that, and she took a seat next to Mrs Scott who was still studying the evening paper's horoscopes. She thought that perhaps Mr Rufus was using the same ploy as herself, that of playing it cool, and this thought cheered her a little. She would feign indifference. So she tried to engage her neighbour in conversation.

'How's your forecast today, Mrs Scott?' she asked. She couldn't have cared less what the stars had in store for Mrs Scott but she wanted to be seen in conversation and its matter was irrelevant.

'This one is for tomorrow,' Mrs Scott said, wishing to be accurate. 'And it's rather good. Very good in fact on the domestic front.'

'D'you have any family?' Mrs Green asked.

'One son. That's all,' Mrs Scott said. 'And he's in Australia. It means that I shall soon have a letter from him. Well it's something to look forward to isn't it,' she said.

'What does mine say?' Mrs Green asked, fearing the conversation would flag.

'What star are you?'

'Scorpio,' Mrs Green said.

'Not a good sign for a woman,' Mrs Scott declared with a Cassandra-like authority. 'Always a sting in the tail. But a very interesting sign nevertheless.'

Mrs Green didn't know how to respond for she had been insulted and flattered in the same breath. 'Well anyway,' she said, 'what does it say?'

'I'll read it to you,' Mrs Scott said. Then with her finger she underlined the words of the forecast. 'You are in for a surprise,' she read. 'It will not be entirely unexpected and it will answer certain questions that have been bothering you of late. Be wary of putting your trust in strangers. Lucky colour, blue. Does that make any sense to you Mrs Green?' Mrs Scott asked.

'No. No sense at all,' Mrs Green said. 'But then I don't really believe in horoscopes.'

'I've lived my life by them,' Mrs Scott said, 'and I've not been sorry.' Then she returned to her paper.

Despite her claimed scepticism, Mrs Green was troubled by her forecast, especially the warning that she should not trust a stranger. Did Mr Rufus fall into that category? And what was the surprise in store? And were those two prophecies connected? But Mr Rufus was no longer a stranger. And he had never given any indication that he was not to be trusted. It couldn't be Mr Rufus, she decided, yet the surprise might well refer to him, and indeed, as the horoscope said, it would not be entirely unexpected. In other words, he might have a proposal in mind. She looked across the table and noticed that both Mr Rufus and Mrs Thackeray were concerned with their dinners, so with a certain relief she turned to hers and ate elegantly since she knew that he could see her. In her mind she scoured her wardrobe for something blue.

While they were waiting for the dessert, Mr Rufus resumed his conversation with Mrs Thackeray.

'But I'm a new boy,' he was saying. 'How am I supposed to know? You tell me about them. Let's go around the table, starting with the horoscope lady.' He deliberately chose Mrs Scott, because moving clockwise, he could leave Mrs Green to the last.

'That's all she is. The horoscope lady,' Mrs Thackeray said. 'She's new too. Came just before you did. I don't know anything more about her.'

'And next to her? The gentleman?'

'That's Jeremy Cross. He's only happy when somebody dies. Then next to him is Jock MacPherson.'

'What about him?'

'What is this?' Mrs Thackeray asked. 'The third degree?' She touched his arm to offset her bullying tone, a gesture not lost on Mrs Green. She wished she knew Mrs Thackeray's birth sign so that she could check on what was in store for her.

Mrs Thackeray did what she could with brief biographies of those around the table. And then it was Mrs Green's turn.

'What about Mrs Green?' Mr Rufus asked.

'I don't like her,' Mrs Thackeray said straight away. 'She's a dark horse that one. She even says so herself.'

'Does she indeed?' Mr Rufus said. 'I don't see anything mysterious about her. In fact I find her quite ordinary. In a pleasant sort of way of course,' he added.

'Has she told you about her Swiss finishing school?' Mrs Thackeray asked.

'Yes. She did,' Mr Rufus said.

'And do you believe her?'

'I see no reason not to. It was the fashionable thing to do at the time. If you had money, of course.'

'Well I think she's making it all up. Showing off,' Mrs Thackeray said. 'And don't ask me why,' she added. 'It's just a feeling I've got.'

Though he didn't voice his agreement, Mrs Thackeray had certainly confirmed a suspicion in his own mind.

The dessert arrived then and their exchange ceased.

After dinner they adjourned to the common lounge for their night drinks. Mrs Green dawdled in the name of 'playing it cool' and when at last she entered the lounge, she found to her relief that Mrs Thackeray was sitting alone and that Mr Rufus was engaged in conversation with the Major and his Jew woman. There was an empty chair beside him, and he half rose and motioned to her to join them and though Mrs Green would never have volunteered any social contact with Mrs Feinberg, she was not going to miss out on Mr Rufus' invitation. So she took the chair next to him and did not notice how Mrs Feinberg trembled.

'Did you have a good time in London?' Mrs Green asked.

'No time for a good time,' Mr Rufus said. 'A consultancy job. And one with a deadline. But I managed it. They did at least have the decency to chauffeur me back.' Then, leaning over, he whispered, 'I missed you.'

Mrs Green was aware of sudden palpitations. She knew their cause, and that cause was an unspeakable joy. But she half feared their effect. She kept very still, and without looking at him, she muttered, 'I missed you too.'

It was then that Mrs Feinberg excused herself, not even waiting for her night drink. The Major was concerned at her sudden departure, though he knew its cause. He had half a mind to go after her, but considered it would be more useful if he stayed in Mrs Green's proximity and possibly picked up some clues in her leprous presence. Mrs Green was glad that the Jew woman had left them, but she was irritated that the Major still held the fort. Could he not see that she and Mr Rufus were in intimate exchange and wanted no eavesdroppers? 'Yes, I did miss you,' she said, and loudly this time so that the Major might take the hint. But he did not budge.

'We all missed you Mr Rufus,' he said mischievously. 'What is it you do on these little jaunts of yours?'

'Just work,' Mr Rufus said. 'Since leaving the bank, I'm called in from time to time for consultancy work. In their London office. I'm glad of it really. Makes me feel less retired. And what about you, Major? Not much consultancy work after the Army, I shouldn't imagine.'

'A retired Major is a retired Major I'm afraid,' the Major said. 'And that's that.' He was not pleased with the turn the conversation had taken. He had not intended to hog Mr Rufus' attention. He merely wanted to eavesdrop. 'And what about you, Mrs Green?' he tried. 'Is there any consultancy work in your department? I suppose it's different for women.'

'Well I never had a proper profession,' she said, glad to be included in their exchange. 'I was simply a wife and mother.'

'And a most noble calling that is,' the Major said, hoping to encourage her to elaborate further on her past.

But Mrs Green felt she had adequately declared herself. There was silence between them.

Shortly Matron came in with their night drinks. She passed around the room with her tray. When she came to Mrs Hughes she paused.

'You won't be wanting one Mrs Hughes,' she said. 'You know what a night drink does to you.' She made no attempt to lower her voice.

Mrs Hughes, already well glued to her chair, seemed to sink further into her upholstered anchorage. She reddened with shame for their was no doubt in her mind that all the residents had overheard, and had drawn their own conclusions. She was enraged, 'Matron,' she whispered, and beckoned her to come close. Matron put her ear close to Mrs Hughes' mouth and this is what she heard. 'I had left you a considerable sum in my will Matron. But now I shall change it. You are a cruel woman, and you won't get a penny.'

It was a lie of course. Mrs Hughes' money would be left to her family, and little Minnie would inherit the larger share. But all the residents knew of Matron's constant legacy expectations and Mrs Hughes saw no reason why she shouldn't be disappointed in advance. An unfriendly word rarely passed Mrs Hughes' lips, but her frailty enraged her and she thought Matron a deserving target. Matron was too astonished to respond, but she had the presence of mind to put a smile on her face as if Mrs Hughes had just told her a joke. In her heart she was fuming, for she believed what Mrs Hughes had told her. She finished her round of drinks and stormed back to her office.

'Whatever did you say to her?' Mr Cross asked Mrs Hughes.

'No more than she deserved,' Mrs Hughes said, which was giving nothing away. Looks were exchanged around the common lounge, but no word was said. In order to break the silence, Jock MacPherson asked Mrs Scott about her horoscope prospects. They were sitting on opposite sides of the room, so Jock MacPherson's voice, never at a pianissimo pitch, boomed across the lounge. And Mrs Scott was bound to boom back.

'I'll read it to you,' she said.

'Let's just have the warnings,' Mrs Green said, having earlier heard of her domestic fortunes.

'Well they're ridiculous, and I never take any notice of them,' Mrs Scott said, and laughed nervously.

'Read them anyway,' MacPherson boomed. 'Just for a laugh.'

Mrs Scott, happy to be centre stage, put down her cocoa and

took her glasses out of her bag. 'Libras,' she read. 'That's me,' she added, 'have been aware for some time of a slight malevolence in the air. They say that every day in this paper,' she laughed again. 'But I never take any notice.' She began to fold the paper.

Jeremy Cross spryly took up his cue. He knew his time would come. And what better moment than this?

'Perhaps you should take notice Mrs Scott,' he said.

'Whatever for?' Mrs Scott bravely maintained her nonchalance.

Everyone in the lounge turned to look at Jeremy Cross, half of those looks begging his silence, and the other half urging him on. But Jeremy Cross never allowed himself to be influenced by anybody. He was his own man and he'd do what he liked.

'Considering the rooms you're occupying,' Mr Cross said.

'What's wrong with my rooms?' Mrs Scott had suddenly lost her indifference to caution.

Another silence, but this time with looks at the floor.

'Their former tenant,' Mr Cross said at last, as he visualised Mrs Scott's name on his list and its cause. 'Shock that proved fatal.'

'It's only a rumour,' Jock MacPherson boomed.

'But there's no smoke without fire,' Mrs Thackeray countered.

'It's idle gossip,' Mrs Hughes pealed from her anchorage.

'You're right Mrs Hughes,' Lady Celia contributed.

Mrs Green had the last word. 'Well rumour or not, I wouldn't sleep in that room if you paid me.'

'What are you all talking about?' Mrs Scott shouted, now quite clearly frightened out of her wits.

Another silence.

'You started it, Mr Cross,' Mrs Green said. 'You finish it.'

Jeremy Cross undeniably had the floor whether he liked it or not. He decided not to mince his words. In any case, he was not given to any form of subtlety in his expression, nor understatement. 'The last occupant, a Miss Bellamy, cut her throat in them,' he said.

Mrs Scott sprang to her feet. Her glasses, bag and perilous horoscope fell to the floor.

'Why didn't anyone tell me?' she shouted. 'No wonder I have feelings of malevolence.' Never henceforth would she ignore her cautions. 'How dare she put me in those rooms?' She made her way towards the door. 'I'll kill her,' she screamed.

She just about made the exit, then clung to the door and fell into a faint. Mr Cross was first on his feet. If Mrs Scott couldn't get to Matron, then Matron would jolly well have to get to her. He rushed to her office.

Mr Rufus was first at Mrs Scott's side. 'It's only a faint,' he said.

'Here, try this,' Mrs Thackeray said as she pulled a bottle of smelling-salts out of her bag.

'The very thing,' Mr Rufus said, unscrewing the bottle and waving it under Mrs Scott's nose. Her eyelids flickered and opened and by the time Matron arrived, she was still prone but recovered. Matron knelt by her side and received an immediate earful. Mrs Scott's temporary coma had in no way diluted her anger. Indeed it seemed to have fuelled it.

'How dare you give me those rooms,' she said. 'I want new quarters immediately.'

'Of course my dear,' Matron said. This was hardly the time to argue or to refute whatever vicious lies had occasioned Mrs Scott's present state. But she more than suspected whose filthy mouth it all came from. She would see that Jeremy Cross in her office. She had seen his survival list behind his wardrobe door often enough and she knew what he was up to. She helped Mrs Scott to her feet and guided her out of the common lounge. She settled her in the armchair in her office and, though she already knew, she asked what it was that was troubling her.

Mrs Scott related Mr Cross's story with her own elaborations. 'Why wasn't I told?' she asked.

'Because it simply isn't true,' Matron said. 'Mr Cross is a malicious liar. He likes to frighten people. Poor Miss Bellamy, who lived very happily in your rooms for many years, died of natural causes. And that's all there is to it. But if you still want to change your rooms, that is easily done.'

'I still want to move,' Mrs Scott said. 'Straight away.'

'I shall see to it,' Matron said. She left the room and instructed one of the maids to move Mrs Scott, lock stock and barrel, into a spare room in the annexe. Then she returned to her office. 'It's arranged,' she said. 'I'll take you to your new quarters. It overlooks the gardens on both sides. I'm sure you'll be very happy there.'

Having installed Mrs Scott, she returned to the lounge in order to call Mr Cross to her office. He followed her, strutting, defiant, but his gait was for the sole benefit of the other residents, in front of whom he could show no weakness. Inside himself he was frightened. Frightened of Matron. Always had been. All his life, any figure in authority had terrified him, starting with his father, who, instead of a tongue in his mouth, had a whip, forked at all times. Matron displayed that same kind of verbal cruelty. She reminded him of his headmaster and the number of times he was called to his study, and the terror of being sent home. Now he feared that Matron would expel him. And where could he go? To which more promising venue could be take his survival list? By the time he reached Matron's office, he was trembling. His strut had wilted, along with his air of defiance.

She did not offer him a chair, and he was afraid to take one of his own accord. So he stood before her, unable to control his shaking, as he watched Matron as Matron watched him. She was half smiling.

'Are you cold, Mr Cross?' she asked.

'No,' he muttered.

'I thought you might be, because you're shivering,' she said. Then, having made her point, she told him to take a seat. She waited for him to get as comfortable as the circumstances allowed, and then she said, 'You've been a naughty boy again, Mr Cross.' Now he was verily back in his headmaster's study, awaiting expulsion. 'You're spreading this rumour again,' she said, 'and you know it's not true. You know that very well.'

He could have told her there and then that he'd seen the cut throat with his own eyes, together with all the blood and damage. And although he knew she was lying, and that she knew that he knew, he was afraid to contradict her. She was a figure in authority, and had the power to do what she wished with him.

'I won't do it again,' he whispered, and he felt the rough blue serge of his school trousers rubbing against his trembling knees.

'This is your very last chance,' she said. 'I want you to go to Mrs Scott and tell her you made it all up. And if ever I hear that you are spreading such a rumour again, I shall have no hesitation in asking you to leave. You may go now,' she said.

He was still trembling as he left her office. He hated Matron and in his mind he forced her name on to his survival list. Matron, for her part, was thinking on the same lines, hoping to add the name of Mr Jeremy Cross in her own satisfied handwriting.

Thirteen

It was the Major and Mrs Feinberg's regular sortie to the village that gave Mr Rufus the idea. Not that he would follow them but that he would do the same, and with Mrs Green. He suggested it after breakfast the following morning. En passant, he admired her blue scarf. Mrs Green was hedging all her bets, and she was convinced that, thus dressed in her lucky colour, the walk was a preamble to the half-expected surprise that Mrs Scott had promised her. Over breakfast that morning, Mrs Scott was happy to whisper the Scorpio forecast for the day, glad that she had a companion in her studies. It simply instructed Mrs Green to take things as they came and not rush to conclusions; by the end of the moon's cycle, everything would become clear. Mrs Green didn't know Mr Rufus' birth sign but she had every intention of wheedling it out of him. Their walk might present an opportunity.

They left The Hollyhocks before the Major and Mrs Feinberg, who had no idea that their example was being followed. They were surprised and disconcerted on entering the tearoom to find their usual table invaded by the enemy. Mrs Feinberg gave an involuntary 'Oh' when she saw them and the Major watched her pale. He squeezed her arm. 'Don't worry my dear,' he said. 'We'll find somewhere else.'

Gently he pulled her away from the door and led her across the road. Mrs Green had not seen them, but Mr Rufus, who was facing the door to the café, had viewed their entrance, their dismay and their withdrawal entire, together with its sound effect. He was more than intrigued. He didn't mention it to Mrs Green, for he instinctively felt that their retreat had to do with his present companion.

'What shall we have?' he said jovially, pleased that he had perhaps stumbled on a clue.

Mrs Green was never short of appetite, and although she had only just put away a cooked breakfast, she said that she fancied a cup of coffee and a cream cake. Mr Rufus hid his disgust and ordered what she wanted. He himself took a cup of coffee.

'What's your favourite food?' he asked, once the waitress had served them.

She answered with no hesitation. 'Roast beef and roast potatoes and Yorkshire pudding. Boring I'm afraid. What's yours?'

'A foreign dish. A German one,' he risked. 'Sauerbraten. That's beef marinated in vinegar, with potato dumplings,' he translated.

'I know that,' she said. 'We had it sometimes at finishing

school. Not my taste at all. Too foreign,' she laughed.

He let it pass and watched her eat her cream bun. It was flirtation time, he decided.

'I do like your blue scarf,' he said. 'That colour really suits you. You should wear it more often.'

Mrs Green smiled, thinking how happy she was to know Mrs Scott, and how much nicer a person she was than that dreadful Mrs Thackeray.

'Thank you,' she said, giving him the nearest she could to a coy look, for modesty was not in her nature.

'Didn't you ever think of marrying again, after your husband died?' he asked.

Mrs Green was mindful of her horoscope. She must take things as they came. She must not rush to conclusions. 'Not really,' she said. 'I had a good marriage and I didn't think I could repeat it. And you?'

'When my wife died,' he said, 'I plunged myself into work. We had no children, so I was very much alone. But since I retired, there's much less work, and I began to feel the need for companionship. But yes, I would most certainly marry again. I am very open to remarriage.'

Take it as it comes, Mrs Green said to herself. So far, it all augured well.

'Would you like another cream cake?' he asked.

'I think not,' Mrs Green said. 'I shan't be able to eat my lunch.'

He paid the bill and they walked slowly back to The Hollyhocks. Mr Rufus knew that flirtation was part and parcel of his programme; it would lead to courtship and eventually a proposal of marriage. The success of this agenda depended entirely on its timing, on choosing the right moment for the onset of each stage. He reckoned that the flirtation period would last some time. Its duration would depend on factors as yet unknown. He recalled the Major's withdrawal from the tearoom and the sound of Mrs Feinberg's dismay. He would find a moment to talk to the Major and seek some clarification.

That moment came after lunch. Mrs Feinberg had retired to her room and the Major was taking a stroll around the gardens. Mrs Green had gone out to do some shopping. She intended to look for a blue dress that would confirm the good fortune that the colour had promised her. So Mr Rufus was alone, and so was the Major. He joined him in the gardens.

'D'you mind if I walk with you?' Mr Rufus asked.

'With pleasure,' the Major said, who was always glad of company.

'I'm sorry you didn't join us in the tearoom this morning.' Mr Rufus came to the point straight away. 'I saw you come in and then go out rather quickly. I hope it had nothing to do with me or my companion.'

The Major was taken off guard. 'Of course not,' he said quickly. He had noticed that Mr Rufus and Mrs Green were constant companions, and although he hated Mrs Green on his own as well as on Miriam's behalf, he did not wish to speak ill of her to her intimate friend. 'Mrs Feinberg and I had certain things to discuss,' he said. 'Private things, and we wished to be on our own. In any case,' he added, 'we had the same thoughts about you.'

'You were right,' Mr Rufus laughed, 'but we took your tearoom. Did you find somewhere else?'

'Yes,' the Major said. 'A little way out of the village. But a cosy little place.' He wasn't going to tell Mr Rufus where it was. He did not wish a run-in with Mrs Green again.

'Seems a very nice woman, that Mrs Feinberg,' Mr Rufus said, digging still, and clearly unsatisfied with the Major's explanation.

'She is indeed,' the Major said.

'Where is she from, originally?'

'From Vienna.' There was no harm in giving her birthplace. That fact was in the public domain. But he sensed that Mr

Rufus was fishing. He would say no more.

'A refugee then,' Mr Rufus said.

That fact too was in the public domain. 'That's right,' the Major said, then he quickly commented on the beauty of the clumps of hydrangeas that they were passing. And thus the subject was changed.

'Did you ever have a garden, Major?' Mr Rufus played along.

'Never had a proper home really,' the Major said. 'Spent all my life in the Army. The mess. That was my home. Then when I was retired, I went to live with my sister. She lived in a flat in Chelsea. No garden there. But I used to walk a lot in public gardens. I enjoy flowers. Then my sister was widowed and she moved out of town, so I came here to The Hollyhocks. And this garden. End of story.'

They walked on a little in silence. Mr Rufus sensed that the Major might well be a mine of information, but he was keeping it close to his chest, so he did not pursue further. They concentrated on the shrubs and the flowers. Mr Rufus was well versed in their names and one by one he passed them to the Major. He felt like a botany tutor giving a lesson to an eager student, for the Major responded well and with a certain excitement, intending to share his newly found language with Miriam on their next garden walk. He was anxious to write down the names so that he wouldn't forget them, so he told Mr Rufus it was time for his siesta, and that he would see him at dinner.

Mr Rufus walked on until he came to a garden bench where he sat and viewed the driveway of the gabled front of the house. He caught sight of a gentleman making his way up the drive, twirling his cane in tune with his jaunty step, and looking up, he saw Lady Celia raise her net curtains, and he heard the distant village clock strike four. He took out his notebook and started to summarise his day's findings. They took up little space. But he was not disheartened. He knew from long experience that information was like a jigsaw. No single piece, however small, was dispensable. Assembly could be long and tedious, but finally there would come a picture.

He noticed Mrs Thackeray walking towards him. She seemed to have it in mind to join him, and when she reached the bench he patted the empty space by his side, by way of invitation. She thanked him and took her seat.

'Where's your constant companion?' she asked with unconcealed sarcasm. 'Don't tell me she's deserted you.'

'I don't think so,' Mr Rufus laughed. 'She's simply gone shopping for the afternoon.' Then, after a pause, 'It's clear you don't like her very much,' he said.

'I already told you that Mr Rufus.' Mrs Thackeray smoothed her skirt, then noticing that her nail polish was chipped, she clenched her fists, ashamed. 'Did she tell you that cock and bull story about her scar?' she asked.

When Mrs Green had first confided in her as to the source of her disfigurement, she had promised to keep her secret. But now she felt she owed her no loyalty, and when Mr Rufus showed more than an interest in her story, she happily broke her earlier promise and told it to him as she had heard it from the horse's mouth.

'Why didn't you believe it?' Mr Rufus asked.

'Simply because the woman is a liar. There's no truth in her at all.' Mrs Thackeray was quite enjoying herself. She did not care that she might be hurting Mr Rufus' feelings in speaking ill of his companion. In any case, she didn't take their relationship very seriously. She was sure that nothing would come of it. Had she herself not been twice bitten, she might even have flirted with him. But she chose to go back to the house. 'I've had my little airing for today,' she said, as if she were an article on a clothes-line. 'I have letters to write.'

It was an excuse that they all made at The Hollyhocks when wishing to be alone. But Mrs Feinberg's Christmas presents lay unused in their drawers and would never see the light of day.

Once Mrs Thackeray had gone, Mr Rufus took out his note-book once more. She had given him a clue, a valuable one, which might well prove to be a central piece of the jigsaw.

At dinner that evening, Mrs Green turned up in a new blue frock, of the bluest blue in the palette. She looked ridiculous, like a blue peter, a signal that she was about to set sail. Indeed in her mind she was, along with her trusted captain, into the far horizon. Mr Rufus rose and took her arm and guided her to the seat next to his. The blue dazzled him and he was glad to seat her by his side, so that it would not continually assail his eye. While she sat beside him, he received only a hint of it, and that was as much as his vision could bear. His notebook jottings confirmed that he must dally a while in the flirtation stage, with a promise that courtship would follow hard upon.

'I love your dress,' he said, not looking at it. 'You took my advice, I see. Blue is indeed your colour.'

'I like to please,' Mrs Green said smiling. Even her smile was blue, an inescapable reflection. 'And what did you do today?' she asked.

He told her the truth. She would find it innocent enough. 'I walked in the gardens,' he said. 'With the Major. We shared our pleasure in the shrubs and flowers. And then Mrs Thackeray came along and we had a little chat.'

'What about?' she asked quickly.

'Nothing specific,' he lied. 'Just the pleasures and no pleasures of old age.'

'Well she doesn't have many pleasures,' Mrs Green said. 'She's too bitter, that woman. Not had much luck with friendships.' She dared to squeeze his arm, and he turned, blue-blinking, to smile at her.

After dinner, Matron came into the common lounge to serve their night drinks. She was wearing her usual peaky Monday look, but now the residents had ceased to notice, and certainly ceased to care. Only Lady Celia took note of it, checking on her

Monday profit, and no longer feeling in the least bit sorry for her.

That evening, contrary to recent custom, and much to Jeremy Cross's relief, Mrs Hughes was amongst the first to retire. Against Matron's now whispered advice, she had taken her Ovaltine and drunk it to its dregs. She had sat for a while, then slowly rose to her feet, leaving the evidence of her night drink on the cushion. She did not bother to hold her handbag behind her, so that her shame was visible to all as she crossed the room very slowly, as if with a certain pride, demonstrating a living proof of what would happen to all of them. Mrs Hughes didn't care any more. She saw no reason to, for she had found a new source of solace, and what's more a pleasurable one, that might hasten her withdrawal from the waiting game. She reached her room and went straight to her cabinet. Over the years that she had been at The Hollyhocks, the family had brought her bottles of cherry brandy for every birthday, Mother's Day, Grandmother's Day, Great-grandmother's Day. She rarely drank, and only to toast one of her family. Thus she had built up a goodly stock, and her cabinet was full. She was glad that she didn't need a corkscrew. A simple twist of the cap was sufficient to allow entry into Lethean waters. She used her Bakelite tooth mug as a glass and filled it to its half measure. And she drank. And she enjoyed. Then she lay back on her bed and, without undressing, she crawled between the sheets and in a moment she was fast asleep. In the morning she awoke, feeling none the worse for wear, and delighted that she was, even to her shoes, already dressed for breakfast. She went downstairs with a song on the fringes of her heart, and consumed a breakfast large enough for two. No one commented on her appearance. Unkempt hair was common enough at breakfast time at The Hollyhocks. But one or two of the residents did notice the smell, and by the end of the week Mrs Hughes found herself alone at the breakfast table, the seats on either side of her conspicuously vacant.

At first, Mrs Hughes confined her cherry brandy tipple to the evenings after supper. For a whole week she had worn the same dress and underwear and the others residents wondered how soon Matron would do something about it. But not until she had been told of the fraying of Mrs Hughes' sheets, worn thin and even torn by the heels of her shoes, did Matron see fit to take action. After all, the sheets were Hollyhocks property, and damage to such property was not to be tolerated. So she went to Mrs Hughes' rooms, while her resident was having breakfast. The smell hit her, a reeking of urine laced with alcohol, and she reeled against the door. Then roughly she opened the windows and stripped the filthy bed. She opened the cabinet door and saw the empty bottles amongst the still abundant stock. That aspect of Mrs Hughes' decline did not worry Matron. Alcohol was not forbidden on the premises, thus Mrs Hughes was not breaking any Hollyhocks rule. But the sheets were a different matter altogether. She dared to look at the mattress on the bed. Fortunately the rubber sheet had fully protected it. But it stank to high heaven. She tore it off the bed, then went down to the kitchen and ordered one of the maids to thoroughly clean and fumigate Mrs Hughes' room. She waited until breakfast was over, then went into the common lounge to arrest the culprit.

She made no secret of it. She actually called Mrs Hughes' name from the door.

'Would you come to my office?' she shouted.

Mrs Hughes was in no way abashed. She peeled herself from her soaked cushion and walked steadily across the room. Her dress was folded into the cleft of her buttocks, and her stockings were wet and crinkled. She left behind her a soft breeze of urine, her calling-card.

Matron did not ask her to sit down in her office. She valued her chairs. But she took her arm, and without a word guided her up the stairs to her rooms. The maids were already at their cleaning, but the bathroom that had been little used in many weeks was still presentable. She led her inside, and still without a word, she ran the hot water and began to undress her resident. She discarded every item of clothing with disgust and then, none too gently, she helped Mrs Hughes into the bath. First, a thorough cleaning, including the hair. Words would come later. Matron's clean-up was rough, but Mrs Hughes did not complain. She was glad that she was giving Matron so much trouble. She even hummed a little as her back was rubbed. When Matron was finished, she helped her out of the bath and roughly dried her. Then peppered her with talcums and sprays that had birthday-accumulated on the bathroom shelf. When she was finished, she looked at her charge, regarding her as a piece of furniture, newly restored, polished and ready to view. Then she remembered the sheets. And spoke her first words.

'You've damaged the sheets, Mrs Hughes,' she said. 'You've gone to bed with your shoes on.'

'That's right,' Mrs Hughes said. 'I've been too tired to undress.'

'Or too drunk, perhaps?' Matron suggested.

Mrs Hughes laughed. 'There's no law against taking a little drink,' she said.

Indeed there wasn't. And Matron didn't care if Mrs Hughes drank herself to death as long as she didn't damage the sheets in the process.

'You must promise me to take your shoes off before you go to bed,' she said. 'And it would help if you washed occasionally and changed your clothes. The other residents are beginning to complain.'

Mrs Hughes was delighted at this news. She knew that they were complaining, not because of her unkempt appearance, or indeed her rancid smell. It was because she was a constant reminder to them all that wetting one's knickers and going to bed with one's shoes on was an essential rule of the waiting game that they were all playing. She herself, wet and dishevelled, embodied the check, before the final mate.

Matron found clean clothes and dressed her. Then she combed her hair, and patted her thinning mane.

'There,' she said. 'Good as new. And keep yourself like that. You can look very pretty if you try.'

But Mrs Hughes was immune to flattery and as soon as Matron was gone, and the maids had finished their spring-clean, she went to her cabinet, unscrewed the cap on a bottle and without evening bothering with her tooth mug, she took a long swig to oblivion. And another. It was not yet ten o'clock in the morning. Thereafter, for the next week or so, Mrs Hughes took her Lethe trip at all hours of the day, and sometimes even at night. But she did remember to take off her shoes. As long as Hollyhocks property was not damaged, Matron would turn a blind eye. She was careful to change her clothes from time to time, but brushing her hair was quite beyond her. She thought it totally unnecessary. Indeed she came to love the tousled matted look. Together with the glowing blush on her cheeks and the dead sparkle in her eyes, she thought she looked much younger than her years. Matron had taken to coming to her room every morning before breakfast. She came to check up on the sheets, and while there, she made sure that Mrs Hughes had cleaned herself up. Then she felt that her matronly duties had been done. Nowadays when Mrs Hughes entered the dining room, the seats beside her were occupied. The smell of alcohol about her person overcame any other odour and was fairly tolerable, though it was the subject of much buzz and rumour in the lounge when Mrs Hughes was absent and happily about her tipple. On the days that Mrs Hughes' relatives visited, Matron made sure that she was clean and presentable, and she would pass her a packet of mints to disguise her cherry-brandy breath. It was important that outsiders carried away a good impression of the home in her charge.

It was Mother's Day. And that day Matron gave Mrs Hughes' room and person a complete overhaul, for visitors were expected. There was post that morning, larger than usual, consisting of a few Mother's Day cards. At breakfast Matron handed them out to those few of her residents who had legitimately earned one. There was a large bunch of roses for Mrs Feinberg from Mark, her son, and though they dominated the breakfast table, most of the residents made a point of ignoring them. Mrs Thackeray, who nowadays missed nothing, noticed that of all people, Mrs Green had received a Mother's Day greeting. She was making quite a production of the opening of the card, carefully putting the envelope to one side. She studied the picture on the card for a while, as if she had never in her life seen it before, but Mrs Thackeray knew that she had examined it well enough, because she had openly snatched the envelope and looked at the post-mark. 'Charing', it said, clearly from the postal collection down the road. Mrs Green had sent the card to herself.

'It's not from your daughter, is it?' Mrs Thackeray asked with feigned surprise.

'Love to the best mother in the world,' Mrs Green read aloud and with absolutely no shame.

'She's got in touch after all these years,' Mrs Thackeray marvelled.

'Does it say where she's living?'

'No,' Mrs Green said with what she hoped would pass as sadness.

'Why don't you look at the postmark then?' Mrs Thackeray suggested gleefully. 'That'll give you some clue.' She inched the envelope back to Mrs Green's hand and she was bound to scrutinise it.

'Why!' she said with sudden pallor. 'It's from here. Charing. She must live in these parts.'

'Then you can expect a visit,' Mrs Thackeray said. 'She might even come today. After all these years.'

'I must ask Mrs Scott to look at my horoscope.' Mrs Green rallied a little, but there was no doubt in her mind, nor in Mrs Thackeray's, that her pitiful deception was unveiled.

The bulk of the post that morning was of course for Mrs Hughes, who was card-celebrated as mother, grandmother and great-grandmother in turn. The residents congratulated her heartily. Their attitude to Mrs Hughes had changed considerably over the last few weeks. There were less and less Minnie-stories to needle them. Mrs Hughes seemed to be engaged in other matters, which could be guessed at by the constant smell on her breath.

'They're all coming to see me today,' she announced.

'Then you must put your best dress on,' Matron said. 'And a bath perhaps,' she added without lowering her voice.

'Perhaps you should have a bath too, Matron,' Mrs Hughes cackled and the residents were astonished at her nerve, that brandy-fuelled insolence, that called for a silent cheer.

Matron pretended that she hadn't heard. 'Is anyone else expecting visitors today?' she asked the room in general.

A few residents put up their timid hands.

'Put your hand up Mrs Green,' Mrs Thackeray said. 'You *might* have somebody.'

Mrs Green ignored her, her bile rising. But the imagined name of Mr John Rufus curbed her fury.

'You may order teas in your rooms,' Matron said, 'and I urge you all to keep your voices down. Some of the residents will be taking their siesta.'

Matron returned to her office. She was furious with Mrs Hughes, that brandy-sodden stinking resident of hers. She did not expect any legacy from that quarter, since Mrs Hughes had relatives in plenty, so she was not obliged to be extra kind to her, or even kind, she thought. She wouldn't bother to see that she cleaned herself up for her visitors. Let them see for themselves what she had to put up with. And smell they certainly would, for Mrs Hughes was already at her cherry tipple at only ten o'clock in the morning. By visiting time she would be reeling.

Matron put a flower display in reception mounted with a Mother's Day card. The display was brought out every year, its plastic make-up newly rinsed and dusted. The visitors began to arrive shortly after lunch. They were laden with flowers and gift-wrapped parcels and most of them wore a guilty look. It had been perhaps a year since some of them had visited, with no excuse of traffic problems for they lived within a stone's throw of The Hollyhocks.

Matron welcomed them in reception. 'It's been a long time,' she said pointedly to those to whom it applied. 'I'm sure your relative will be glad to know she's not been forgotten.'

'Oh shut up,' one of the gentleman visitors said under his breath. He had come to see his mother for the first time since last Mother's Day. His bunch of flowers was the largest, as were his packages.

'You know the way of course,' Matron said. 'Or have you forgotten? In case you have, you'll find the names on the doors.'

The visitors trooped up the stairs like a pack of admonished schoolchildren and Matron returned to her office.

It was a Monday, and the hush-money lay in an envelope on her desk. Monday was never a good day for Matron, especially this Monday coupled as it was with Mother's Day and all the extra work that it called for. She was particularly depressed this day. Mrs Hughes' barb still rankled. She had never been so insulted. She as Matron was not *supposed* to be insulted. It was her prerogative to insult others, and she would not stand for such insurrection. She would give Mrs Hughes a good talking-to in the morning. She thought she might catch up on a little sleep before Mr Venables arrived and to help herself, she took a small measure of whisky from her cabinet. She dozed off pretty quickly and was not in reception to welcome the Hughes tribe, who found her absence faintly offensive. They needed no directions to Mrs Hughes' room, being weekly visitors. But they were nervous. Recently they had noticed a deterioration in her condition. They had all been on holiday and thus had not visited her for almost a month. They were frightened that her condition might have worsened.

Their fears were confirmed on entering the room. Firstly its smell, secondly, its chaos, though their effects were simultaneous. Yet its tenant looked well enough. Her cheeks were rosy, too healthy looking for a high blood pressure, and she was laughing most of the time. Her daughter put it down to a delight in seeing them after such a long time, her granddaughter could see at once that her granny had turned into a lush, and little Minnie thought that her great-grandmother was simply daft. And each in their way, was right.

'Your room hasn't been cleaned, Mother,' the daughter said.

'It was cleaned this morning,' Mrs Hughes giggled. 'That's what Matron calls cleaning.'

'What's happened, Granny?' the granddaughter said.

'Nothing's happened. Come. All of you give me a kiss.'

They hugged her then and in proximity, the laced smell was intolerable.

'You smell,' Minnie said.

That was enough for the daughter. She went straight to Matron's office. She tapped lightly on the door, but there was no reply. So she went straight inside. Matron was lying on the couch. Her mouth was open and she was snoring. This sight did not improve the daughter's temper. What right had she to be sleeping when her mother's room was filthy and its tenant stank to high heaven?

'Matron,' she screamed.

Matron practically flew off the couch. She was in the middle of a dark dream featuring Mr Venables and with the cry, she thought he had materialised in her office. So it was with a certain relief that she saw that the caller was a woman, and slowly recognising her as Mrs Hughes' daughter, she knew what she had come for. The daughter made no apology for waking her. She had no right to be asleep while on duty and she came to the point straight away.

'Have you seen the state of my mother's rooms?' she said, 'and have you noticed by any chance the state of my mother?'

Matron straightened herself. 'Sit down,' she said. 'It's a long story.' She sat herself down and rubbed the sleep out of her eyes. Then she leaned forward, as if she was about to tell a story to a stubborn child. 'It all started a few weeks ago,' she said, 'when your mother became incontinent. Very often when that happens, the person becomes quiet, withdrawn, docile in a way. I'm afraid your mother did nothing of the sort. She seems to have gone a bit wild. She doesn't always clean herself and she rarely changes her clothes. And of course, as you must have realised, she's taken to drink.'

In telling the story as it was, the total truth of it, Matron had taken the wind out of the daughter's sails.

'But surely Matron,' the daughter's voice was less strident now, 'you could see that she's clean and tidy and that she doesn't drink.'

'She's not my only resident you know,' Matron said. 'We do what we can. Her room is cleaned every day. Her sheets are changed,' she added pointedly. 'As to the drink, your mother is too old to become an alcoholic. Besides, I have the impression that it makes her happy. And what's wrong with that? Would you rather see her sitting in a chair all day like a vegetable?'

By now, the daughter was completely deflated. She had never taken to Matron, but she had to admit that she was talking sense. 'How long can this go on?' she said helplessly.

'Who knows?' Matron said. 'But when she goes, she'll go happy. With all her family around her. Which is more than I can say for most of my residents.'

She felt that she had acquitted herself well, and was entitled to ask the daughter to leave. She still had a little time to prepare for her miserable Venables encounter.

'Thank you Matron,' the daughter said. 'I don't feel any easier, but I do see your point.'

Matron opened the door for her. 'Come as often as you can,' she said.

When she had gone, Matron went straight to her cabinet. She deserved a drink, she thought. She poured herself a small whisky fortifying herself against her next appointment.

Upstairs in Mrs Hughes' room, the daughter opened the door on a silence, broken only by her mother's occasional giggling. She was now openly at the cherry-brandy bottle.

'I'll have some of that,' the daughter said.

'So will I,' said the granddaughter.

'So will I,' said Minnie.

'No you won't,' Mrs Hughes snapped. 'None of you. It's mine.' She grabbed the bottle and clasped it to her chest. Her lifeline.

This was a new mother, a new granny. A new great-grandmother. They stared at her, disbelieving. And sat in silence. 'Tell great-granny what happened to you in school yesterday,' the granddaughter said after a while as she pushed little Minnie to Mrs Hughes' side.

'I don't want to know what happened to you in school,' Mrs Hughes said. 'I don't want to know anything about you.'

'Granny!' the granddaughter said, astonished.

'Nor you either,' Mrs Hughes said. 'Not any of you. And I want you to go. All of you.' She took a swig from the bottle to swallow the lump in her throat. 'And I don't want to see any of you again.' She put the bottle on the table, her heart breaking.

'You can't mean that, Mother,' the daughter said. She went across to her and tried to hold her.

Mrs Hughes pushed her away 'Go away,' she whispered. 'All of you.' And she giggled with a giggle that had nothing to do with pleasure. 'Please go,' she said again.

They tried to kiss her goodbye, but she turned her face away. When little Minnie went towards her, she actually pushed her aside. They went to the door. The three of them, bewildered and full of sorrow.

'We'll come tomorrow,' the daughter said.

But for Mrs Hughes, tomorrow never came. Quite simply, she wanted no tomorrow, or any of the tomorrows to come. For no tomorrow could be near enough to see little Minnie as a young woman, to go to her wedding, to delight in her firstborn. And if there were no tomorrows that were near enough for that, then today would have to do.

She finished the bottle and would have opened another, had she been able to make it to the cabinet. But her legs were too unsteady to take her. She shifted over to her bed, and sitting down, she thoroughly wet the counterpane. She had just about enough strength to pull back the duvet and crawl inside. Bugger the sheets, she thought, as she dragged her shoes under the blanket. She cradled her legs up to her chest, and simply willed herself to die.

That evening when she didn't appear for supper, Matron went to her rooms. She found her cradled, foetus-like and peaceful. She had died from the most natural cause of all, the simple wish to resign from the waiting game, and that night before he went to bed, Jeremy Cross inscribed her name on the back of his wardrobe door.

Fourteen

Matron went back to her waiting list and still no gentlemen had materialised. She had vacancies to fill. Mrs Hughes had to be replaced, and poor Miss Bellamy. Regarding the latter, she was confident that Jeremy Cross would henceforth hold his tongue. She wrote off to the two youngest ladies on her list, one of seventy-five years, the other of seventy-eight, and enquired whether they were still interested in joining in the waiting game. Within the week came two affirmative replies and Matron was able to report to the board that she had a full house. She looked around her residents in the common lounge and found them all fit and hearty, none of them threatening 'natural causes'. She dared to hope that she would not have to consider her waiting list for some time to come. She was fully staffed and all of them were satisfactory, and were it not for her regular Monday visitor, she would have been content. But Mr Venables was a blight on her horizon and she could never hope for its removal.

Like the rest of the dear and undear departed, the name of Mrs Hughes was never mentioned in the lounge. Any more than was Mrs Webber's, Mrs Primple's or poor Miss Bellamy's. It was as if the residents had cancelled out their previous existence lest to acknowledge it would only serve to pinpoint their own survival, that term that reeked of mortality. Which was just as well, for one of the new residents, a Mrs Harvey, answered to the name of Minnie, but all the old-timers addressed her as if they'd never in their lives heard the name before.

Mrs Harvey, at seventy-five the younger of the two new girls, despite her age and three former marriages, was still on the hunt, and on arrival at The Hollyhocks she cased the joint and found the pickings far from ample. She noted that Mr Rufus was clearly engaged with Mrs Green, that the Major never let Mrs Feinberg out of his sight, and that Jeremy Cross was beyond anybody's pickings. That left the solitary Jock MacPherson. It wasn't as if Minnie Harvey had much of a choice, so she settled for Jock and made a play for him. She would have stood a better chance had she been a sprig of heather, or a thistle perhaps, which would at least have given them something in common. But Jock MacPherson had neither time nor inclination for a relationship. His sights were elsewhere, unrelated to man or woman. He did not even bother to avoid Mrs Harvey because he was totally unaware that she was stalking him. Besides, he had important things to put his mind to. Only that morning he had turned on his radio and heard confirmation of a rumour that had been noised for some time. Parliament was about to hold a full-scale debate on Scottish devolution. He cheered when he heard the news and did a little jig in his pyjamas. He had to go to London. He had to go to Parliament and listen to the debate. And he had to make his own voice heard.

He packed a bag and ordered a car to take him to the station. Matron tried to dissuade him from going. 'Where will you stay?' she asked him.

'In a hotel,' he said. 'And I have friends in London. They'll all be going to the debate.'

She noted the fervour in his eye and she knew that nothing would stop him. 'You must have your breakfast first,' she said. She took his arm and walked him to the dining room.

'Mr MacPherson is going to London,' she announced. 'On his own,' she added, in the hope that others might dissuade him.

'I'll go with you if you like,' Mrs Harvey volunteered straight away.

'You're very kind to offer,' Jock MacPherson said. He would have used her name but he couldn't remember it.

'You'll be lonely in a big place like London,' Mrs Harvey persisted.

'I shall have my cause for company,' he said.

Mrs Harvey was not put out. She didn't consider cause as competition. She would wait for his return from London where hopefully he would have left his cause behind.

After breakfast, Matron saw him to his cab. 'When will you be back?' she asked.

'Tomorrow night perhaps,' he said. 'I'm only going for the debate.'

'Enjoy yourself,' she said as she bundled him into the taxi and noticed how frail he was.

But Jock MacPherson was feeling anything but frail. He was

buoyed up with expectancy. He dared to hope that home rule for Scotland might well come in his lifetime. He overtipped the taxi driver and took a first-class return to Victoria. On arrival, he booked into the station hotel, smartened himself up and went to the bar and ordered a stiff whisky. Not that he needed it to put him into the Gaelic mode, for he rarely dwelt outside it. He experienced a moment of regret that he had not packed his kilt for his parliamentary attendance and he ordered a second whisky to lift his spirits. He thought he might take a leisurely stroll to Westminster as a sort of dummy run for the real thing on the following day.

He set out briskly, high on the whisky's after-taste. On reaching Buckingham Palace, he found a bench and rested himself a while. He turned his back on Her Majesty's residence. He would not acknowledge it. Perhaps on the following day, if all went well, he would face it with a certain gratitude. He rested for about half an hour, then made his way down Birdcage Walk. When the Houses of Parliament were within his sight, he rested again on a bench alongside the Abbey. He heard shouting, too raucous to decipher the actual words, and he saw banners raised, too distant for his vision to decode their messages. But in his heart he knew that they were singing for Scotland. It was a dress rehearsal for the morrow, he thought, and he couldn't have come at a better time. He was anxious to join the crowd, but conscious too of a racing of his heartbeat in response to that glorious patriotic fervour. He forced himself to rest on the bench, and catching the tune from the distance, he joined in the singing of 'Scotland the Brave'. He heard the echo of bagpipes and he could hardly contain his joy. Still he sat there, despite his itching feet. Then the singing stopped for a while, and in its interval he rose and steeled himself. He walked slowly and carefully towards the banners and the source of the renewed singing. All his life he had waited for a moment as hopeful as this one and he wasn't going to rush headlong into the crowd to savour it. For now, nearing his target, he saw that it was indeed a crowd, young and old, raucous with fervour, or so he hoped, though he suspected that that fervour might well have been fuelled by Scotland's liquid spirits. He saw police forming a cordon around the demonstrators, and from a distance they looked benign enough, for the crowd, though noisy, were cheerful. He wanted to run to join them, but mindful of his age and the dignity that that age required, he walked at a measured and slow pace as he recalled his service in the regiment of Scots Guards so many years ago. Eventually he reached the square, and threaded his way behind the police cordon and through the crowds they had been sent to control. He was pushed and shoved, though not urgently. He had meant to make his way to the back of the throng which seemed to be largely composed of people of his own generation, glowing and silent. But he found himself shoved to the front alongside a banner whose legend was outside his line of vision. He craned his neck forward and managed to read 'Home Rule for Scotland Now'. Then he felt safe and happy in his surroundings. He noticed that those alongside him, the banner holders, were young. They could have been his grandchildren. They were heavily heather-tattooed and earringed and he was delighted that the hunger for national independence still prevailed. He was standing next to the end-holder of the banner, a man slightly older than the other bearers and looking distinctly uncomfortable. He turned to MacPherson.

'Hey Jock,' he said unknowingly using his addressee's name. 'Will ye hold this banner for me a while. I'm bursting for a wee pee.' He thrust the handle into Jock's hand and disappeared amongst the crowd.

Jock held the handle aloft. A tingle started in his arms and soon suffused his whole body with a surge of pride. He was in the forefront of the battle and again he regretted not wearing his kilt. For there were kilts all around him, and sporrans too and

the women sported thistles in their hats or heather in their
lapels. The crowd began to sing again, this time, 'Loch
Lomond', and Jock joined in heartily, even managing a descant
here and there, his body trembling with a maudlin joy. He
couldn't remember when he had last been so happy.

Suddenly there was a pressing movement from behind and
the crowd were forced forward so that the frontline banner
holders were perilously touching the serried ranks of the police
cordon. There was a second surge from behind and cries of
'Sod off, you fascist scum.' Fights broke out at the back of the
crowd and Jock was faintly anxious, but relieved that he himself was in the front line. He heard shouts of abuse and again
the crowd surged, so that it was difficult to keep the banner
steady, that banner which proclaimed nothing but an innocent
yearning for home. He stubbornly held on to its handle, determined to remain part of the protest. But soon enough, in a
final shove, he found himself in the none too friendly embrace
of a policeman.

'That's enough,' the policeman yelled, snatching the handle
from his hand. He gripped him under the armpit. 'An old man
like you should know better,' he said.

'What are you doing to me?' Jock MacPherson spluttered,
feeling himself dragged along the pavement.

'I'm arresting you for disturbance of the peace. You don't
have to say . . .' His words were lost in the angry indignant
shouts of the crowd.

'I can walk,' he said with dignity. 'You don't have to drag
me.' He watched as the rest of his banner fell to the ground and
all its bearers embraced in a boys-in-blue huddle. Only Jock
MacPherson had a personal escort. They were herded towards
the Abbey, then bundled into a police van.

I must visit the Abbey tomorrow, Jock MacPherson thought
and its rich portals were his last tourist view as the van doors
closed after him.

He found himself amongst a group of now subdued protest-
ers, presumably the sharers of his banner which gave them
something in common. But he did not attempt conversation
with them. The presence of two policemen on each side of the
van signalled that silence was expedient. The van was win-
dowless so there was no way in which its inmates could sense
its location. But the ride lasted only a short while. It pulled up
sharply and the rear doors were opened from the outside.
Then, cordoned by the police, the group were ushered inside
the station.

They were each charged separately and all of them for disturbance of the peace. None of them denied it. For them it was
a virtue, almost a pleasure to disturb the peace on behalf of
Scotland's independence.

When Jock MacPherson's turn came, he, like the others,
made no denial. He was taken to a room and fingerprinted.
They gave him a rag to wipe the ink off his fingers and he was
glad that the stains refused to budge. He considered them the
marks of his stigmata. He was then profile-photographed. I
now have a police record, he thought to himself, a record on
behalf of my beloved land. He was told that he would appear
before the magistrates at some time on the following morning
and that he would spend the night in the cells. He was thrilled.
He would shortly qualify as a martyr, but he was saddened by
the fact that he would miss the debate that had been the
supreme purpose of his visit.

'I'll miss the debate,' he said indignantly.

'You can have it in your cells,' the officer told him. 'Come on
Grandad,' he said, and taking his arm, he led him down a
flight of stairs to the incarceration chambers.

There were already half a dozen or so men in the cell that
Jock was assigned to. His escort gently led him inside.

'Settle down men,' he said to the general assembly. 'You've
got a long wait.'

Jock MacPherson looked at his watch. It was only four-thirty. He wished he'd brought his pipe or had something to read. One of the men offered him a cigarette. He took it gladly and sat on a bunk that seemed to be the only vacant one. The man sat by his side and struck a match for him.

'This is a pretty mess we're in,' Jock MacPherson said. 'And for doing nothing at all.'

'Just our bad luck,' the man said. 'I'm Ian.' He put out his hand.

'I'm Jock,' Jock MacPherson said.

'This is Jock lads,' Ian announced to the other men. 'Come down from Scotland, did you?' he asked.

'No. Just out of London. Place in Kent.' He didn't want to expand on the nature of that place. They might begin to pity him or to take his protest less seriously.

'Have you told them there where you are?' another man asked. 'You're allowed a phone call.'

'I'm not expected back till tomorrow,' Jock said. When he'd been offered the call, he'd refused. He had no intention of announcing his martyrdom down the wire and to the sole ear of Matron. He would announce it on his return to the company in general, preferably in the dining room when all were assembled.

'Don't be too sure they'll let you out tomorrow,' Ian said. 'They could give you a week. Or a fine. Or both.'

'Don't listen to him, Grandad,' another man said. 'They'll let you off with a caution. You'll have a police record though,' he laughed. 'Something to tell your grandchildren.'

They all seemed so unruffled, so indifferent to their plight as if it were part and parcel of their day's work.

'Have you been in this predicament before?' Jock asked.

'Most of us, yes.' Ian answered for them. 'But not here. My first time in London. But we've done plenty in Glasgow.'

Jock wondered whether their 'plenty' was all on Scotland's behalf but he refrained from enquiry.

One of the men pulled a pack of cards from his pocket, and others, pairs of dice. They had clearly come prepared. Jock had nothing except his thoughts, and the preparation of the tale he would tell around The Hollyhocks' table. He lay back on the bunk. He was suddenly very tired. His long walk to Parliament that morning, though now it seemed years ago, and that interminable standing outside the House, shifting his own weight and that of the banner from side to side, all these exertions had left him exhausted. Very soon he was fast asleep. Ian covered him with the blanket provided, then he squatted on the floor to join in a game of craps. At six o'clock the warder brought in food that passed for supper. Jock was still fast asleep, but the other men saw fit to wake him for he would get no more food till the morning. 'Wakey wakey,' they shouted, then shoved him gently. Jock opened his eyes and quickly closed them again. For a moment he'd seen men about him and a grey wall behind them and he thought he was in a dream. But a further shove woke him again as did the call of food. He felt hungry and he sat up on the bunk and looked around him and thought himself still in a dream. Even while he was eating, he could not locate himself. He wondered what he was doing in this strange place that looked fearfully like a prison, and who all these men were and where had they come from. And why was he suddenly eating baked beans, a food he hadn't tasted since childhood? One of the men was playing a mouth organ. He recognised the tune and, like the beans, it was a reminder of his childhood, of the Scottish glens where he had played as a boy. He felt safer now, back in a known place, but he couldn't understand why it was so enclosed and why there were grown men where there were always children. 'Go back to sleep Grandad,' he heard one of the men say and he let himself be tucked into the blanket again, and lullabied back into the dream that was no longer a dream for him but an uncertain reality.

When he awoke next morning, he felt refreshed after his long sleep and he looked forward to the football game that his father had promised to take him to. He noticed that he had wet his bunk, but his mother would understand. She would put it down to excitement. There was porridge for breakfast too, his favourite food, though his mother had forgotten the toast.

As they led him out of the cell, he had a sudden realisation of where he was, and why and how. And he regretted that he had paid out good money for a decent bed in a hotel when he had failed to make use of it. He recalled that he was to appear before the magistrate that morning. He hoped the hearing would be short and would still leave him time to attend part of the debate. With his comrades, for that's how he thought of them now – comrades-in-arms – he was led to the anteroom of the court chamber. They were to be tried singly, and to be called in alphabetical order. He didn't know the surnames of his companions so he didn't know how soon he would be called. He waited for what seemed a long time and it was after eleven that he heard the first name. Its sound lifted his spirits. MacBarnes. His turn would come soon. But it was after twelve and they'd still only reached MacDonald. What with the break for lunch it was just after four o'clock, well beyond debate time, when the letter P was finally acknowledged. Jock MacPherson, he heard, and for a moment he thought he must answer to the school register. 'Here sir,' he said. But as he was placed in the dock, he was rudely shipped back to his present reality.

'Jock MacPherson,' he heard, and he cursed the capital P of his name and knew that tardy letter had caused him to miss the event which had brought him to London in the first place. There were three mouths on the desk in front of him, and he noticed that one of them moved.

'You are charged with causing a breach of the peace. How do you plead? Guilty or not guilty?'

He thought he was watching television. 'Guilty I suppose,' he said.

He watched the three mouths swivel to each other and open and shut in turn. Then he saw the camera turn on himself and for its benefit he put on a remorseful face. Then there was a picture of his mother in the gallery, praying for his deliverance. And his father put a protective hand on her shoulder.

'Fined thirty-five pounds,' one of the mouths snapped. 'And bound over to keep the peace.'

He smiled joyfully because he thought it was expected of him and went to join his parents in celebration. But there were few people in court and certainly no camera or gallery. He was led to where he must pay his fine and his belongings were returned to him. It was not until he found himself in the street that he accepted the fact that he was no longer a little boy.

He took a taxi back to the hotel, changed his clothes and reluctantly paid his bill. He managed to catch the five-thirty train and he arrived at The Hollyhocks in time for dinner.

Which was the setting he had envisaged for his tale. He took the seat next to Mrs Harvey, not of his deliberate choosing but simply because she had pointed it out to him and drawn it back for his occupation. He saw no point in refusing it. Matron was ladling out the soup.

'How was the debate, Mr MacPherson?' she asked.

He paused, waiting for silence. 'I didn't hear it,' he said.

'Why ever not?' Mrs Thackeray asked. 'Couldn't you get in?'

'No. I could have found a seat,' he said, 'but I was elsewhere.'

'Elsewhere?' Matron asked. 'Where was that?'

'In goal,' he said. 'I spent the night in gaol.'

He let it fall on to the table as Matron dropped the ladle into the tureen. Mrs Harvey drew her chair closer to his. She was in ecstasy. She had often fancied herself as a gangster's moll and never in her life had she been so close to its realisation. The table was agog with curiosity. An event had evented and though they had to experience it at second hand, it was still better than no event at all.

'Let me finish serving the soup first,' Matron said. 'We don't want it to get cold.'

The serving gave Jock time for rehearsal, although he had already rehearsed his telling on the train journey, and sometimes out loud, much to the curiosity and concern of his fellow passengers. He could hardly wait to begin. But he was suddenly hungry. He realised he'd not properly eaten since his breakfast of the day before. He vaguely remembered some beans and porridge, but he could not put them into any context. So he insisted on having his soup before he embarked on his tale. Then, partially satisfied, he began. He told his story in meticulous detail and it pleased him that he could achieve such itemised recall. The residents managed an occasional forkful of food during Jock MacPherson's pauses and of these there were many, to lend suspense and drama to his narration. He too paused to eat at times, and by the time the pudding was served, he had reached his court appearance. He would keep them waiting for the verdict, he decided, and he took time over his dessert.

Well he wouldn't be hanged, Mrs Harvey thought, which put paid to her presence at the gallows, weeping at his feet. Let out on bail was the most she could hope for, in which case she could comfort him pending his trial. She moved her chair closer so that her knees nudged his. But Jock MacPherson didn't even feel the nudge, so intent was he on rehearsing the final verdict. He was aware that it would be something of an anti-climax and he wondered how he could dress such a letdown in the clothes of martyrdom.

'I had my fingerprints taken,' he said. 'Both hands. And my photograph. Both sides of my face. I've got a police record,' he said proudly. He hoped that his cause would be satisfied with that. He took a last mouthful of pudding. 'Then I was fined,' he said. 'Thirty-five pounds. And bound over to keep the peace.'

Mrs Harvey stifled her disappointment. All he had was a police record which called for little show of devotion or sacrifice. Still, it would have to do. Her late mother had disapproved of all her marriages, more on principle than argument, and if she knew that Jock MacPherson was in her daughter's present sights, she would have had apoplexy. Mrs Harvey took some pleasure in that.

When they adjourned to the common lounge for their night drinks, all of them vied to sit next to Jock MacPherson. For he was their star, their celebrity.

'Did you *feel* guilty?' Mrs Green asked, salivating. She looked across at Mr Rufus ensuring that he appreciated the intelligence of her question.

'Guilty of what?' Jock MacPherson asked. His answer confirmed the banality of the question.

Mrs Green sulked and moved her chair away. 'It's vandalism. That's what I call it,' she said crossly. 'All these demonstrations. They're just an excuse for violence.'

Jock MacPherson rose from his seat and walked over to where Mrs Green was sitting. He looked as if he might strike her. Mr Rufus half rose in case a defence of some kind was called for and Mrs Thackeray watched the proceedings with an excited anticipation that Mrs Green would finally get her comeuppance. She moved her chair slightly so that she could get a better view.

She saw how Mr MacPherson came to a halt a few inches from Mrs Green's chair. He bent over towards her, his face almost touching hers.

'Have *you* ever had a cause, Mrs Green?' he said. 'Ever in your life? A cause? A cause worth dying for?'

Mrs Thackeray caught sight of Mr Rufus who was seen to rise slightly in his seat, straining his ear for her answer, and Mrs Thackeray wondered why it was so important that he should hear her reply.

'*Any* cause?' Jock MacPherson repeated.

'I believe in England,' she said lamely.

He turned his back on her with contempt. 'Very safe,' he said. 'Safer than Scotland.'

He did not return to his seat but announced to the general assembly that he was very tired after his day's exertions and that he was ready for sleep. The residents encouraged him for they needed his absence before they could indulge in gossip.

'Well done, Mr MacPherson,' Mr Rufus said and there was a general cheer from the assembly.

He smiled at them, satisfied. When he reached the door, he turned and they noticed a childlike smile wash over his countenance.

'I have to go to bed now,' he said, 'because I have to get up early in the morning. My mother's taking me to the dentist.'

A stunned silence shocked the room for some time after his departure. All of them had heard his exit line and only one conclusion could be drawn. At this point Mrs Harvey entirely abandoned her strategy. It was clear that Jock MacPherson could never be part of her future, for the state of second childhood was irrevocable. His parting shot had done more than astonish them. It had cast the whole of his adventure story in doubt. Had he imagined it all? Had he indeed travelled to London, let alone spent a night in a police cell? All of them doubted it now, until Mr Rufus intervened.

'I believe him,' he said. 'I believe he did spend the night in gaol. And I think that that experience, which must have been terrible for a man of his age, I think that that experience unhinged his mind a little. But after a good night's sleep, he should be himself again.'

As it turned out, Mr Rufus was right, if only in part. Mr MacPherson had indeed been brought to confusion in his prison cell. But a good night's sleep was not going to reverse that irrevocable step he'd taken into his boyhood. And the following morning, when all were seated at breakfast, Mr MacPherson's chair was shriekingly unoccupied. Jeremy Cross happily envisaged a further name behind his wardrobe door. They waited, dawdling with their food, pretending not to be waiting for anything at all. Then the plaintive sound of bagpipes was heard and the tune of 'Flowers of the Forest', the piper's lament, wafted down the stairway. And within its melody came Jock MacPherson, dressed in his full Scottish regalia, his kilt, his plaid socks, his brogues, his sporran, his tassels, his cape, his pipes bellowing his heart out. He was going home, our hero. Home to Scotland. And on the way, he was going round the bend.

Fifteen

Over the next few days Matron kept a close watch on Mr
MacPherson. His condition disturbed her. He wore his Scottish
emblems night and day, refusing to abandon them even for
sleep. After a week, he had become what Matron termed a
'management problem'. She would have to find another home,
one that specialised in Mr MacPherson's condition. She would
be sorry to lose him. In all the years he had been at The
Hollyhocks, he had never given her any trouble. She would
miss him. She went to her office to make the appropriate
phone calls.

She settled him with little difficulty in the most reputable home in the area. She would take him there herself. She packed his clothes, together with his personal belongings. And he watched her.

'Am I going back to school?' he asked. 'When does term start? And don't forget my tuck box.'

Matron became his mother for his sake, and answered all his questions. He followed her like a lamb, the bagpipes swinging from his plaided shoulder. It was early in the morning when she took him from The Hollyhocks. A time when no one was about, because she did not want to call attention to his departure. She would announce it at breakfast. The whole truth of it.

She had ordered a car to take them to The Harbour, as his new home was called. A place for shelter, for mooring, a name that lent hope to a continuation of life's journey. But it was a misnomer. The Harbour was not for mooring; it was for permanent anchorage. It was but another venue at which to play the waiting game. But at The Harbour, the game was more fun. Because its participants saw it only as a game, exactly like those games they played in the cradle, in the nursery or in school, or on the playing field, each site depending on the limits of their recall.

She helped the new Matron settle her charge in his room.

'It's good to be back in school,' he said. 'See you at Christmas, Mother dear.' He stuck out his cheek for a kiss, and Matron obliged, tousling his hair. On her way back to The Hollyhocks, she did her level best to stop crying.

She announced Mr MacPherson's departure at breakfast, and gave its reasons. She assured them all that he was happily settled at The Harbour assuming that they would be concerned with his welfare. But Jock MacPherson had already, by necessity, been forgotten and if occasionally he was recalled, it was because of his police record which was now, in their eyes, total fantasy. Jeremy Cross wondered whether it would be justifiable to add Jock MacPherson's name to his list. He knew it was slightly unethical, but after all, anyone who landed up in The Harbour was as good as dead anyway. He would think about it. Perhaps he would inscribe his name in brackets. Those parentheses would give the name a certain licit ambiguity. Yes. He would do just that after breakfast.

In the common lounge, Mrs Scott was studying the day's horoscopes. Over the weeks she had turned many of the residents on to star-gazing, and she was looked upon as the expert in the field. The new girl, Mrs Harvey, having recently barked up the wrong tree, was still open to forecast as to her chances, though looking round, she had to admit that she had exhausted all possibilities. Her eye fell on Jeremy Cross as he was leaving the lounge to amend his list and she asked Mrs Scott, who by now knew everybody's birth sign, what his star was.

'Gemini,' Mrs Scott said without hesitation. 'And a typical one.' Mrs Harvey didn't now what a typical Gemini was and she didn't care, but she asked for his horoscope none the less, for it was tangential to her own. 'Gemini,' Mrs Scott read out. 'A new chapter is beginning in your life and you will be in a position to demand what you want.'

Mrs Harvey rather wished that she were a Gemini herself, for that forecast would have suited her very nicely. With little enthusiasm she asked for her own. The Pisces forecast.

Mrs Scott was on stage once more. 'Pisces are prone to do too many things at once,' she read. 'Decisions are out of your hands. But be patient.'

'It's all a lot of rubbish,' Mrs Harvey said under her breath. Yet she half believed it. It was up to Mr Cross to decide what he wanted and it was faintly possible he didn't want her good self. 'I don't want him anyway,' she said, again under her breath. 'It's only because there's absolutely nobody else.'

The Hollyhocks was the third home she'd tested, spending a few months at each previous one, where the pickings were even leaner. She did not have the strength to move again. She would have to settle on remaining single for the rest of her life. It was not a happy prospect. But she must not give up hope. To give up hope was to begin to die. Jock MacPherson's quarters had to be filled and it might well be by a knight in shining armour. Meanwhile she would keep up her appearance and her regular appointments with the Hair and Handcare Parlour. Mrs Harvey would fight the good fight, no matter how many fell by the wayside.

Upstairs in his quarters Jeremy Cross had just finished inscribing the bracketed Mr MacPherson on the back of his wardrobe door. He stepped back to admire his handiwork and as he did so, he felt a sudden shooting pain in his ribs.

'No!' he shouted to his four walls. 'Absolutely not!'

He rang his bell for Matron, then slowly he sat down on his bed holding his chest and willing the pain to ease. Which it did, quite suddenly, so that by the time Matron arrived, he felt well again. But Matron insisted on calling the doctor and she ordered him to bed straight away. As he lay there, waiting for the doctor to arrive, he gloated a little, celebrating his survival. No doubt Matron would subject him to the 'tray in the room' routine for a few days, while those downstairs in the common lounge would whisper and draw their false conclusions. Then after a few days he would appear, dapper and well, at the break-fast table, and disappoint them all.

But that was not to be. The doctor insisted that he go to hospital for a series of tests.

'Just to make sure,' he said.

He booked him into a private ward at the Dover Infirmary, and by evening he was installed in his private room, with a tele-vision, and a tray of haute cuisine at his side. They had taped his chest with four wires all attached to a small recording device that would monitor his heartbeat and its variations over twenty-four hours. There was nothing he had to do except lie there. He was in hospital simply to be seen to. He rang for the nurse and ordered newspapers. That was the extent of his reading. In all his life he had probably read no more than four or five books. But he devoured newspapers. They were in no way threatening. Their pages did not stretch into the hundreds and load you with guilt if you didn't read them all. You could pick and choose from a newspaper according to your personal taste. He liked the obituaries best, and after those, the news. He didn't bother with leader articles or any commentaries. He had his own opinions and he didn't need anyone else to confirm them. There was a phone on his bedside table. He knew it would never ring and he himself would never use it since he had no one to call. He had had few friends in his life and he had made it his business to outlive them all. So he didn't need a telephone. But its very presence irritated him. He had to admit to himself that it drew attention to the emptiness of his life and that perhaps the pursuit of survival was not the main purpose of living. And he realised that all his life, he had done nothing else. As a boy, he had weathered all the dropouts in his class, and as a man he had kept his jobs while others around him fell by the wayside. With such a survival purpose in mind, he could never afford to make friends or to risk an intimate relationship. He would not allow himself to regret it, especially now in the autumn of his days, else it would totally negate his past. Yet he would be happier if they took the telephone away and he looked at it with such loathing that the telephone trembled and shivered with a mighty ring. Jeremy Cross jumped in his bed, and didn't dare to think of the frenzied pattern his heart was recording. He let it ring a few times while his palpitations slowed. Then he picked up the receiver.

'Hello?' he said.

'Mr Williams?' a woman's voice asked.

'No,' he said flatly.

'Oh I'm sorry,' the woman said, 'I must have the wrong number.'

He put down the receiver and he felt a pricking behind his eyes. Then a tear on his cheek, and more tears as he realised exactly what he was. A wrong number. Everybody's wrong number. Beginning with his mother who had wanted a little girl. Now he couldn't stop crying, realising that it had been many many years since he had shed a tear. Not even at his mother's funeral so many years ago, for she had never forgiven him for his gender. That was the wrongest number of all.

When the phone rang again shortly afterwards, he picked up the receiver with regret. 'You've got the wrong number,' he said, even before he had heard any voice on the other end of the line.

'Mr Cross?' he heard.

He recognised Matron's voice.

'How are you feeling?' she asked.

He did not answer immediately. It took him a little time to realise that there was actually somebody outside of himself who cared about him, or at least pretended to, and that in itself was better than total indifference.

'I'm fine thank you Matron,' he said at last. Then he couldn't resist it. 'I shall outlive you all,' he said.

'I've been in touch with the doctors,' Matron told him. 'They're awaiting results of all the tests. Then we shall have to see. Just be patient Mr Cross,' she added. 'I'm sure there's nothing to worry about.'

He thanked her for ringing and meant it. Now the presence of the telephone did not bother him. He heard how his heartbeat had settled, and he lay back happily to watch television.

The results of all the tests that Mr Cross was subjected to necessitated a longer stay in hospital than was anticipated. He did not enquire as to the reasons why, nor did he question his subsequent treatments. Or what the treatments were for. He simply didn't want to know. He took the pills they gave him and offered his arm for pulse and blood pressure and his other arm for the taking of blood. He gave of himself willingly in the knowledge that he was being seen to.

Over the next week, Matron telephoned every day. She asked the same questions and wished him the same progress. Her phrasing never varied. Her call had become routine. Yet he was glad of it. It justified the presence of a telephone on his table.

During his second week in hospital, he had a visitor. There was a knock on his door. He wondered who it could be. Nurses never knocked. Nor doctors. So it had to be Matron. He could think of no one else. So he called 'Come in,' as he straightened his pyjama-top and put an expression of welcome on his face.

But it wasn't Matron. It was Mrs Harvey who, that morning, as on every other morning, had listened to Mrs Scott's reading of her Pisces horoscope. 'In pursuit of your wish, grab the bull by the horns,' it had advised her. 'This opportunity is unlikely to occur again.'

She had gone straight to her room, smartened herself up and ordered a cab to take her to the local station. Once there, she booked a ticket to Dover, and only when she was settled in a corner seat did she consider what she was doing and how she should go about it. She rehearsed a few opening remarks, but since such remarks depended entirely upon the patient's reaction to her visit, she would have to play it by ear.

In the foyer of the hospital there was a shop, displaying overpriced flowers and extravagant chocolates and cakes. She thought she might buy him a little something, but on seeing the prices she decided that a gift would be a little too forward. She took the lift to his room and dawdled a little while outside his door. She was nervous. She was aware that a nurse was watching her, so she had to stop prevaricating and knock boldly on his door. When she heard his 'Come in,' she hesitated again and had the nurse not been eyeing her, she might well have turned tail and gone straight back to The Hollyhocks. The nurse started to walk towards her. She was trapped. She had nowhere to go except through his door.

'Hello Mr Cross,' she said, watching his face carefully as he watched hers. It registered little else but astonishment. There was no hint of pleasure or welcome in his features, so she responded to his show of surprise.

'You weren't expecting me,' she said, inching her way towards the bed.

He managed a smile then, but it was not meant for her. He was smiling to himself, wondering what on earth was the woman's name. He knew it was a Hollyhocks face. And a new one. He recalled too that that face had once tried to outlast him in the common lounge when everyone else had gone to bed. But fatigue had got the better of her. Or was he confusing her with someone else? Whatever, he wondered why she had come, or more specifically, what she was after. She drew up a chair to the bedside. 'How are you feeling?' she asked tenderly and she actually laid her hand on the covering sheet. Mr Cross felt trapped and cornered. She had a look on her face that suggested she might get into the bed beside him. He inched himself squarely into the middle to scotch that possibility. He wished he could remember her name.

'What's the news at The Hollyhocks?' he asked. He felt he ought to initiate some safe conversation.

'No news at all,' Mrs Harvey said. 'Nothing ever happens there. It's a very dull place. As a matter of fact,' she whispered, leaning towards him, 'I came here for a little excitement.'

My God, Jeremy Cross thought, this woman is actually flirting with me and he dreaded to think what mischief this encounter was doing to his heartbeat. She was not good for him, whatever her name was, and he wished to God that she would go away.

'I'm feeling very tired,' he said. 'I'm supposed to have a sleep every afternoon. That's what the doctors say.' He hoped she would take the hint and leave.

But she did neither. 'Oh you go to sleep,' she said. 'I'll wait. It'll be nice for you to have someone to wake up to.'

He was stupefied by her boldness. 'I can't sleep if I know someone's watching me,' he tried.

'I won't watch you,' she persisted. 'Promise,' she added with a flirtatious smile.

'I'd rather you went,' he said. He had to spell it out for her once and for all.

'As you wish,' she said. She took hold of his hand, and in such a grip that he thought she might have it in mind to take it with her. Her touch felt like snakeskin.

'I'll come again,' she threatened. 'You need company from time to time.'

He pulled his hand away and turned over as if to go to sleep. 'Thank you for coming,' he muttered into the sheets, not caring whether or not she heard. He lay still, waiting to hear her foot-steps cross the room and the closing of the door. At last he heard it, and he sighed with relief. Then sitting up once more in bed, he decided that his visitor, whatever she was called, was a person for whom he would gladly be the wrong number. He set to wondering why she had come. And what she was after. She was a gold-digger, he decided. She had heard that he was a man of means and that he had no relatives, and that it was rumoured that his health was poor and that she was going to hook him before it was too late. Hence her visit, and possibly more to come. He smiled to himself. If she had the audacity to come again, he would tell her, en passant of course, that he was a homosexual, and had been so all his life. It was worth a try. It was a small price to pay for his future peace.

Mrs Harvey had left the hospital severely disappointed. But she was not one to give up so easily. She recalled her horoscope. 'Grab the bull by the horns. This opportunity is unlikely to occur again.' That was the forecast only for today. Tomorrow it might be too late. She decided to hang around in Dover for a while, to visit the castle perhaps, and then to have a cup of tea, and afterwards, having given him enough time to sleep, she would make a return visit and exploit her forecast to the full. 'I'm a brazen hussy,' she said to herself, recalling the term with which her mother had labelled her throughout her girl-hood. But she had never cared, and she wasn't going to care now. At seven o'clock, having done the castle and had her tea, she made her way back to the hospital. This time, she didn't even bother to knock on his door. She walked straight in and took her seat beside the bed. At first Mr Cross thought he was dreaming. Or rather, nightmaring.

'You're back,' he spluttered.

'Looks like it,' she smiled, her hand sidling along the bed-clothes.

'Look,' he said. He still couldn't remember her name.

'Call me Minnie,' she interrupted him.

'Look Minnie,' he said, grateful for some label. 'I think it's very kind of you to visit me. Very kind indeed. And all the way to Dover! But *twice* in one day. I don't understand it. I don't understand it at all.'

'I thought you might like company,' she said. She thought she might try sulking. It usually worked with an ungiving man. But she sensed that Mr Cross might be sublimely indifferent to sulks, as he would be to tears. She put on a brave and brazen face. 'In any case, I could do with a little company myself.'

'But you have company at The Hollyhocks,' he said.

'Just a lot of old women,' she said with contempt. 'There are no real men there. And that's the company I like to keep. Always have done. All my life.'

This was undeniably his cue, Mr Cross thought. And the declaration of his homosexual proclivities sprang to his lips. He took a deep breath and wondered what it would sound like.

'I have to tell you Minnie,' he said. 'I'm a homosexual. I've been that way all my life.'

Mrs Harvey laughed. 'I know you are my dear. I knew it when I first saw you. It's pretty obvious to anybody.'

He could well have crowned her. How dare she. He was sorely tempted to deny it. To confess that it was only a ploy to get rid of her. To claim that he had had hundreds of relationships with women in his time and that he thought that all queers were perverts. He wondered what antics his heartbeat was up to.

'But I'm only looking for companionship,' Mrs Harvey prattled on. 'At our age, who cares what your preferences are? That side of things doesn't really matter any more.'

He turned on her. 'It matters to me,' he almost shouted. 'Minnie,' he said. Again he wished he knew her full name because he was about to insult her and send her on her brazen way and a mere Christian name sat awkwardly with rudeness. But he ploughed on, taking care not to look at her. 'I have absolutely nothing to offer you,' he said. 'In fact, I don't like you very much. And I want you to go. Immediately. Or I shall ring for the nurse and she shall put you out.'

Mrs Harvey rose from her chair, trembling with rage. 'I know where I'm not wanted,' she said. She went to the door and turned. 'I hope you die,' she hissed.

She stood outside his door for a while, shivering. She had never been so grossly insulted. She did not regret her parting shot. She had meant it sincerely. It would be embarrassing to have to see him again. So she hoped that he would die in hospital. And soon.

As she sat on the train on her return journey, she cursed Mrs Scott and her mumbo-jumbo and vowed that she would never take the bull by the horns again.

When the nurse took Mr Cross's blood pressure later that evening she noted that it had risen, as had his pulse rate. She gave him a sedative.

'Did your visitor upset you in any way?' she asked.

'She most certainly did,' he told her.

'Then I won't let her in again,' the nurse said.

'Don't worry,' Mr Cross smiled. 'I don't think she'll be coming.'

He went to sleep shortly afterwards and happily dreamed that he had inscribed her name, whatever it was, on the back of his wardrobe door.

After another week and further tests, Jeremy Cross was discharged from hospital with a clean bill of health. Matron had ordered a car to fetch him home. He looked forward to his return to The Hollyhocks and he was not in the least bit worried about the stories that Minnie something had probably circulated in his absence. He reckoned that he had won their little battle and he knew that she knew it too. When he entered the common lounge, he was given a polite welcome. He had clearly not been much missed. He noted that the Minnie woman was absent. He supposed that she was too embarrassed to face him. But he did get a large welcome from Mr Rufus who had just entered the lounge, and, taking her cue, Mrs Green rose from her chair and echoed her pleasure at his recovery. At dinner that evening, Minnie's chair was vacant. He wondered where she was. It was Mrs Thackeray who asked Matron for the whereabouts of Mrs Harvey.

'She has a headache,' Matron said. 'She's asked for a tray in her room.'

Jeremy Cross smiled to himself. God was occasionally good.

That evening, Matron had invited an expert on ageing to come to talk to her residents. Occasionally she would arrange an evening with a special guest for an informal debate in the common lounge. Though she had been offered a number of lecturers from the agency that she used, she had problems in choosing a suitable subject. Her last had been one on the mysteries of the East, but the lecturer had been so boring and so lacking in mystery himself, he was unable to transfer it to his subject. The meeting had broken up early. Some of the residents had even walked out during the lecture. Those who stayed, did so out of pity. That meeting had been some months ago, and Matron had been wary of organising another. But when the agency offered her an expert on the process of ageing, she sensed that it was a subject that would appeal to everybody. She was right. For when they adjourned to the common lounge after dinner, with the exception of Mrs Harvey, she could boast a full house. The lecturer had not yet arrived, so the night drinks were served. Shortly they heard the bell in reception, and Matron went out to greet the visiting expert. A silence fell in the common lounge as they waited for his entry. And when it came, there was a general sigh all around.

Matron introduced him. 'This is Mr Roberts,' she said gamely. They stared at him. This so-called expert on ageing was all of twenty-five years old. Matron viewed him with pity. He was going to have a very rough ride indeed.

Mr Roberts sat down nervously in the chair that Matron offered him, but he refused the coffee that came with the chair. He was jumpy and he wanted to get the whole business over and done with. He smelt the hostility in the room, and the contempt. He thought he'd better come clean straight away.

'Ladies and gentlemen,' he began. 'Thank you for asking me to come and speak to you tonight. Now I am well aware that everybody in this room knows a damn sight more about ageing than I do.' It was a clever opening gambit. With his confession, he'd taken the wind out of their disdainful sails. They tittered, and some even clapped, grateful for his ready acknowledgement of their superiority. Matron was pleased. It might turn out to be a good evening after all.

'So what am I going to talk about?' Mr Roberts went on. 'I have done a study on ageing and I have interviewed hundreds of people like your good selves. And I want to tell you about the conclusions I have drawn from these studies and ask you if I've got it right or wrong. In other words, I want your opinions, I want your wisdom. In a way, I have come here for selfish reasons. I have come to learn. Will you help me?'

Now they were completely won over. But not Mr Rufus, nor Mr Cross, who both thought that Mr Roberts was a cunning young bastard, and neither had any intention of giving him the benefit of their acquired wisdom. But they listened, curious to see if he could get away with it.

He began by telling them the story of an ageing lady – he was careful not to use the word 'old' – who had confided in him that her life began in earnest at eighty. It was not until then that she had rid herself of domestic responsibilities. Her husband had died and her two children were comfortably married.

'Now tell me,' he said, affecting a chatty intimate manner, 'does that story resonate with any of you?'

There was a silence before Mrs Thackeray saw fit to argue. 'What's the point in life beginning at eighty,' she asked, 'if you no longer have the strength to enjoy it?'

'That's a very good point,' Mr Roberts said. 'I'm grateful for it. Any more contributions?' A note of desperation had crept into his voice and it was not lost on the residents.

'Personally,' Mrs Green piped up, more for the benefit of Mr Rufus than for that of the lecturer, 'I rather enjoyed looking after my husband and daughter. I miss those responsibilities.'

'I'm sorry but I don't believe you,' Mrs Thackeray said.

'Well I know you were pretty glad to get rid of *your* husband. You told me so yourself,' Mrs Green said.

'You made that up. I told you no such thing.' Mrs Thackeray was enraged.

'You're losing your memory. That's your trouble,' Mrs Green said.

Mr Roberts sat back. The floor was no longer his, and he was deeply grateful to pass it over. The room was agog with excitement, as spectators at a cock-fight, or in this case, a hen-fight, but just as vicious.

'And what about your daughter, that so-called lovely daughter of yours whom you say you miss?' Mrs Thackeray was about to play her trump card. 'That daughter who hasn't talked to you in forty years.' She allowed a pause. 'That daughter who gave you that scar on your face.'

First blood to Mrs Thackeray, the spectators thought. And they waited for Mrs Green's riposte. Over the past months, interest in Mrs Green's scar had evaporated, but now at its mention, and possibly ugly provenance, curiosity was renewed. Mr Rufus especially was seen to prick up his ears, though he squeezed Mrs Green's arm as a public gesture of support. Matron thought for a moment that she should call a halt to the hostilities but she was enjoying it much too much and she, like the others, was itching to learn about the scar. When it was clear that Mrs Green had nothing to say, Mrs Thackeray offered the explanation they were all waiting for. 'Her daughter,' she announced, 'that one whom she misses looking after, her daughter once told her she wished her mother was dead, and she threw a saucepan at her and caught her on the cheek. I could tell you a lot more too,' she added meaningfully. And though the ringside would have relished 'a lot more too', Matron decided to call a halt.

'That's enough ladies,' she said. 'What must poor Mr Roberts think of you?'

Poor Mr Roberts, who had been very happy on the sidelines, was now obliged to take the platform once more. The residents began to dislike him. His presence forbade the continuation of an argument that threatened to develop into an exciting shooting-match. They wished he'd go back to where he came from. As he opened his mouth to speak, Mrs Thackeray added her coda. And it was well above a whisper. 'To say nothing of that Swiss finishing school of hers.'

'What Swiss finishing school?' Lady Celia suddenly gave voice. She knew a thing or two about Swiss finishing schools, from genuine personal experience.

'Ask her,' Mrs Thackeray said.

The ceasefire had been broken and Mr Roberts leaned back once more. Matron made no further attempt to intervene. Her curiosity about the Swiss finishing school got the better of her.

'What was the name of your school?' Lady Celia demanded with some authority.

'I can't remember off hand,' Mrs Green was bound to admit.

'You're losing your memory. That's your trouble.' Mrs Thackeray paid her back in kind.

Mrs Green didn't know what to do. She sensed that nobody in the room was on her side except perhaps dear Mr Rufus, who kept squeezing her arm. She looked around helplessly. Then she decided that the only course open to her was tears. In her life of deceit and denial, tears had proved to be a useful weapon and with much rehearsal she had perfected their means of production. She let them fall, without using a handkerchief to stem them. She wanted her helplessness clearly visible. She would play the victim and hope for their pity and eventually their turning against her attacker.

But Lady Celia was now well into the fray, and she was not so easily disarmed.

'Whereabout in Switzerland was it?' she insisted. 'The German, the French or the Italian region?'

'The German,' Mrs Green offered. 'Near Zürich.'

'German,' Lady Celia said with disdain. She donated to the word far more syllables than it phonetically merited, which rendering encapsulated her contempt for the whole nation. Lady Celia was known to have lost sundry relatives in both the First and Second World Wars. She was not likely to find that nation or its so-called finishing schools worthy of her consideration. 'I didn't know that there were finishing schools in Zürich,' she said.

Mrs Green wished that she could faint. But apart from her fury, she felt perfectly fit, so she cried more audibly and hoped for the best.

'Crocodile tears,' Mrs Thackeray muttered.

At this point Matron again called the residents to order. But nobody wanted to listen to Mr Roberts any more and his twenty-odd-year-old geriatric experience. Mr Roberts was more than happy to oblige them, having decided that in future he would address his geriatric lecture to classes of sixth-formers. Matron recognised that Mr Roberts had been a mistake and she hoped he'd have the decency to refuse his fee. She offered him a cup of coffee and a cake in case he had some embarrassment to swallow.

By now Lady Celia was well into her stride. She rarely took part in common lounge discussion, but any subject tangential to Germany clearly loosened her tongue. And forked it too.

'Finishing schools,' she said in disbelief. 'What do the Germans know about finesse? About elegance? About etiquette? A finishing-*off* school more likely. They had plenty of those.'

'I have to agree with you there, Lady Celia.' The Major had suddenly joined the fray. He put his arm around Mrs Feinberg's shoulder, declaring themselves a united front.

'I'm of the same opinion,' Mrs Thackeray declared, though she had never in her life given the matter a thought, but if the target was Mrs Green, she was happy to shaft her arrow in that direction.

'Well there's good and bad in every race,' Mrs Scott, who felt she ought to join in the discussion, said. But she made a note to reread the day's horoscopes to ascertain whether the evening's fiasco had been forecast.

It was then that Mr Rufus spoke, and in order to emphasise his defence of Mrs Green he rose from his seat.

'I don't see any point in this discussion,' he said. 'If my good friend Mrs Green says that she went to a finishing school in Zürich, there's absolutely no reason to disbelieve her. She can surely be forgiven for having forgotten its name.'

This sober contribution served to stem Mrs Green's tears and she took his hand tenderly as he sat down beside her. It also silenced them all.

Except for Jeremy Cross who until now had held his tongue during the whole exchange. But he could not forgo an opportunity to demolish Lady Celia, his arch enemy of years' standing, who threatened to outlive them all. He opened his mouth to speak, and held it open for a little while, so that those around him would note that he was about to declare.

'I think you are deeply intolerant Lady Celia,' he said. 'Just because you're titled, you think you have a divine right to ride rough-shod over everybody else.'

There was a gasp around the common lounge. No one had ever dared to speak so boldly to Lady Celia. With her title she was assumed to be beyond criticism. Yet they were all inwardly delighted that she was about to be pulled down a peg or two.

'It's the trouble with all of your class,' Mr Cross went on. 'You think you're so special. But you're no better than any of us. You and your chinless kind.'

They were words he had saved up for years, ever since coming to The Hollyhocks, and he was glad that they were out while there was still time, though it had never occurred to Mr Cross that he didn't have all the time in the world.

'It's time somebody told you . . .' He had a lot more to say and his mouth was moving. He felt it, but he couldn't hear the sounds. On discharge from the hospital, he had been given a clean bill of health. Yet he slumped to the floor, astonished. Then the sounds came back, matching his mouth's movements.

'No!' he shouted. 'Absolutely no!' He was by no means the last bottle on the wall. He stared at Lady Celia with loathing. 'It's not fair,' he whimpered. 'You're older than me.' Then the pain seized him and, fair or not, he resigned from the waiting game.

That evening there was no competition as to who would be the last to leave the lounge. It was, as usual, Jeremy Cross. But this time, in a box.

Sixteen

While Mr Cross was being belatedly seen to, Mr Roberts made a stealthy exit. He didn't ask for his fee. He reckoned he had been paid handsomely in the form of a pretty good story that he could tell to his sixth-form audiences, with his own embroidery. Lady Celia, temporarily ruffled, gave her studied opinion that Mr Cross deserved to die for speaking ill of the ruling classes. And to this, Mrs Thackeray was heard to say 'Bollocks'. When Mrs Harvey heard the news, she thanked God that He had answered her prayer. And so promptly. But Matron didn't know what to think. She had never particularly liked Mr Cross, but a dead body was somehow unaccusable. She had had it removed to the morgue immediately, as if, in his corporal absence, he would no longer disturb her. She went up to his room and gently packed his clothes away. The row of his empty shoes upset her profoundly and she didn't know why. For a long time she stared at his list at the back of his wardrobe door. In its crooked way, it was a history of The Hollyhocks since his arrival. She felt it should be preserved. Like an archive. She read it slowly and knew it was somehow incomplete. Then carefully she inscribed his name on the bottom of the list. And alongside it, as cause of death, she wrote, 'great expectations'.

It was time for Lady Celia's monthly journey to London. To the sherry in Lady Priscilla's drawing room and an update on their nefarious activities. She herself had nothing to report apart from the confirmation of the ferret's regular Monday call. Lady Priscilla announced two more profitable clients. A transvestite judge, and a member of the Cabinet who was particularly fond of little boys. The ferret had found them both.

'What a treasure he is,' Lady Celia said, as she sipped her sherry.

'But Lord Welland has died,' Lady Priscilla said. It didn't represent a loss of income, for his widow had agreed to continue the payments rather than see her faithless husband's reputation sullied.

'Aren't women strange,' Lady Celia said, having forgotten that she herself had done exactly the same.

'And thank God for that,' Lady Priscilla giggled, 'else we would both be out of profit.' And she refilled their sherry glasses. 'There's something I must tell you,' she said. 'The ferret wants to talk to us. Both of us together. I've asked him to join us for a sherry. He should be here soon.'

'What does he want to talk to us about?' Lady Celia asked.

'I fear he wants a larger cut,' Lady Priscilla said. 'Why else should he want to speak to us?'

'We can't do without him,' Lady Celia said.

'But at the same time,' Lady Priscilla argued, 'where could he go?'

'He could go it alone. Take our clients. We couldn't stop him.'

'But *we* have the connections,' Lady Celia said. 'Or at least you do.'

'I don't like it,' Lady Priscilla said. 'He might even stoop to blackmail.'

Neither lady thought that funny, and they sipped their sherry very seriously.

As four o'clock chimed on the heirloom clock in the hall, the doorbell was heard and the maid introduced the punctual ferret. He was invited to sit down and a glass of sherry was put into his hand. He would happily have done without it. A can of lager would have been more to his taste. He held the two ladies in utter contempt, and viewed their tipple likewise. But because of them he made a good living, and contempt was a small price to pay.

'You wanted to talk to us?' Lady Priscilla asked, when she deemed he'd drunk enough sherry to cover his ration. For the two ladies held the ferret in equal contempt.

'I want to ask a favour,' he said. 'A favour that would be in your interest too.'

That request could have applied to anything. 'What is that?' Lady Priscilla asked tentatively.

'I'd like a car,' he said. 'A little one would do. I have sciatica, and walking troubles me sometimes. I have to stand around a lot in this job and it would be helpful if I had somewhere to sit.'

Lady Priscilla was on the point of offering him a motorbike, which she felt was far more in line with his class, but Lady Celia thought they had got off rather lightly. Hastily she agreed.

'I've seen a nice one at my local garage,' the ferret said. 'It's only five years old, with low mileage. I can get it for two thousand.'

The poor devil's not even asking for a new one, Lady Celia thought. And Lady Priscilla's long-held opinion that the ferret was deeply working-class was confirmed.

'We'll leave it to you,' Lady Priscilla said, 'if you think it's a good buy. Try it out and let me know. Then we'll see to writing a cheque.'

'Thank you very much,' the ferret said and he put down his half-finished sherry on the table.

'Anything else to report?' Lady Priscilla asked. 'Did you follow up that bishop I told you about?'

'It's all in hand Lady Priscilla,' he said, and he turned to Lady Celia and actually winked at her.

She was affronted but she could not afford to take offence. 'Who's this bishop?' she asked when the ferret had gone.

'It's early days yet,' Lady Priscilla said, 'but I picked up a hint from Edwige Schloman, you know, that foreign salon crawler. It seems he's up to no good.'

'What sort of no good?'

'No good good enough for us. Anyway, the ferret's on to it. It could be a big one. And I will, as usual my dear, keep you informed. Now where shall we dine?'

Every month when Lady Celia visited London, it was their custom to dine at a restaurant of their choice.

'I think tonight we could splash out a little,' Lady Priscilla said. 'We've got off lightly with the ferret. We should celebrate. What d'you say to dining at the Savoy?'

'I think that's a splendid idea,' Lady Celia said.

Lady Priscilla rang for her valet and instructed him to book a table. 'Make sure it's in the centre,' she said. Then to Lady Celia in a whisper, 'We want to see and be seen. We'll put the meal on expenses as usual.' She talked like a law-abiding citizen who regularly paid her taxes, though neither lady had ever filled in a tax form. But they were not above claiming expenses on an income undeclared.

They refuelled themselves with more sherry, then Lady Priscilla suggested a short siesta before dinner. The two chaises longues in the drawing room would suit their purposes and shortly their gentle snores, staccatoed with alcohol, echoed into the hall, so that the maid forbore to collect the drinks tray. The seven o'clock heirloom chimes stirred them awake, simultaneously. They blinked at each other and thought that two women who were able to snore together must be very good friends indeed. They spruced themselves up, Savoy-fitting, then Lady Priscilla called for her chauffeur.

Their table was perfectly placed. Spot in the centre with unrestricted viewing on all sides. The Savoy dining room offered good pickings for their trade. It was possible to note who was dining with whom and in what state of intimacy. And more profitable, who was *not* dining with whom and who was the interloper. Lady Priscilla had a highly practised eye and though she appeared to be staring you in the face, she was in fact doing a three hundred and sixty degree optical orbit of her surroundings.

'Nothing of interest so far,' she concluded. 'But it's still early and there are empty tables.'

Lady Celia, on the other hand, made no effort to conceal her curiosity, and she actually swivelled her head to case the joint openly. And her eye fell on one table, and she quickly turned away.

'I've found someone,' she said. 'But it's of no interest to us. But personally, I'm curious.'

Lady Priscilla had a better view of the table that had roused her interest and Lady Celia told her friend where it was located, describing its tenants as precisely as she could.

'I can see them,' Lady Priscilla said. 'He's in his seventies, and she's about the same. Who are they?'

'I don't know who the woman is,' Lady Celia said, 'but he's Mr Rufus. He lives at The Hollyhocks. And he often comes up to town. But who's the woman? It can't be his wife. He's widowed.'

'His mistress?' Lady Priscilla suggested, 'though she's a bit long in the tooth for that, isn't she.'

'Do they look intimate to you?' Lady Celia asked.

'They seem to be engaged in very serious conversation,' Lady Priscilla said. 'They're too solemn to be lovers, and too talkative to be man and wife. I'll go to the cloakroom and on my way, I'll eavesdrop a little. Meanwhile don't let him see you. But first, let's order.'

She called the waiter over, and they ordered the set menu. Neither lady was particularly interested in cuisine and to order a set menu was time-saving as well as less expensive. The house white would be adequate with their fish, and once that was settled, Lady Priscilla anxiously needed the cloakroom. Lady Celia did not turn around to watch her. She didn't need to. She had a view in the mirror along one wall and through it she could monitor her friend's passage.

When in reach of Mr Rufus' table, Lady Priscilla dropped her handbag and quickly stooped to pick it up. But she spent an inordinate time on the floor, but had to rise when a waiter approached to offer help. And all the time, Mr Rufus, bless him, had not allowed his conversation to be interrupted. Lady Priscilla then made her way to the cloakroom which she didn't need, allowed a little time for her sojourn there, then returned the way she had gone, dawdling almost imperceptibly at Mr Rufus' table. At last she joined her friend just as their soup was being served.

'Not very interesting I'm afraid,' she said. 'I could only catch a little. He was saying that it would soon be over. He had a few loose ends to tie up. And on my way back, I heard the woman say, But it's been one of the most interesting ones you've done.

And he said, And the most terrible. Does any of that mean anything to you?' she asked.

'No, nothing,' Lady Celia said. But in truth it was a little more than nothing. It meant that Mr Rufus was not in the least bit what he seemed. She didn't share this opinion with her friend. It was all too complicated, and in any case, Mr Rufus was not a potential client.

'I think they're about to leave,' Lady Priscilla said. 'He's just called for the bill. He'll have to pass us to get out, I'm afraid.'

'Well it can't be helped,' Lady Celia said. 'There's no reason why he shouldn't be here. Nor I for that matter.'

'They're getting up,' Lady Priscilla said.

Lady Celia watched their approach through the mirror, and through the mirror she noticed that Mr Rufus had noticed her likewise. She watched him hesitate and he actually paled. She turned her face then, to force him to acknowledge her.

'Why, Lady Celia,' he said. His voice was steady. 'This is a surprise.'

'This is my friend, Lady Waterson.' She hoped it would lead to the naming of his own guest. But although the woman stood meekly by his side, he made no attempt at an introduction.

'Well I shall miss my train,' he said quickly. 'I'll see you later perhaps.'

Then he was gone. He obviously couldn't get away quickly enough.

'That man's got something to hide,' Lady Priscilla said. 'He's keeping her a secret all right. D'you think he's worth investigating?'

'Not much money I'm afraid,' Lady Celia said. 'And nothing to lose.' But in her own mind, she wasn't too sure.

The spare tables slowly filled up, and after a quick look around, Lady Priscilla assured her friend that there were no interesting pickings. 'Next month we'll dine at the Ritz,' she said. 'That's where I discovered Lord Popple.'

'Any news of him?' Lady Celia asked. 'He must wonder why he was so suddenly let off the hook.'

'I saw him a month ago at Lady Julia's salon. We had a most amicable chat. He's carrying on as before, I gather. But we were right to drop him. When he dies, we might well pick up on his widow.'

'Unless she dies first,' Lady Celia said.

'The way I'm told he's carrying on,' Lady Priscilla declared, 'I think that's highly unlikely.'

Lady Celia caught the last train back to The Hollyhocks. She wanted to avoid the possibility of running into Mr Rufus. There were only a few people dawdling in the common lounge. With the passing of Jeremy Cross, there was no longer any competition in the last-to-leave race. There was no sign of Mr Rufus. He had already gone to bed with his secrets. But at breakfast the following morning, Lady Celia asked him if he had enjoyed his Savoy dinner. And the question was audible enough to be received by Mrs Green who was sitting next to him. Again he paled. 'Very much thank you,' he said.

'And your companion?' Lady Celia pursued. 'Did she enjoy it too?'

'I'm sure she did,' he said weakly.

Lady Celia left it at that, as she noted Mrs Green's puckered frown, but she could not hear the hastily mumbled conversation between them.

After breakfast Mr Rufus was seen to take Mrs Green's arm and lead her into the garden. She had clearly demanded an explanation.

'An old colleague of mine,' Mr Rufus told her. 'Retired now. We worked in the bank together. She's widowed, a bit lonely I suspect.' Then he realised that Mrs Green was widowed too, or so she said, but she was certainly lonely, so according to his story both women had equal qualifications for his attention. He therefore added a disqualifying rider. 'She's going to settle in

Canada,' he said with sudden inspiration. 'She's going to live with her son. It was a kind of farewell dinner.'

Mrs Green dared to squeeze his arm. She considered they were back in business.

'You're a pretty little thing, you know,' he said. He thought that a little flirtation was called for, a nurturing of some intimacy that would allow for the questions he needed to ask her. 'I thought Lady Celia very rude regarding that finishing school. I mean, even if you'd never been there, she had no right to subject you to cross-examination. I've often lied about where I've been. Everybody does.' He was trying to make it easy for her.

She laughed. 'You're right,' she said, encouraged. 'I never went to one. It was just a silly show-off.'

'I'll keep your little secret,' he said, satisfied. He continued with his flirtations. They clearly paid off. Slowly she would reveal herself to him. If pushed, he would go as far as proposing marriage, but he hoped that such a proposal would not be necessary. 'What do you say to having dinner with me this evening? We can take a cab into Canterbury. I know a good fish restaurant there.'

Mrs Green was by now convinced that all was over bar the confetti. 'That would be wonderful,' she said.

They almost skipped back to The Hollyhocks so that Mr Rufus could reserve a table.

The Major and Mrs Feinberg had taken advantage of Mrs Green's garden stroll and had gone to their favourite tearoom in the village. Over the weeks that had passed, there had been no improvement in Mrs Feinberg's condition. She still retired frequently to her rooms and rarely took part in any communal gathering. But her dependence on the Major, that safety valve of hers, had increased and was laced with deep affection. She loved being by his side, and sometimes she wished they shared a little cottage together, far far away from The Hollyhocks and its disturbing virus. He must have read her thoughts.

'We could move out of The Hollyhocks,' he said suddenly, as soon as they had been served.

She was silent. Now that he had proposed it, seductive as it was, it smelt somehow of abdication. Mrs Feinberg was not one to surrender. Neither was the Major but no progress had been made in finding a connection with the worm-eaten Mrs Green. And there seemed little likelihood of discovering it. The Major, too, was aware of the impediment, but he took the plunge nevertheless.

'Miriam,' he said, taking her hand. He squeezed it hard as if he were injecting himself with courage. 'Miriam,' he said again, 'Will you marry me?'

It was not an unexpected question, yet it came as a surprise, and she was at a loss as to how to answer it. She did not want to refuse him, but in her heart she felt the suggestion ill-timed, as if the shadow of unfinished business hung over it. That remarriage would be a new life that could not be embarked upon until a former life was settled. She gave her thoughts to the Major and he could not help but agree.

'But it isn't no,' he said. 'I could have hope?'

She squeezed his hand in turn. 'Of course,' she said.

As was their custom, they dawdled their way back to The Hollyhocks. Both were elated in the knowledge that a happier life could be in store.

'We will get to the bottom of it,' the Major said with confidence. 'I feel it in the air.'

They were passing through a wooded glade, and for some reason both paused at the same time. It might have been to view the carpet of bluebells that heralded the spring. Or it might have been the silence that they both wished to savour, a silence that would have been broken by footfall. Or rather it was because both sensed that a pause was opportune for whatever would fill it. When he took her in his arms it seemed timely and in season, and his gentle kiss, a sealing of their union. Safe, so safe, was how Mrs Feinberg felt as she nestled in that secure shelter that he had offered to give her for the rest of her life.

At lunch, she had sufficient courage to sit right next to Mrs Green who lost no time in telling her of her evening assignment with Mr Rufus. Loud enough too, to pierce the ears of Mrs Thackeray and Lady Celia, who both silently wished that she would choke on her evening-out fishbones.

In the common lounge after lunch, Matron announced that the following day the garden of a stately home nearby was being thrown open to the public in all its springtime splendour. She suggested it might be a pleasant outing for them and that she would order a minibus if enough residents wished to go. They were enthusiastic. All had been injected by the hopeful spring air.

'Shall we go?' Mrs Green asked Mr Rufus. 'It should be fun.'

'I have some work to finish off on this consultancy,' he said. 'But you go, my dear, and when you come back, you can tell me all about it.'

'I'll do that,' she said happily. 'I've always loved gardens.'

All the residents expressed a wish to go on the outing. All except Mrs Scott who declared that she had to wait for the evening paper and her horoscope before she could make a decision. But by evening Matron had a full complement of sightseers with the exception of Mr Rufus who, as he told her, had a deadline to meet.

Mrs Green insisted on entering the common lounge before dinner along with her companion, to confirm that they were dining elsewhere. And Mrs Scott was gratified that she was wearing blue, however that horrendous colour ill-suited her. She was convinced that she would have a lucky evening. The darkness lifted on Mrs Feinberg's heart as the couple left the lounge and at dinner that evening, she unashamedly held the Major's hand under the table.

At breakfast on the following morning, none of the residents showed any interest in Mrs Green's night out. But she was going to tell them about it anyway. She even persuaded Mr Rufus to join in her account.

'We started off with oysters,' she said slyly. She hoped that they fully understood the significance of that choice and its aphrodisiac overtones. And in case they didn't, she actually winked at them.

'Whitstable oysters,' Mr Rufus said, knowing their provenance irrelevant, but he felt he had to contribute something.

'And what was the delicious wine we had with it, John?'

'A chablis,' Mr Rufus said. 'Very dry.' He wondered whether his partner was going to go through the whole menu. For his part, he couldn't recall it. He remembered eating fish of a kind but he had been too intent on his probings to savour whatever it was he was eating. He had wished she wasn't stuffing herself so heartily, and thus would have paid more attention to his questions. But on the whole it had been a profitable evening. The bill had astonished him. She had insisted on cocktails and a post-prandial brandy. But he would claim it all on expenses. She had by now reached the main course and reminded him that he had ordered salmon. She herself had sampled the sole. By the time she reached the dessert, having itemised each of the accompanying vegetables, the residents were no longer listening. Indeed, other conversations had started up during her account, and the puddings and their ornaments fell on deaf ears. Mrs Thackeray was pumping Lady Celia on her Savoy encounter. Mrs Scott was apprising Mrs Harvey of her day's forecast. 'Don't try to do too much at once,' it advised. Mrs Harvey wondered how that injunction could apply to somebody who was doing absolutely nothing at all. During Mrs Green's account, the Major and Mrs Feinberg had been silent, their hands clasped under the table, but the Major had sensed a burning rage in his companion which he feared might well explode. Which it did, and in the middle of Mrs Green's crème caramel and the sweet hock that had washed it down.

'Oh do shut up Mrs Green,' Mrs Feinberg exploded.

The others around the table stopped mid-sentence and silence was allowed for the dear Mrs Feinberg's detonation.

'Nobody is interested in what you had for dinner,' she said. 'Nobody is interested in a single thing that you do. You are a total bore and you'd do us all a favour if you would shut your mouth.' She was trembling with rage, yet she squeezed the Major's hand, and he was convinced that her outburst had done her a power of good.

'Well done,' he whispered.

Poor Mrs Green was silenced and she looked to Mr Rufus for support.

He gave it lamely. 'I think that was uncalled for, Mrs Feinberg,' he said, although she had spoken on his behalf as well. 'Mrs Green was only trying to share a pleasant experience.' It was the best that he could do.

But Mrs Feinberg had no intention of apologising and certainly not of leaving the table. Uncalled for or not, what she had said was deeply called for in herself, and she felt strangely content. She thought that her outburst had been the first step towards her recovery.

Matron came in to announce that the minibus would be collecting them in half an hour's time.

'I don't feel like going,' Mrs Green whispered to Mr Rufus.

'But you must go my dear,' he said. 'You must show them all that you won't be beaten. In any case, I depend on you to tell me all about it when you come back. I don't know about the others,' he said flirtatiously, 'but I *love* your stories.'

'You're right,' she said, suddenly defiant. 'I'll show them.'

Mr Rufus went out on to the drive to see the minibus off. He noticed that Mrs Green was sitting alone and he was not surprised. He didn't envy her her morning's outing. As the bus drew away, he saw that Matron was making her way down the aisle. He hoped that she was making for the empty seat at Mrs Green's side, but the bus drove out of sight while she was still on her way.

Matron did indeed sit beside her, so that her isolation would be less conspicuous.

'You didn't tell us what Mr Rufus had for pudding,' she laughed.

Mrs Green was put considerably at her ease, and Matron stayed by her side all morning. She sensed that Mrs Green was a wealthy woman. A ship-owner's widow could hardly be short of a few pennies. A small bequest would not be out of order. Then she automatically thought of the disgusting Mr Venables, but she was determined not to let that thought spoil her day.

The garden was already crowded. There were no guides and the visitors were left to their own devices. Several watchmen were placed around the lawns and beds, to ensure that cuttings were not purloined. Not that that was in the minds of any of the Hollyhocks, for none of them had their own gardens to cultivate. They were content to enjoy the splendid bouquets and to rest occasionally on the benches amply provided on the paths. Apart from Mrs Green and Matron, almost all of the residents walked alone. It seemed that in such sumptuous surroundings, no company was needed. But the Major and Mrs Feinberg were soldered together. After her outburst at breakfast, Mrs Feinberg was in spirited mood.

'I think I'm beginning to discard her,' she said.

'You couldn't make me more happy,' the Major told her.

A tea-tent had been set up at the end of the garden and the Major suggested a little refreshment. It seemed that the others had the same goal in mind and when the couple arrived, the tables in the tent resembled a gathering in the Hollyhocks dining room. Matron still stuck nobly at Mrs Green's side. Lady Celia automatically took the seat at the head of the table,

and Mrs Thackeray offered to bring her her tea and teacake.
She was still curious about Mr Rufus and his companion at the
Savoy, hoping that it signalled the end of the liaison with Mrs
Green. She had questions to ask, and she knew Lady Celia to be
tight-lipped when occasion demanded. So she grovelled in
bringing her tea and cake. Since her appalling connection with
Mr Thurlow, she had learned that to become master, one had
first to play the servant. She laid the tea in front of her. 'Is
there anything else you would like?' she asked.

'Thank you,' Lady Celia said. 'This will do nicely.'

Mrs Thackeray sat at her side. The servant ploy was over.

'What was she like, this companion of Mr Rufus?' she began.

'Why are you so interested?' Lady Celia asked.

'I simply don't think that Mr Rufus is what he says he is.
Any more than Mrs Green.'

'Then they make a very good pair,' Lady Celia said, and with
such finality that Mrs Thackeray was obliged to abandon the
master role that she had held for but one brief question.

'D'you ever go up to London?' Lady Celia asked wishing to
change the subject entirely.

'Not often,' Mrs Thackeray said, sourly recalling her last visit
when she had shopped for her trousseau. Since that time,
London had lost its appeal. 'I don't have any reason to go
there,' she said.

That seemed to put an end to the subject and Lady Celia
couldn't be bothered to think of another.

'I think we should think of making tracks,' Matron said. 'It's
almost lunchtime.'

They finished their tea and trooped towards the exit and the
minibus that awaited them. At the gate there was a small shop
for the sale of souvenir postcards of the flower arrangements.
They all went inside and inspected the pictures. They were
tempted to buy, just for souvenirs, to remind them of the
outing. But they dithered. Where would they put them, but in

that chest of theirs that held those things that would never come in handy? But they bought them all the same. If for nothing else, they could be used in a round of 'Snap'. At least it would make a change from the waiting game.

When the minibus had pulled out of The Hollyhocks' drive, Mr Rufus had returned to reception. He sat down for a while to control his excited anticipation. The coast was clear. But for the maids, The Hollyhocks was empty. He made sure that they were in the kitchens and that the rooms had already been cleaned. Then he made his way upstairs.

Outside Mrs Green's door he paused, and took out of his pocket a bunch of various keys. It took him a little time to find one that fitted; shortly he was inside the room. He recalled the last time he had been there and the acrid taste of the wine she had offered him. He suddenly felt very sorry for her. But there was a duty to be done and he could not afford emotional involvement.

He set to work. Only one drawer of the tallboy was locked and he had little difficulty in opening it. It revealed many of the treasures that he had been seeking. He took his working camera out of his pocket and with infinite care he photographed every sheet of treacherous evidence. Then he replaced all that he had found, and locked the tallboy drawer. He did likewise to the door of her room. Then he went to his own and what was left of the morning was spent in delighted perusal of his findings.

He heard the minibus draw up on the driveway and he hurried downstairs to greet them in reception. Mrs Green was the last to alight having been seated at the back of the bus. She looked glum and miserable, but when she saw him her face creased into smiles. He walked towards her and in front of them all, he embraced her and kissed her almost on the lips. A Judas kiss, he thought, if ever there was one.

Seventeen

The next day was a Sunday. Not one of the Hollyhocks was a churchgoer. In general they felt that, since God had ignored them for most of their lives, there was little point, and even less wisdom, in reminding Him that they were still around. In the common lounge after breakfast, Mrs Scott was surrounded by the Sunday papers, each of which gave a full week's forecast to every sign. The residents waited patiently for their individual predictions. Since Mrs Scott's arrival, clairvoyance had become a Sunday morning routine at The Hollyhocks. Each resident listened earnestly to what was in store for the week, and having heard, each one declared it mumbo-jumbo. Mrs Scott read out the star signs in turn. All of them, curiously, had one forecast in common. From Capricorn to Sagittarius, right through the zodiac, every sign was promised a big surprise.

'It will take place here, in The Hollyhocks, next week some time,' Mrs Scott elucidated. 'A communal surprise for everybody.'

'Is the surprise good or bad?' Mrs Green asked.

'It could be either,' Mrs Scott told her. 'All that it means is that an event will occur that will astonish us all.'

They all looked at each other, wondering which one of them would be responsible for such a bolt from the blue. But all they saw in each face was the sure promise of mundane predictability.

'We'll just have to wait,' Mrs Thackeray said. 'It'll be something to look forward to.'

'Or not,' Lady Celia said.

But good or bad, they were promised an event of sorts, a happening that would break up the monotonous tenor of their days.

'I can't wait for it,' Mr Rufus said.

'Neither can I,' Mrs Green echoed, for whatever her John said, she felt she had to confirm.

After all the horoscopes were read, it was time for mid-morning coffee. The village tearoom was closed on a Sunday, so the Major and Mrs Feinberg were obliged to take a turn on the lawns. The elation that had followed Mrs Feinberg's outburst at Mrs Green was now diluted and her confidence was undermined. She would have preferred to retire to her quarters, but the Major persuaded her to resist that temptation. He took her arm and led her into the garden.

'She might follow us,' Mrs Feinberg said.

'I think after yesterday,' the Major said, 'she will avoid us as carefully as we avoid her.'

The Major was right. Mrs Green had thought to invite Mr Rufus to take a garden turn, but on seeing its occupants she decided it better to stay where she was.

'Shall we walk a little?' Mr Rufus suggested.

'Let's stay here,' she said, 'and have our coffee quietly.'

They were sitting in an isolated corner of the lounge, a spot that Mrs Green had deliberately commandeered for their privacy. The after-taste of his public kiss of the day before still lingered on her lips, and she wondered if there would be a follow-up. Brazenly she took his hand. 'It was so wonderful coming back from the flower-show yesterday,' she said.

'I was very glad to see you,' he said. 'I missed you, you know. And I'm going to miss you again, I'm afraid.'

'I'm not going anywhere,' she said.

'But I am. I have to go up to town again. But I promise you it's the last time. I can tie up all the business by this evening. I'll probably be late, but I'll see you first thing in the morning.'

'Would you like me to come with you to the station?' she said. 'It'll be fun for me, waving you goodbye.' She talked like a child and for a moment he once more felt sorry for her.

'If you like,' he said. 'I've a taxi coming in half an hour.'

'I'll be ready,' she said, and she left him to go to her room to put on something blue.

He held her hand in the taxi and felt like a heel. He would be glad when tomorrow was over. She stood on the station waving the train out of the platform. She was thinking that this would be the very last time that they would be apart. During the next week he would propose to her. She expected it and thought it inevitable and therefore it could be no part of the so-called surprise that Mrs Scott had promised them. She felt very superior to them all. Especially to that Jew-woman who next week would be obliged to grovel to her with congratulations.

When she returned to The Hollyhocks, she went straight to her quarters. She did not wish to mix with the others. She felt

them unworthy of her company. Once in her room, she locked
the door and unlocked the drawer of her tallboy. She took out
the files, the letters and the certificates, and she studied them,
although she knew them all by heart. She was sorely tempted to
destroy them, to put them to the torch so that not one shred of
evidence remained. But she had first to make sure of her future
before she could negate her past. By the end of next week she
could look forward to a splendid conflagration. Why, she might
even set The Hollyhocks on fire, thus confirming Mrs Scott's
mumbo-jumbo surprises.

On the train, Mr Rufus was studying that same evidence.
What with all the proof and the witnesses already gathered
over the years, it was more than enough to convict her. He took
a large whisky from the first-class trolley service, to celebrate
the end of his mission.

When he reached Waterloo, he took a cab directly to the
offices of his superiors. Once settled, they ordered the in-house
lunch and at once set to work. By seven o'clock they had sifted
all the final evidence, and made full arrangements for the show-
down. Then Mr Rufus went home to his flat in Belgravia where
his wife had prepared dinner.

It was a celebratory dinner that night. Over the years,
Margaret had shared the case and its frequent setbacks with her
patient and determined husband.

'You'll need a holiday after this,' she said, as he was decant-
ing the claret.

'I thought we might go to Wales again,' he said. 'Stay in that
lovely hotel on the lake. Do a little fishing perhaps. And we
could take our golf clubs.'

'I'm in favour of all of that,' Margaret said. 'It seems years
since we've spent some solid time together.'

They dawdled over their pre-prandial drinks. 'From tomorrow, I can stop being an old codger in an old-age home. And
thank God for that,' he said.

'I'll drink to that,' his wife said.

'Home tomorrow for good.' Her husband raised his glass.

'Until the next time,' Margaret laughed.

He took the last train back to The Hollyhocks. He prayed that she would not be waiting up for him, hovering in the common lounge in her hideous blue. He didn't think he could face her. Tomorrow would be a difficult enough day. He longed for it to be over.

Mercifully the lounge was empty when he arrived. No one was about and he went upstairs to his rooms dreading her sudden blue appearance on the landing. But he made his quarters safely. Once inside, he studied the room for the first time. He had never bothered to examine it, assured that his stay would be temporary. He had regarded it as a mere hotel bedroom. But now he viewed it differently. He saw it through the eyes of a true resident. The chest filled with might-come-in-handy relics, and aides-mémoire that were no aid at all, a pile of clobber left for relatives, who would irritably discard it all to sort, or pause and occasionally wonder. Then the dressing table with its glass top framing a family snapshot history, a birth, a wedding, a picnic perhaps. The silver-backed hairbrush with its bird's-nest tuft of grey hairs, the matching hand-mirror, rusted around its rim. The powder-box, the ornate empty scent bottle and the hairpins scattered on the powder dust. And the wardrobe, now too large for one's reduced apparel and hangers, empty and ashamed. And the bed, that final resting place. The room was their last port of call in the waiting game. John Rufus now looked at it in that new light, with the eyes of Mrs Thackeray, Mrs Scott, Mrs Harvey and the rest, not forgetting Mrs Green, an exception perhaps, because she was not going to die in that bed, but in a far less comfortable place, with perhaps a wooden hairbrush as a luxury.

Before going to bed, he packed the few clothes that he had brought with him, and his toilet requirements. He wanted no

delay in his leaving. He looked at his watch. It was well past
midnight. One more day and it would all be over.

In the morning, Matron stirred in her bed and knew it was
a Monday even before she opened her eyes. In her sleep, Mr
Venables had become her routine Sunday nightmare and, as on
every Monday morning, she rose from her bed and wished him
dead. She dressed and went downstairs to supervise the kitchen.
Breakfast was almost ready and most of the residents were
waiting in the dining room. Mrs Green kept an empty chair
beside her, and her eye on the dining-room door. When he
entered, she signalled him to her side. His heart sank, knowing
that he had to switch to the flirtatious mode and to retain that
shame until mid-afternoon. He smiled and made his way
towards her.

'Did you finish all your business?' she asked.

'Yes,' he said. It was a relief to tell her the truth for once. He
had finished his business, though it was not the bank business
that Mrs Green imagined. 'Did you miss me?' he teased her.

'Very much,' she said. Then after a pause, 'There's a fair in
Canterbury this afternoon. An antiques fair. Would you like to
go?'

He was careful not to be too prompt with his refusal. 'Not
really,' he said. 'I'm not very interested in antiques. In any case,
it looks as if it's going to rain. Why don't we stay in this afternoon? We could have a game of gin rummy. And then perhaps,
this evening,' he suggested cunningly, 'we could go into
Canterbury for dinner.' He envisaged the dinner Mrs Green
would be having that evening and its menu would be dull and
standard, and its location far from Canterbury. Again a surge of
pity threatened, but he knew he had only to recall the horrific
evidence he had collected, and that pity would ferment into
rage.

'You have organised my whole day,' Mrs Green said brightly.
Then in a whisper, 'You make me very happy.'

He wondered how happy the thought of him would make her by the time the day was over. 'We could take a little stroll this morning though,' he suggested. 'I think the rain will keep off for the time being.'

Mrs Green was more than ready for a stroll. The open air allowed for more privacy than the common lounge and she fully expected some declaration of intent from her loved one. But she would not get that declaration until the afternoon, and it was highly unlikely that it would be to her taste.

'It must be a short walk though,' Mr Rufus said. 'Just to the village and back. I have a few letters to write before lunch. You know, thank you letters, to all those who helped me in my latest assignment.'

What a polite man he is, Mrs Green thought. 'Of course you must,' she said. 'I would do exactly the same.'

'Now a brisk walk,' he said, 'to tone up our muscles.'

'To strengthen our thighs,' Mrs Green said, hoping to lead him into areas of verbal excitement.

He played along. 'And to gird our loins,' he said.

We are well and truly in business, Mrs Green decided. But on their walk to the village, he said no more. Halfway there, she tried again.

'Are your loins girded?' she dared.

Mr Rufus was non-committal. 'Getting along,' he said.

'Mine are,' she laughed.

But it led nowhere. Again he was silent and filled with disgust.

At the village he guided her into a quick U-turn. She could have done with a bit of a rest, for the walk had been largely uphill, but Mr Rufus was in a hurry. She wanted to continue their conversation, one-sided as it might be, but she had no breath for the hot phrases that wet her lips.

It was downhill on the way back. He took her arm and squeezed it. 'I look forward to our game of gin rummy,' he said. 'But I have to warn you, I'm a champion.'

'You're a champion in everything,' Mrs Green said.

For the rest of the way they walked in silence, he squeezing her arm from time to time to keep up with his flirtations. Gestures were easier than words. As they entered the common lounge Mr Rufus noticed how quickly Mrs Feinberg left. He was unsurprised by the hostility between them, for, unlike Mrs Feinberg, he knew its cause, a cause so coincidental that it stretched credulity. He settled Mrs Green in the corner of the lounge. 'I'm off to write my letters,' he said. 'I'll see you at lunch.'

But he had no letters to write. His urgent and most pressing job was to go to Matron's office and come clean.

He knocked on her door.

'Come in,' he heard.

He stood inside her door and watched her sorting papers on her desk. He waited until she was done then he took the chair she gestured towards him.

'How can I help you Mr Rufus?' she asked.

'I need to talk to you urgently Matron,' he said. 'And it may take a little time.'

'I'm not busy,' she said. She was curious. Always had been about Mr Rufus. Something about him didn't fit. Above all his appearance. He was nowhere near ready for an old people's home. Perhaps what he had to say would explain the enigma of his person. She leaned forward on her desk. 'I'm listening,' she said.

He took a deep preliminary breath. 'First of all,' he said, 'my name is not John Rufus. It's Ivor Kennedy.'

In her long years at The Hollyhocks, Matron had encountered this false identity syndrome several times before. She tolerated it, sensing perhaps that once one qualified for the waiting game, it was expedient to pretend to be somebody else, so that the Angel of Death might be fooled. But that was clearly not Mr Rufus' intent, or Mr Kennedy's, as he now declared himself.

'Why did you give me a false name when you registered?' she asked.

'Because of this,' he said. He handed her his badge and identity tag.

She scanned it, astonished, then read its legend aloud. 'Ivor Kennedy. Inspector. Scotland Yard War Crimes Commission.' She was nervous. Was she under investigation? And had he been sent to The Hollyhocks for that purpose? And did that purpose have something to do with Mr Venables? She knew that her face was white with fear, and that he could not ignore her shivering.

'It's all right Matron,' he assured her. 'It has absolutely nothing to do with you. I can assure you that what I have to tell you will in no way harm the wonderful reputation of The Hollyhocks. Which it justly deserves, I may add. In fact, it will certainly put The Hollyhocks on the map.'

Matron didn't know what he was talking about, but she was relieved that he had attributed her pallor to her fear of The Hollyhocks' repute, and she felt her colour return. Let off the Venables hook, at least for the time being, she felt she needed a drink, and she offered one to Mr Kennedy.

'You've quite shocked me Mr Ruf . . . Mr Kennedy,' she said. 'I think we could both do with a pick-me-up.' She went to her cabinet and poured two small measures of whisky. He took his gratefully. It would help him along with his tale.

'You quite took me in Mr Kennedy, when you registered,' Matron said.

'So did Mrs Green, I'm afraid.'

'Mrs Green?'

Then his story began. He told her everything that she needed to know. From time to time she gasped in disbelief, and at one point in his story she gave a little cry of horror.

When his tale was done, and its telling had taken well over half an hour, he allowed Matron to refill his glass. Hers too. They both needed a breathing space.

'I have to ask your co-operation in this,' Mr Kennedy said. He then itemised the business she had to attend to. As soon as Mrs Green's rooms were free, she was to pack all her belongings and store them in her office. He would meantime make it his business to keep Mrs Green downstairs. The police would arrive at The Hollyhocks round about four o'clock.

That time rang a terrible bell in Matron's ear. Whatever was she to do with Mr Venables? He would surely understand that she was otherwise engaged and would come back later to claim his due. But this was no time to worry about that. She had first to obey Mr Kennedy's instructions. She felt suddenly very important, a key figure in the programme, and she could not deny that she was looking forward to it.

'I must quietly pack her things,' she said, 'and bring them down to my office.' She repeated Mr Kennedy's instructions. 'Should I hide them?'

'No,' Mr Kennedy said. 'That won't be necessary. They will be taken away before she sees them. Then when the police arrive,' Mr Kennedy went on, 'and are settled here in your office, I want you to send for Mrs Green. She will be in the lounge, and I shall be with her. We will then both come to your office and in less than ten minutes, it will all be over.'

'I will have to offer some explanation to my residents,' Matron said.

'Wait until we have gone,' he told her. 'Then you can tell them all that I have told you.' He smiled at her. 'I'm grateful for your co-operation Matron,' he said. 'I'll take this opportunity to say goodbye, since I shall be off with the rest of them. And when the coast is clear, could you also instruct the maid to bring my cases down at the same time?'

'Leave it all to me,' Matron said.

They shook hands. Matron's was trembling with an excitement that equalled her horror. At the door he turned. 'I don't know about the others,' he said, 'but I do know for sure that

Mrs Feinberg is indeed Mrs Feinberg and of all the residents in The Hollyhocks, she will be the happiest to see the back of Mrs Green.'

Matron had been told to keep her mouth firmly shut until it was all over. When that time came, she would call them all together, and stressing her own part in the proceedings, she would tell them the whole horrific story.

Mr Kennedy returned to his room and stayed there until the lunch bell sounded. He put on his tired flirtatious smile, and went downstairs to the dining room. As he expected, she was already seated, with the reserved empty chair beside her. He went to join her. He kept his face well away from hers. He did not want her to smell the whisky on his breath. But she caught it and it pleased her. She assumed he had taken it to give him courage to voice his proposal which she fully expected before the end of the day.

'You were right about the rain,' she said. 'There's quite a storm brewing.'

'Not very good for the antiques fair,' he said. 'Though I suppose they'll have a marquee.'

The soup arrived and he dawdled with it. It was one o'clock and he wanted to stretch the lunch hour. The idea of playing gin rummy for three solid hours appalled him. He ate slowly urging Mrs Green to do the same.

'It's much healthier,' he said. 'We have to keep fit.'

'Absolutely,' she said, sensing what he wished her to keep fit for.

So they took their time, the pair of them, and they were the last to leave the dining room. He looked at his watch. Two o'clock. He hoped they'd come on time.

'Let's take our coffee,' he said, 'and then we can settle down to a game.'

They sat themselves in a corner of the lounge. The rain was beating down on the windowpanes. No resident would venture out of doors in such weather. There would be a full house in the common lounge for the rest of the day. They lingered over their coffee, then Mr Kennedy crossed the room to the side-board and took a new pack of cards out of the drawer. He shuffled them like a professional casino croupier. 'I'll keep the score,' he said, and they started to play.

After a series of ten games, he had lost nine. He wasn't allow-ing her to win. Indeed, he fought hard to hold his own. It was just that she was such a cunning player and obviously at some time of her life, and he could guess when, she had put in a lot of practice. The time passed quickly and when he looked at his watch, it was just after three. And then the unforeseen happened.

'I think I'll go upstairs,' she said, 'and have a little siesta. I need to be bright and awake for our dinner tonight.'

'You can't go,' he said, rather too desperately. Then, in a more measured tone, 'You can't leave me without a chance of fighting back. That would be too cruel. Please don't go,' be begged. He couldn't allow her to go to her room. She would see that it had been stripped, and she might well do a skip. No, he had to keep her by his side. If pushed, he would even propose marriage to her. 'I want you to stay,' he said touching her arm.

She thought it would be folly to absent herself at such an ardent moment.

'Of course I'll give you a chance,' she said. 'Though I promise you I will not be beaten.'

He sighed with relief and dealt the cards once more.

'You play very well,' he said. 'Where did you learn?'

'My husband was a great card-player,' she said. 'We played a lot together, especially when I was pregnant. It passed the waiting time.'

'Well he certainly was a very good teacher,' Mr Kennedy said. He tried to win the next game. And the following. But she managed to outwit him each time.

'You're too good for me,' he said. Surreptitiously he looked at his watch. A quarter to four. Two more games at the most and it would all be over. 'Just one more,' he said. 'Then you can have your siesta.' He dealt the cards very slowly and he took time over his play, hovering and dithering over which card he should offer. As he played his last, he heard the four o'clock chimes from the village clock. They had to be here. He would plead for just one more game.

Upstairs in her room, Lady Celia raised her net curtains. And she was astonished to see two police cars parked below her window. But not as astonished as was the ferret, who rattled up the drive in his pathetic four-wheeler and pulled up sharply at the sight of them. The stationary car trembled with his fear. With a crash of gears he went quickly into reverse, and before Lady Celia could reckon on the loss of two hundred and fifty pounds in their weekly takings, he was out of the driveway with wisps of gravel smoke in his wake.

Downstairs in the full-house lounge, as Mrs Green was yet again threatening a siesta, and Mr Kennedy was on the perilous verge of a marriage proposal, one of the kitchen maids mercifully made an entrance. She made straight for Mrs Green and whispered, 'Matron wants to see you in her office.'

'Whatever for?' Mrs Green said. She was clearly nervous.

'I don't know,' the maid said. 'I don't think it's very important.' Matron had clearly coached her. Mrs Green hesitated.

'Would you like me to come with you, my dear?' Mr Kennedy said.

'Oh, would you be so kind? I don't know why, but I'm always nervous of this sort of thing. It's like being called to the headmistress's study.'

He took her arm and guided her out of the room. At the door, he was seen to put his arm around her shoulder. Nobody particularly noticed their exit and conversation, such as it was, and the odd siesta, were not interrupted. Mrs Scott gathered up her knitting and put her bag on the floor.

'The evening paper must have arrived,' she said and she went into reception to collect the latest horoscopes. Through the front door she could see the exciting evidence of the law, and she rushed back into the lounge to tell of her findings.

'There are two police cars in the driveway,' she announced excitedly.

The residents stirred.

'D'you think this is the surprise, Mrs Scott?' one of them asked. 'The one in all our horoscopes?'

'I think perhaps it is,' Mrs Scott said with a certain triumph.

Conversation ceased, and those who dozed were aroused by the smell of an event that was eventing and was not to be missed. Slowly they all trooped into reception. The Major and Mrs Feinberg were the first in line for they were seated nearest the door. Then came all the others, and Lady Celia too, down from her rooms to see what all the fuss was about. They gathered in a group in reception. And there they waited. Whatever was eventing, they knew was taking place behind Matron's office door, and they stared at it, determined to wait there until it opened. They were silent, sensing that the goings-on behind that door called for a certain solemnity. And indeed, those goings-on were solemn and serious enough.

When Mr Kennedy and Mrs Green had left the lounge, he had kept his arm firmly around her shoulder until they reached Matron's door. And even then, while opening it for her, he maintained his protective gesture. But once inside Matron's office, he considered that his six years' investigative work with all its ups and downs, its moments of hope and equal moments of despair, was now at an end. He had done his part of the job. Now it was up to others to pick up the pieces. So he dropped his hand from her shoulder. And moreover left her side. Matron was seated at her desk, and he took up his stand behind her. He had clearly defected.

Mrs Green was flanked by two uniformed police officers, one

of whom was a woman. In the corner stood another man of the law, by his isolation and beribboned uniform clearly one of a higher rank. It was he who took Mrs Green's arm and stood her in front of Matron's desk.

Mrs Green felt her knees weaken, and a hot trickle of liquid rinsed her legs. She started to cry. Not so much because she had been found out and her past discovered, but because of the method they had used to trap her. She felt the imprint of Mr Kennedy's, her John's, treacherous hand on her shoulder, and she knew it was not an engagement ring that he'd intended to offer her, but in its stead, a pair of handcuffs. She stared at him with loathing. She knew she would have time, and too much of it, to recap on his deception, to squirm in the recall of her own advances and expectations. All that would come later. But for the moment, blind hatred would do.

Then the much beribboned policeman spoke. 'Heidi Schloss,' he said, loud and clear, and with perfect pronunciation. 'I am arresting you on the charge of murder and conspiracy to murder three thousand Jewish women and children at the extermination camp of Birkenau, Auschwitz, between November 1942 and May 1944. You do not have to say anything at this time, but anything you say will be . . .' And so on and so forth.

But she wasn't listening. She was too stunned by hearing that name. That name that she had forfeited so many years ago, that name of which she was so proud and of which she still was, and would be for the rest of her life. That true German name of Aryan purity. When she heard it now, she mourned that she had ever forsaken it. There was some relief, even a joy in hearing it again, even though it came out of a mouth that would condemn her. In that holy name, she felt she had to make a stand.

'If Hitler had won the war, you lot would have gone to Auschwitz too,' she said.

'But he didn't, did he?' This whisper from Matron who could not resist the temptation.

Mrs Green stared at Mr Kennedy, willing him to look at her. At last he did, as the handcuffs were secured around her wrists. His face was expressionless. At most it stated that his duty had been done.

The two lesser police officers stood either side of her, and taking each arm, they moved towards the door. It was that sight of the three of them in line that first stunned the gaggle of silent residents assembled in reception. For an instant the group paused on the threshold, as if for a photo-call, then they walked slowly towards the front door. When the back of them was in full view, a loud scream broke the silence. It came from Mrs Feinberg.

'Heidi Schloss,' she yelled. Then she fell on the Major's arm. Mr Kennedy, emerging from Matron's office, turned towards her and smiled.

'You may very well be right, Mrs Feinberg,' he said.

Matron went to the doorway to see the back of them. She refrained from waving. It seemed inappropriate, and as soon as the arm of the law had swept the gravel, she returned to the astonished reception.

'What happened, Matron?' was the general question.

'Go into the lounge. I'll be with you shortly. Then I'll tell you everything.'

But first she had to attend to Mrs Feinberg who, wilting on the Major's arm, was close to collapse. She took her arm, and the Major the other and together they helped her into the dining room where there was a sofa alongside one wall. The Major laid her down, while Matron fetched a glass of brandy.

'I'm all right,' Mrs Feinberg said. 'I'm more than all right,' and though there were tears in her eyes, she offered a half-smile. Matron put the brandy to her lips.

'I think she's part of your story,' the Major said, and very gently he pushed up the sleeve of her cardigan.

'I know,' Matron said. 'Mr Rufus told me.' The Major wouldn't have known about Mr Kennedy, so she stuck to his Hollyhocks name.

'It was the back of her,' Mrs Feinberg was anxious to tell them. 'Just seeing the back of her between those two policemen. That's how I always saw her. The back of her, between two guards. Those fat legs of hers, and the sensible shoes.' She sighed. 'I'm glad I didn't recognise her before. I would have killed her. Killed her for my father, my mother and my three little sisters.' Then she started to cry in earnest.

'You must rest now,' Matron said. 'You've had quite a shock.'

'I'll stay with her,' the Major said. He sat himself down at the end of the couch, and took Mrs Feinberg's hand, and kissed it. 'You're free now,' he whispered.

Matron then went into the common lounge to tell her story. She was rather looking forward to it. It was the most exciting event that had happened at The Hollyhocks since she had taken up her post over fifteen years ago. The residents sat like good children, upright in their chairs, waiting for their lesson. Matron sat herself central in the lounge.

'It all began this morning,' she said. 'Before this morning, I knew nothing about it. Nothing at all. It was after breakfast when Mr Kennedy came to my office.'

'Mr Kennedy?' some queried.

'Well,' Matron smiled, greatly enjoying herself, 'you all thought he was Mr Rufus. And so did I. Retired bank manager from Manchester. Well, he wasn't. Far from it. He wasn't from Manchester, and he certainly wasn't retired.'

'What was he then?' Mrs Scott asked. If he'd given a false identity, and no doubt a false birth sign, she had misread his horoscope, and she was very cross with his deception. It cast doubt on her expertise.

'His name was actually Ivor Kennedy,' Matron went on. She

allowed a pause to herald her first piece of surprising information. Then, 'He was an inspector at Scotland Yard. He worked
for the War Crimes Commission. His job was to track down war
criminals.' A nervous sigh of excitement crossed the room in
anticipation of what cloak and dagger scenario was to come. 'He
has been working on Mrs Green's case for almost six years.'

'Case?' Mrs Harvey asked. 'What case?'

'The case of Heidi Schloss,' Matron announced dramatically.
'That was her real name. The one we knew as Mrs Green. Mr
Kennedy told me how it all started. It was in Edinburgh where
Mrs Green was living. She had been married long before. To a
German. But it only lasted two or three months. She never had
any children. At the time when Mr Kennedy tracked her down,
she was living with a woman called Mathilda, and they'd been
together for twenty-five years. Then Mrs Green fell in love
with another woman.' A sigh, laced with giggles, scored this last
revelation. 'So she threw Mathilda out of the house. I suppose
after twenty-five years, poor Mathilda was pretty upset. And
she wanted revenge. In other words, she shopped her.' Matron
was quoting Mr Kennedy, for the verb 'to shop' was unknown
to her. And likewise, she presumed, to her residents. 'She
decided to tell on her. They'd lived together for so long that
Mathilda knew some of Mrs Green's secrets. And they were
terrible. So she went to the police. But there was a lot she
didn't know. That's when our Mr Kennedy was called in.'
Matron now considered that she owned the inspector, having
looked after him for a few weeks, whatever he called himself.
'And for the last six years,' she went on, 'he's been all over the
world interviewing survivors.'

'Survivors of what?' Mrs Scott asked.

'Well that's the whole point,' Matron said. 'Our Mrs Green
turns out to be Heidi Schloss, one of the commanders at
Auschwitz concentration camp, and she personally sent three
thousand or more women and children to the gas chambers.'

'The murderer,' Mrs Thackeray shrieked. 'I always suspected that woman.'

'So did I,' Lady Celia said. But she hadn't. Not a bit. But if she had, she would most certainly have put the ferret on to the case. And she deeply regretted allowing such a profitable fish to slip through her net.

'But why did Mr Rufus, or whatever his name was, why did he come to The Hollyhocks? And actually stay here?' Mrs Scott wanted to know.

'He was tying up loose ends. He hoped to get some leads from the culprit herself. That's why he seemed so friendly with her.'

'Friendly?' Mrs Thackeray scoffed. 'A bit more than that, I thought. He practically proposed to her.'

'Mr Kennedy is a respectable married man,' Matron said. 'He has a wife, two children and five grandchildren.'

'Did he get anything out of her?' Lady Celia asked.

'Only that she'd never been to a Swiss finishing school.'

'I could have told him that,' Mrs Thackeray sneered.

'He did find some private papers though,' Matron said. 'He went to her rooms, that day we visited the gardens. They more or less confirmed everything that was already known. So this morning he came to my office and came clean. We arranged for her arrest.'

'What did she say?' More than one resident asked the question.

'They told her what the charges were, and she didn't deny them. She looked daggers at Mr Kennedy as you can imagine. And between you and me,' Matron lowered her voice, 'she wet herself.'

'Serves her right,' Mrs Thackeray said, though they all knew that a pair of wet knickers was in no way a payment for three thousand innocent souls. 'Did she say anything at all?'

'Yes. She said that if Hitler had won the war, all of us would have gone the same way. So they took her away. You saw the rest of it. There'll be a trial. Mr Kennedy say she'll get life.'

'It's a pity they've abolished hanging,' Mrs Thackeray said. 'And by the way, what about that scar on her face? She told me her daughter threw a saucepan at her.'

'It was a saucepan all right,' Matron said. 'But it wasn't her daughter who threw it. She didn't have a daughter. It was poor old Mathilda when she was thrown out of their house.'

'Good old Mathilda,' Mrs Harvey said.

'What a terrible story,' Lady Celia concluded, and that judgement silenced them for a while.

Then Mrs Scott spoke. 'How did Mrs Feinberg know her name?' she asked.

'That's another story,' Matron said. 'And almost unbelievable.'

The residents leaned forward. Their silent attention was flattering and Matron was going to milk the Feinberg story dry.

'You may have noticed,' she began, 'that Mrs Feinberg never wears short sleeves.' She herself had never noticed it, but the fact added drama to her tale. She let them wonder for a while. Then she began again. 'There's a number tatooed on her arm. She was a prisoner in Auschwitz. She and her family. She survived, but her mother, father and three sisters went to the gas ovens. Heidi Schloss, our Mrs Green, sent them there.' She paused again. Mrs Scott gave another cry of horror and Matron let it echo for a while. 'Mrs Feinberg was always uneasy in Mrs Green's company,' Matron said, 'but she couldn't figure out why. Until this morning. And it all came back to her.'

'Poor Mrs Feinberg,' Mrs Thackeray said. 'Where is she now?'

'She's resting,' Matron said. 'The Major is with her.'

Another silence, this time broken by Lady Celia. 'D'you think, Matron, we could all have a drink? A proper drink. I think we all need one.'

'A good idea,' Matron said, since it was Lady Celia who had suggested it. 'We'll drink a toast to Mrs Feinberg.'

'And a farewell to whatever her name was,' Mrs Scott said.

Matron took herself off to the kitchen. On her way, she heard the village clock strike six. And she recalled that it was a Monday, and Mr Venables had not put in an appearance. Perhaps he had seen the police cars in the drive, and had turned his crooked tail. She dared to hope that she had seen the last of him.

Eighteen

And she most certainly had. For Mr Venables would never darken her office door again. He had made that quite clear to Ladies Priscilla and Celia on the latter's subsequent visit to London. He swore that he wouldn't put a foot or a retread tyre on that Hollyhocks gravel ever again. The place was spooked, he said. Once the law had visited it, it was bugged. He was not prepared to take the risk.

They had to give in to him. Matron's contribution was not so great a loss, and they'd had a fair run with her. So they agreed to let her off the hook.

Mrs Green, or Heidi Schloss, as she was, with the help of the newspapers, now nationally known, was remanded in custody until the date of the trial which was fixed for three months hence. So the residents had to wait for its outcome. The papers had given only meagre particulars of the offender, but amongst those was her true birthdate. Mrs Scott set to reading her horoscope, and after some weeks she forecast that the murderer's future promised to be bleak. Which all of the residents could have told her anyway.

Once more there was a full house at The Hollyhocks. Mr Kennedy had been right. Fräulein Schloss had put the home on the map, and Matron's waiting list had lengthened considerably, and was punctuated by a respectable number of masculine names. What was more, two months of four o'clock Mondays had passed with no sign of Mr Venables. Matron was content.

After the arrest of Heidi Schloss, Mrs Feinberg had fallen into moods that either leapt into delight or dipped into despair. The Major never left her side. Mark, her son, came often to visit her since she was too unwell to risk the journey to London. Matron knew that her recovery would take time, that perhaps it was only now, after over fifty years of grieving, that she would be able for the first time to truly mourn.

'Time will heal,' the Major kept telling his charge.

Between them they added up to over one hundred and fifty-two years, but both in their affection for each other were willing to give time, time.

Downstairs in the lounge, Heidi Schloss was the nightly topic of conversation. The residents never tired of maligning her, not in front of the Major and Mrs Feinberg in case a reminder of her story would be painful. But in their absence, it was Fräulein talk. All other ex-residents of The Hollyhocks were forgotten. They had to be put out of one's mind simply because they had died. It was as if they had let the side down and thus did not merit recall. The names of Mrs Webber, Mrs

Hughes, Mrs Primple, Mr Cross and even poor Miss Bellamy were never uttered. Mr Thurlow merited an occasional snide reference, and so did Jock MacPherson, who according to reports, was still in the land of the bagpipe living. But the Fräulein was absolutely undead, and it was unlikely she would ever be forgotten. She had become the legend of The Hollyhocks and perhaps in the years to come, a plaque would appear on the door, declaring that 'the murderess slept here'. Mrs Scott never let up on her readings and there was never a shortage of willing ears.

One morning after breakfast, a week before Mrs Green's trial, she was doling out the forecasts for her followers. It was Mrs Thackeray's turn. Under Sagittarius.

'It seems you're in for another surprise,' Mrs Scott told her. 'I was right before, wasn't I?' she said.

None of them had forgotten that pre-arrest forecast and since that time, Mrs Scott had been taken far more seriously.

'Well I hope it's a nice surprise,' Mrs Thackeray said. 'I could do with one.'

Of late, she had been feeling very low. Mrs Green's departure had left her with no one to bully. And the rage that the late Mr Thackeray had engendered so many years ago still festered in her bones. She needed another target. Another battleground. She would go to the Thackeray vault, she decided, and in its seething contemplation, she would healingly detonate.

It was a fine day, and a slow and measured walk to the cemetery would serve to fuel her rage, and thus augment the relief she would feel on reaching her target. She had to walk through the village to reach the road that led to the church. She would have stopped at the teashop to fortify herself with some refreshment, but through the window she could see the Major and Mrs Feinberg holding hands across one of the tables. She hurried on, envy augmenting her rage. In time she reached the road at the village end.

It wasn't Mrs Thackeray's fault. As always, before crossing the road, she mouthed that maternal mantra of her childhood. 'Look right, look left and right again.' It wasn't her fault. It was just her bad luck, and no doubt the surprise that Mrs Scott had promised her, that the oncoming car, fresh from Paris and the ferry, and yet unacclimatised, was driving on the wrong side of the road. Poor Mrs Thackeray. It wasn't her fault at all.

'I did look, Mummy, I promise I did,' she said, as she passed out on the kerbside.

A screaming ambulance took her to the hospital and within the hour, Matron was at her bedside. She held her hand.

'You're going to be all right, Mrs Thackeray,' she said, although the doctor had whispered that there was no hope of recovery.

'Where's Mr Thackeray?' Mrs Thackeray asked.

'He's dead, my dear,' Matron said.

'Where's dead? Is it far?'

She was soon to find out.

Matron went back to her waiting list. But first to the common lounge where, to their half-mast sorrow, she broke the news to her residents. Very soon Mrs Thackeray would be forgotten like all the others; in the meantime, they had a funeral to look forward to and a party-wake afterwards. Matron knew that her residents, whose lives were a little short on silver linings, would welcome any diversion on offer.

She went back to her office and her list. Mrs Thackeray's rooms were some of the finest in the house. They overlooked the gardens on both sides, and because of the view she had paid a little extra for her keep. Their future tenant would be similarly obliged. The waiting game, she thought, could be played by any number of players, but more often than not, it was a sad solitaire. So she scanned her list for a gentleman who was unbusily doing it on his own. The name of Anthony Carstairs struck her as class. A retired headmaster from Sussex. At least he claimed to be so. After her experience with Mrs Green and Mr Rufus, Matron was wary of the declarations made on the registration form. But neither Mr Rufus nor Mrs Green had given any trouble. Indeed, they had caused an event of memorable proportions. She looked once more at her list and then she made her decision. She would write a letter to Mr Anthony Carstairs, enclosing an invitation to play the waiting game.

Now you can order superb titles directly from Abacus

☐ Autobiopsy	Bernice Rubens	£6.99
☐ Brothers	Bernice Rubens	£7.99
☐ The Elected Member	Bernice Rubens	£6.99
☐ Mr Wakefield's Crusade	Bernice Rubens	£6.99
☐ Our Father	Bernice Rubens	£6.99
☐ Yesterday in the Back Lane	Bernice Rubens	£6.99

─────────── ⬭ABACUS⬭ ───────────

Please allow for postage and packing: **Free UK delivery.**
Europe: add 25% of retail price; Rest of World: 45% of retail price.

To order any of the above or any other Abacus titles, please call our credit card orderline or fill in this coupon and send/fax it to:

Abacus, 250 Western Avenue, London, W3 6XZ, UK.
Fax 0181 324 5678   Telephone 0181 324 5517

☐ I enclose a UK bank cheque made payable to Abacus for £ . . . .
☐ Please charge £ . . . . . . to my Access, Visa, Delta, Switch Card No.

☐☐☐☐☐☐☐☐☐☐☐☐☐☐☐☐☐☐☐☐☐☐

Expiry Date ☐☐☐☐   Switch Issue No. ☐☐

NAME (Block letters please) . . . .

ADDRESS . . . .

. . . .

. . . .

Postcode . . . . Telephone . . . .

Signature . . . .

Please allow 28 days for delivery within the UK. Offer subject to price and availability.

Please do not send any further mailings from companies carefully selected by Abacus ☐